THE BOOK

The author, Ines Sachs, and her husband make the decision to live out the dream of life in the sunny south of France. In this book, she affectionately describes, with a large dose of humour, their emigration: how a dream becomes a plan (not for nothing is she married to a project manager), the minor difficulties and major hurdles that need to be overcome, and ultimately, the arrival in their new homeland, which doesn't go nearly as smoothly as they had imagined.

A book for all Francophiles. And a rich treasure trove of experience for anyone who, like them, wants to turn the dream of moving to France into reality.

THE AUTHOR

Ines Sachs was born near Dresden in 1972. She was a successful event manager and head of communications before she and her husband decided to turn their backs on Germany and live a life under the sun of Southern France.

Ines is very interested in interacting with her readers and therefore welcomes any contact via her homepage.

https://ines-sachs.de/en

Ines Sachs

APÉRO AT NOON

The Adventure of Moving to France

The original version
APÉRO UM ZWÖLF
VON ZWEIEN, DIE AUSZOGEN IN FRANKREICH
ZU LEBEN
published in German in 2022

1st edition

Author: Ines Sachs
First publication: 2023 as e-book
Cover illustration: Ines Sachs
Copyright © 2023 Ines Sachs
Copyright of the English translation © 2023 Ines Sachs
ISBN: 9798866117642
Independently published

The work, including its parts, is protected by copyright. The author is responsible for the contents. Any exploitation is not permitted without her consent. Publication and distribution are carried out on behalf of the author, who can be contacted at: https://ines-sachs.de/en.

for
my husband Christian,
who has gone along with all this nonsense and is still going along with it. Although, actually, it's more me who has gone along with all his nonsense and is still going along with it.

TABLE OF CONTENTS

Part 1: From Dream to Plan 1
  Singapore 2
  The Decision 5
  The Quest for the Perfect Town 9
  The Shock 14
  The Flexible Interpretation of the Verb "produire" 18
Part 2: We Move 23
  Seek and ye Shall Find – or not 24
  There's Already a File on it 40
  The Paradox of Madame Pinel 45
  I Rent a Flat 48
  We Have Something to Tell you 57
  Flat Handover 68
  Hard Work 81
  Clearance Sale 89
  It's Always a Case of Some Losses 103
  Jean Reno and the Apple 108
Part 3: Arrived 111
  A Stormy First Night 112
  Moving in with Obstacles 116
  After the Move Comes the Next Move 131
  Of a Thousand and One Little Things 135
  Apéro at Noon… 152
  Waterfalls – and other Challenges 163
  The Never-ending Story of the Car Registration 174
  Coffee Party 192
  Amongst Immigrants 204
  Lost in Translation 210
  Feeling Like a German 224
  Epilogue 230

PART 1:
FROM DREAM TO PLAN

SINGAPORE

How does one start a book?

With the beginning, of course.

Yes, but where is the beginning? When you want to tell something that subtly started sometime in life and, strictly speaking, is not finished to this day. Well, I suppose I'd better just get started.

So, my story begins in Singapore, more precisely at Singapore airport. You're right, dear reader, this is quite a stretch. But I have to start somewhere. So why not there?

We had spent two exciting weeks in Singapore. Why we were there is irrelevant. Suffice to say, my husband had briefly been there for business before, and the city had impressed him. So, we had explored it in detail and were waiting at the airport for our return flight. We still had some Singapore dollars left. And as exchanging a few dollars made no sense, we wanted to spend them quickly. We were just thinking of a few kilos of chocolate as emergency supply for the long flight, when we stumbled upon the displays in front of a bookshop. There was something that jumped out at us. On the cover of a book, a silhouette of a hammock stretched between two palms and above it the lettering "The 4-Hour Work Week" (by Timothy Ferriss). It was worth giving up our remaining dollars for this.

And that's where it all began.

Before you rush off to buy the above-mentioned book, I must warn you. It was just the trigger that started certain thought processes in us. It did not help to get us to France. Nevertheless, I highly recommend this book to you.

The flight from Singapore to Frankfurt took 13 hours. Christian started reading in the boarding area, and by the time we landed, he had finished it in a quick read. Later, he read it again, but slowly and thoughtfully. In between, he kept telling me what he had read. When he finally put it down, my anticipation had been built up so much that I couldn't wait to start reading it. We discussed every chapter and shared our thoughts.

For some time, we had both been dissatisfied in our jobs. We both worked irresponsibly hard, were stressed and had to force ourselves every morning to get up and drive to the office. The fun of the job was long gone. And yet, when I started with my boss, I had told him I would stay as long as I enjoyed the job.

So far, we had arranged our lives pretty much like everyone else. We had well-paying jobs, owned a flat, and spent our money as a reward for hard work. We were trying to get pregnant. Not because we necessarily wanted a child, but because it was simply time. All our friends around us had already "laid eggs" at least once, as Christian likes to say. Our mothers kept asking us when they would finally become grandmothers. We felt a certain pressure. And since the job was no longer fun, but paid well, that was the best time for maternity leave. Mother Nature knew better. We didn't have a child. In retrospect, I must admit, thank God! We were not ready for it and our motives were definitely the wrong ones. I was relieved when we later decided to become permanently happy non-parents.

Now, that book had crossed our path and caused us to think about the basis of our decisions. A continuation-as-before was no longer possible. But what did we want at all? And wanting is all well and good, but what could we actually do? What were we really good at? What did we want to do with our lives, what did we want to achieve?

We asked ourselves these and similar questions in the following weeks and months. We read countless books, attended seminars and lectures. It was not a lightbulb moment, but a slow development. We often sat together for hours, brainstormed, discussed, looked for solutions. And we searched for our purpose, for the reason for our existence.

It was a wonderful time. We spent an incredible amount of time together. For the first time in our lives, we talked about our dreams and fears. Yes, ok, we had talked before and thought we knew roughly what the other wanted. But we had never done before so intensely and deeply as we did now. And one or two things we took for granted turned out to be not quite right or no longer up to date. Our relationship could only benefit from it.

Come on, be honest, hand on heart, when was the last time you've talked to your partner about such things? Do you really know exactly what he or she hopes for in life? I think you should talk!

THE DECISION

The outcome of this months-long introspection was this decision: We wanted to live by the sea in the sunny south. Forever!

There are people who simply rush headlong towards the first best goal, quickly find their way around everywhere and, if they no longer like it there, simply fly elsewhere on a whim. They settle in quickly and let go just as fast. They take life lightly. You know the sort of person I mean, don't you? Well… We are not this kind of people. We need preparation. But if you are such a person, you can be sure of my admiration. And you may skip this chapter. If you're anything like us, keep reading!

"Sunny south" and "by the sea" was admittedly still somewhat unspecific. So, we now searched the world map for all countries with sea access and made a list. My husband loves Excel lists and is capable of creating the most complex formulas. I freely admit, when these formulas exceed a certain length and contain more than one IF, then I'm out. That's too exhausting for me. I'm more of the gut-driven type. For me, it would be entirely sufficient to list a handful of criteria that one can easily research and compare. I would then leave the rest of the decision to my gut. But my husband needs this. Without in-depth research, which he at least and to my greatest relief takes on himself, and without his Excel matrix, the man makes no decision. So, I had to endure it.

In a brainstorming session, we established our criteria such as political stability, low crime rate, good infrastructure, fast accessibility, and a dozen more. Then we sorted them by importance. With what? Of course, with an Excel matrix! Gradually, we filled this list. We read the information on Wikipedia, watched videos about the countries on YouTube. We found such exciting things as the Big Mac Index, which records the price for a Big Mac in all countries where there is a McDonald's, which allows you to get an idea of the price level. We also found Numbeo, where you can compare the cost of living in many cities worldwide. Take the home town, where you know the prices, and compare them with Marseille, for example, to estimate the budget you'll need in your new life after emigrating.

One of our criteria was the language. We were looking for a country where a language was spoken that we could already speak or would easily learn. So, our selection was reduced to all the English, French, German and Spanish-speaking countries in the world.

Another criterion was the climate. It should be sunny and warm. Countries like Greenland, Iceland, Norway, and so on were therefore eliminated from our list. The right language was spoken in the UK, but the weather…

And then there was the topic of accessibility. We had family in Germany and wanted to be quickly on-site for our German business partners in the future. So, an international airport with regular flights to Germany was a must. Also, the duration of the flight and the time difference should ideally not be too dramatic.

With every criterion that we examined, more and more countries were eliminated from our list. It happened that in the end, only a handful of countries were left. To you, dear reader, I can say, these were precisely the countries that I had long selected with the help of my gut and without lengthy research. But you don't necessarily have to rub that in my husband's face. We now scrutinised these countries very closely. Most of them we already knew from previous travels and therefore had a pretty good idea about them. Those we didn't know yet were to be visited on our next holiday.

After all the remaining countries were examined, we evaluated the criteria, and this resulted in a ranking. Now, guess which country was the winner!

France is number 1!

I admit, our subconscious may have played a little trick on us. In the end, one tends to opt for the familiar, which reduces the risk of getting cold feet. But honestly, France really does offer – almost – everything the heart desires. But I don't need to explain that to you. You wouldn't be reading this if you hadn't already decided on France, right?

We had often been to France before, had lived and worked there. Christian was, having spent several years going to school in Paris and therefore speaking fluent French, predestined for jobs in France. His first job after university was in France – back then without me, later ones always had something to do with France. So, it was inevitable that I would eventually end up in France with him. But those were work-related stays without self-determination over space and time. All in the north and all limited in time.

That was good schooling and preparation. By now we both spoke fluent French. We knew and liked the French. And when we were in Germany, we were often drawn to France on our holidays, but then to the south. Thus, over time, we had practically travelled the entire southern coast of France and had a rough idea where we would like it best. So, you see, we were biased.

So, what exactly were the aspects in the favour of France in our eyes?

To you, who are reading this book, I probably don't need to explain the reasons. You simply want it, it feels right, and that should say it all. But unfortunately, that's not how it works. Family and friends, to whom you later announce your decision to emigrate, want to know the motives. And you'd better come up with good ones so they can't unsettle you with their thousands of ifs and buts.

Here are our most important reasons for immigrating to France:

- France is part of the EU, and as an EU citizen, one can settle here without having to ask anyone for permission. There are no complicated, lengthy or even expensive immigration processes. Setting up a company as a European is not a problem.
- France is a highly developed country, and the level of infrastructure is comparable to that in our home country.
- France is a democracy and politically stable. Strikes and protests happen everywhere, and we were already familiar with those from the past.
- It has access to the sea, and even offers a variety that is hard to find elsewhere: the Mediterranean, the Atlantic, the Channel coast, each offering a different picture, so there's something for every taste.
- It is easily accessible. The Mediterranean coast has 3 major airports: Nice, Marseille, Montpellier. There are regular flight connections to all major European cities, and the flight duration is short. There is no time difference.
- The Mediterranean coast offers exactly the right climate. And it has dreamy beaches.
- The crime rate is reasonable.
- A language is spoken here that we could already speak.
- We already knew how life in France works and were familiar with French administration.
- And not to forget: the wine, the food…

The dice were cast; we wanted to go to the Mediterranean in southern France. Now all we had to do was "simply" find out which place would become our new home.

THE QUEST FOR THE PERFECT TOWN

On the French Mediterranean coast, there are three regions that offer an international airport. As previously mentioned, these are Nice, Marseille and Montpellier. It was important to us to be able to travel quickly to Germany, both privately and for business. So, we had to choose one of these regions. This decision was made quicker than you might think. I had expected that another Excel matrix would be necessary, but I was wrong. Nice and the Côte d'Azur were far too expensive for us. So, they were immediately eliminated. The landscape around Montpellier was too flat, and thus too boring for us.

So, Marseille it is!

Our choice of this region was chatted through for 5 minutes. We drew a virtual 1-hour radius around the airport of Marseille using Google Maps and were quite surprised to see that we could even reach Toulon to the east. To the west, we could reach as far as Arles. We were less interested in the interior of the country, we wanted to stay near the coast. In case you're also interested in this region, let me mention at this point that the reality looked a bit different. You can't drive from Toulon to the Marseille airport in one hour. We've tried it, it's not possible. Except maybe on Sundays at 3 o'clock in the morning.

Now it was finally time for an Excel spreadsheet again. We made a list of all the towns and villages that fell within this radius. Now we diligently collected information on the internet for all these places and filled them into our list. Of course, we had also set criteria here and prioritised them. In the first step, we were only interested in collecting facts such as population size, property prices, number of supermarkets, hospitals, doctors etc., to find out which places could theoretically be considered for us on paper, or rather, on the Excel sheet. For Marseille, we had selected individual *arrondissements*, such as the 8th *arrondissement*, which we treated as independent places in our list. This was work for the weekends, and even I found some enjoyment in it, although research is usually not my thing. We could even walk through the streets virtually with Google Street View and look around in every neighbourhood. At the end of this research phase, we had a well-filled database and a – theoretical – order of places that could be suitable for us as places to live. However, there are criteria that cannot be found out on the internet, such as charm, feeling at home, and last but not least, the actual price level. These now had to be completed live and in colour on site. And finally, my gut got a say as well.

We had booked a holiday flat in Bandol, right by the sea. For two weeks we wanted to explore all the places on our list intensively. The aim was to have found the perfect place to live by the end of these two weeks. Or at least something that came very close to it.

The task was to find out for each of these places whether we could imagine living there. What did it feel like to walk through the alleys? Was it clean? Were there neighbourhoods that were to be avoided at all costs? How much did parking in the centre cost? What were the prices in the restaurants? Were the restaurants open all year round? And so on and so forth. One place per day. No, it definitely wasn't a holiday, it was really hard work.

We quickly covered the west of Marseille. Fos-sur-Mer lay under an unbearable petroleum stench. I can't imagine how the people who live there can stand it. We had hardly arrived there when we wanted to leave again. And we did. Why waste time exploring a place you can't stand the smell of. Martigues was on the way back, we didn't even bother to look at it. We just assumed that it would stink there just as much due to its proximity to the Étang de Berre and Fos-sur-Mer. It was eliminated. Perhaps unjustly, who knows? It might have outdone all the others because of its unbeatable proximity to the airport. But is too much proximity such a good thing?

We had planned two days for Marseille. We already knew Marseille from previous trips to the area. But we had been tourists and – as tourists do – had only focused on the tourist highlights around the historic city centre and the port. As a potential resident, you have very different demands than a tourist. That's why the districts that the tourists appreciate so much were excluded for us from the start. But we didn't know the other *arrondissements* at all. We made up for this now and discovered that even in this million-plus-metropolis there were corners where life was quite pleasant, with surprisingly little city noise and even less crime. The 8th, 9th and 10th *arrondissements* held their own in our list. Especially the 8th had taken our fancy and led the list for a long time, until… well, until we found something better.

Anyone who knows the area a bit has probably also heard of Cassis, or has even been there themselves. Cassis is a dreamily beautiful little town. But unfortunately, many thousands of others know this too. Accordingly, property prices are set high. We could not and did not want to afford that. Not to mention the fact that in summer the town is overrun with tourists.

Aubagne was a very hot candidate on paper. It was located strategically perfect to Marseille and the motorway, had unbeatably good infrastructure and a pretty historic city centre. Property prices here were relatively low and there were countless property adverts for year-round rentals. So, was it perfect for us? Unfortunately not. It was not by the sea. But it remained on the list, and it held its own in the top ranks.

After a day's break, which we'd snuck for ourselves in Fos-sur-Mer, and which we spent stretched out on the beach, we decided to move on to Toulon next. We weren't familiar with the city. It had never enticed us for a holiday. On paper, Toulon seemed the next best candidate due to its good infrastructure, and we were curious to see how this French naval base would appear to us. In short, we didn't like it. Our gut instincts said no. We tried hard and spent an entire day trying to find the charming side of Toulon. There must be one, I don't want to do the city an injustice, but we found nothing to convince us.

So, we thought that having Toulon nearby and being able to use its infrastructure, without actually living there, could perhaps be an idea. So, we explored the surrounding area. Unfortunately, without success. We liked one small town, but it was too expensive. The next one lacked a beach, and another one further on had a beach but otherwise had nothing to offer.

Sanary is a small, sunlit town, which, for a few years, was the capital of German literature in exile. With the rise of Nazism in the early 1930s, a great number of German writers and intellectuals left Germany and settled in Sanary-sur-Mer. It has been a temporary safe haven for those whose lives were at risk in Nazi Germany. The playwright Bertolt Brecht, the writers Thomas Mann, Lion Feuchtwanger, Stefan Zweig and Arnold Zweig and many more sought and found exile in Sanary. We too fell in love with this town immediately. Unfortunately, despite all our good will and optimistic calculations, Sanary couldn't climb up our list. The infrastructure was simply too meagre.

Bandol was our base camp during these two weeks of exploration. We liked it here. We felt at ease here. We would have loved to keep our holiday apartment permanently, with its beautiful view of the sea and direct access to a small beach. But we didn't seriously consider it. A pure holiday resort was out of the question for us. We would be completely alone in winter. Not to mention, the flat couldn't be heated. Absolutely out of the question. And Bandol itself didn't make it to the front ranks of our list, because here too, the infrastructure was insufficient. In all these smaller places, it was the supermarket and medical care that were lacking. And what took Bandol out of the game for good was the omnipresent train, as the railway line runs very close to the town or even partly in it. As it could be heard at night, that was a no-go for us.

We could still vaguely remember La Ciotat. During one of our previous holidays in Cassis, we had driven through here once and a motorcyclist had crashed into the back of our car, denting our bumper and boot. We had remembered the town as not very appealing and were accordingly sceptical when we now came here to scout it as a potential place to live. Our surprise was all the greater when it pushed its way to the top of our list. The town centre was charming, the beaches were quite narrow, but numerous, and it somehow felt good.

At the end of these two weeks, we had a clear winner... Drumroll... Ta-daa!... La Ciotat! Followed by Marseille 8e and Aubagne.

I would like to point out here that this is our very personal selection. Connectivity and infrastructure were very important to us. You might have other criteria. Make your own list and explore the places that you're considering. Only you know what feels good for you. Or perhaps you're one of those enviable people who don't need a list at all and just let their gut instincts guide them. Even then, I still recommend that you do a minimum of preliminary research so that at least you know which places to show your gut.

The Shock

During our research tour through the towns around Marseille, we didn't just extensively explore all the places, but also found ourselves stopping in front of every estate agent's shop window that advertised rental properties. We wanted to get an idea of how many rental flats there were and what kind of space one could get for what price.

As we stood in front of another such shop window in Sanary, the estate agent came out and approached us. She clearly couldn't have much to do at that moment. We should come in for a moment and tell her what we were looking for. This felt a little awkward to us, as we weren't ready for this yet. We hadn't even decided on a place. So, we told her that we'd like to move to the area, though not until next year, and that we were currently on a research tour. Hearing our accent, she recognised we were foreigners and asked us where we were from. When she heard we were from Germany, she was absolutely delighted and began to tell us about the German artists who had lived here in Sanary in the 1930s. We finally had to rein her in to get back to the main topic. And then she asked us:

"So, you'll be moving here from Germany? Do you have a French income?"

We shook our heads in unison.

"Ah!" she said significantly, giving us a worried look. "That could be difficult."

Our faces were a picture of bewilderment, forcing her to elaborate. She handed us a sheet and said:

"We at ORPI require our future tenants to provide proof of French income at least three times the monthly rent. It's a must. And look here, it says you must provide the last three payslips and an employment contract. Also, the last two tax statements. And of course, these documents must be French; otherwise, we can't verify their authenticity."

Christian, sitting next to me, audibly drew in breath but forgot to exhale. The punch had hit home. I asked:

"How do we rent a flat if we can't provide these proof documents? We have enough financial means to pay the rent, even six months in advance if necessary."

Then an apparent lifeline came to her:

"You need a guarantor!"

"A guarantor?" Christian asked. Not because he hadn't understood what she'd said, but because he couldn't believe it. We had been out of the school or university age, when parents still need to vouch for you, for decades. And now we were supposed to find someone, preferably a French national, who would act as a guarantor for us. This person would then need to prove a sufficiently high income in our stead, provide all these beautiful proofs, and then in a worst-case scenario, pay our rent if we couldn't – or didn't want to.

"Have you no family members who could vouch for you?" she asked us in all seriousness. Well, we did have family, of course. But apart from not wanting to ask anyone for such a favour, they all lived in Germany and had German income. That wouldn't get us any further. And we didn't have anyone with a French income whom we could ask such a question.

She looked at us pityingly, slowly shook her head and said:

"Then it won't work, *désolée*. At least not with us."

The last part of her sentence made me prick up my ears. Did that mean this was not handled the same way everywhere? Were there estate agents who had a solution for this? So I asked her:

"What do you mean by 'not with us'?"

"Well, there are a few landlords who accept what's known as a *caution bancaire*. You have to deposit a certain amount of money in a bank account, which is tied up for the duration of the rental contract, and the bank provides the guarantee for any unpaid rent. When you find a rental property you like, you have to ask the agent if the landlord accepts this", she explained.

"How much would one need to deposit with the bank?", I enquired.

"There is no rule. The amount is freely negotiated between the tenant and the landlord. It can be between 6 and 36 months rent. On average, it's 18 months rent. But that's negotiable."

Now it was my turn to hold my breath. We thanked the friendly agent, who wished us a "*Bon courage*" as we left, and we half-stumbled out of the *agence*. We had something to think about.

If we assumed a monthly rent of 1,000 Euros to make the calculations easier, that would be 18,000 Euros, which we would have to deposit in one go. And it would sit there, uninterestingly and tied up, for as long as we lived in the flat, and perhaps even a few months beyond, until the landlord finally released the money. On top of this, at the signing of the rental agreement, we also had to pay the first month's rent, the agent's fee, and the standard deposit of three months' rent. That would put us easily at 23,000 Euros, which we were supposed to just conjure up. And the cost of the move wasn't even included yet. There had to be another solution!

Firstly, we decided to confirm this information. From then on, we didn't just stand in front of the estate agents' shop windows, we went inside to find out under what extraordinary circumstances they would rent a flat to us foreigners without French income. It turned out that one or two agents would indeed apply this *caution bancaire* in our case. So that was at least a feasible solution, even though we didn't like it very much, as we didn't want to have that much money tied up.

To our relief, we also found out that there were indeed agents who were fine with foreign income, as long as it was high enough. And we got the tip to try and rent directly from a private individual. Mind you, this advice came from an estate agent. However, it was one of those who thought it was *'impossible'*, and thus knew that he wouldn't be able to rent us a flat through his agency. Despite this, he was excited about our immigration project and thought it was great that there were people who wanted to move to "his" country. So, he thought long and hard about whether he could help us in some way. Finally, he scribbled "scloger.com" and "pap.fr" on a piece of paper and said: "Maybe you'll find something here. *Bonne chance!*"

We definitely needed both luck and courage now, and not just a little.

Just a note on this. In the meantime, we've learned that there's no legal basis for the documents actually having to be French. According to the law, foreign documents must also be accepted. The landlord or agent can request that the documents be translated into French. But the source of income can certainly also come from abroad and be proven with foreign documents.

This was already the case at the time we were looking for a flat. Unfortunately, it's just that as a prospective tenant, you don't have the power to assert your rights. If you point it out to an agent, well then, they just don't have any suitable flats available. Insisting on your rights doesn't get you anywhere here. If agents prefer documents from France because they can verify their authenticity, that's their prerogative, and it's understandable at that. You have no choice but to accept the situation as it is, and make the best of it.

The Flexible Interpretation of the Verb "produire"

Making the best out of it. Yes, but how? We were stuck. The estate agents had told us which documents they needed in order to let us rent a flat. In this, we had recognised a pattern. We realised that we could rule out several of the agents right from the start. There are very few independent agents in France, most belong to a group, or rather, a franchise. We had found that particularly the large franchise groups, which, much to our dismay, had numerous agencies, tended to have the strictest rules. Thus, all agencies of the groups Orpi, Foncia, and Fnaim were out of the question for us. There was no point even trying with them. What remained wasn't much.

Out of the few that were open to us, only a small fraction was willing to accept documents that were not in French. These were the ones we needed to find.

But there was another problem. We didn't want to go for that *caution bancaire*. We didn't want to have so much money tied up. What if we needed it? That could really only be the last resort. So, we needed an *agence* that would accept foreign documents, without additionally requiring this annoying *caution bancaire*.

However… at the time the rent would start, we would no longer have a valid employment contract. Our jobs couldn't be done from France or from a home office. We had planned to quit. We intended to become self-employed and had already started on the side. We had a company in Germany and were currently checking whether and how we could transfer it to France. This company had not been in existence for very long, and there were no annual financial statements or tax returns from previous years, which would have shown sufficient income. So, we couldn't use these as proof of income for the apartment hunt. We had enough financial cushion to survive for quite a while even without any income. We had calculated all that. Paying the rent was no problem. But without proof of income, we wouldn't get a flat. What now? Good advice was dearly needed.

For weeks we puzzled away. We tried to see if we could get a furnished flat with a one-year lease. But that wasn't possible either without income proofs. The exact same proofs were required for the one-year contracts, and the conditions regarding the income were the same as well. So that was no alternative. A holiday home, perhaps? And simply rent it for a long time? That wasn't possible either. Holiday homes can only be rented for a maximum of 90 days at a stretch. So, we would have had to move every 3 months. The rent would have blown our budget during the high season. And what was to become of our furniture and belongings during this time? We would have had to put them in storage. That would have been a solution, but we didn't really like it. We were going in circles. Over and over again we told ourselves, there must be a solution, we can afford the rent, and we will pay it. And over and over again we pulled out the sheets with the lists of documents that the estate agents had given us. We went through them hundreds of times to see if we had overlooked anything. It was exasperating. We found nothing.

As we sat once again frustrated and at a loss in front of these sheets, staring at the individual points, my gaze drifted away. Away from the list items towards the little sentence that was above the points:

"*Veuillez produire les justificatifs suivants*" it said there. *Produire*? Produce? We were supposed to produce the proofs? We laughed. We joked about it. Yes, of course, we would produce proofs, we would produce lots of proofs. We could produce anything. Give us a print shop, and we would produce tonnes of proofs. One crazy idea followed another. We got so carried away that we ended up laughing uncontrollably. We spluttered, we gasped for air, tears streamed from our eyes. The hyperventilation didn't stop us from producing more crazy ideas. There it was again, that word! Yes, we wanted to produce. And how! We wanted to produce tons. It went back and forth like this for what felt like an eternity until we collapsed exhausted onto the sofa. We couldn't go on. Okay, let's call it a day. We couldn't think clearly anymore anyway. How about a bit of telly?

These were not serious thoughts. We wanted to forget them. But we couldn't. In the following days and weeks, this terrible word *produire* kept cropping up. It haunted our thoughts. Neither of us dared to say it. Each of us thought, 'Couldn't we perhaps… But no, that's completely unthinkable!' Like cats, we tiptoed around the cream pot. Neither of us dared to say it first. We weren't "ready" for this step. And yet the thought stubbornly lodged in a corner of our brains, grinning at us cheekily from its corner.

Time passed. Our project continued to progress. In the meantime, we had put our flat up for sale – speaking of burning all bridges or all ships, that sort of thing – and two serious potential buyers had emerged. And these potential buyers had the audacity to ask us about our move-out date. Move out? Us? Um, when are we moving out? Um, we haven't given that any thought yet, ahem, um, when would you like to move in? In two months? IN TWO MONTHS?! Sh…! Take a deep breath! Don't panic! We'll figure it out. Somehow.

Should we now let the buyers off the hook, just because we still hadn't found a solution for our "provable" problem? Crisis meeting! It was time to say it out loud. I did it. We would produce the appropriate proof for these pesky estate agents. They practically left us no other choice. After all, we could present our employment contracts in their original form. Both were unlimited, had a sufficiently high salary and were far, far away from any probationary period. We wouldn't have to mention that we had already terminated them if no one would ask us. Christian's latest payslips were still "fresh" enough, they would do. The fact that no new ones would follow, we didn't have to mention if no one would ask us. Is withholding information already punishable? I know, I know… It was borderline. Very borderline from a legal point of view. But strictly speaking, not at all. They only ever asked about the past. The latest payslips, the last tax statement were requested. Not once was it mentioned that one had to swear an affidavit or somehow prove that one would still be employed at the start of the rental period. The only thing to do was to follow precisely the wording of these proof documents lists. Nothing more and nothing less. We decided to do just that. The rest was silence.

Yet, we should still get the opportunity to actually produce proof ourselves. How this came about, you will find out in the chapter "I Rent a Flat".

PART 2: WE MOVE

Seek and ye Shall Find – or Not

It stood before me like Mount Everest, the task titled "Renting an apartment". Indeed, I was really apprehensive about it. This task had been looming into view for several weeks now. I had been working on its predecessors like "Setting a date for viewing apartments" and "Scanning apartment ads and arranging viewing appointments" for the last two weeks. With moderate success. Setting the date was easy. Contacting the landlords and estate agents seemed to be all the more difficult.

I systematically combed through all possible property platforms and also the websites of the estate agents for suitable apartments. There were quite a few that we liked. For each of the advertisements in question, I had written to the provider with my prepared little text, in which I briefly introduced us and explained why we liked their apartment so much. In perfect French, of course. Each time I mentioned the date when I would be on site and asked for a viewing appointment.

Quite simply, they didn't think it necessary to reply to me. For some of the ads, I noticed after some time that the ads had disappeared. So, they probably weren't up-to-date anymore. Two at least briefly and succinctly answered "*C'est loué*", it's rented. The rest kept quiet.

Even repeated follow-ups by email and chasing by phone didn't help. Most of the time, the person responsible for the rental was just not there. They promised to pass on my message, and he or she would call me back later. This then unfortunately never happened.

The results were disheartening.
Contacted: 52
Viewing appointments: 2

So, I had two appointments. The first one was a private rental, which I had found on leboncoin, the French classified ads equivalent of Gumtree. The very friendly gentleman, Henri, was even kind enough to send me photos and the floor plan of the apartment. He was keen to show me the apartment, but he had to inform me right away that he had "*déjà un dossier dessus*" (already a file on it). I was so thrilled to have a genuine viewing appointment that I didn't inquire further. I would find out more about this *dossier* later on.

The second appointment was kind of a last resort. It was a furnished flat, but it could allegedly be adapted to the tenant's wishes and rented long term. As I said, pure desperation.

That was the state of affairs when our project plan kindly but firmly reminded me that I now had to book a hotel in Aubagne. Easy. I can book hotels. I just mustn't start thinking about why I was booking this hotel room and what I would have to do once I was there.

This is where a good project plan pays off. Because once it's in place and all tasks are defined, all that's left is to just go for it. No more pondering over the Why. Just do it. The only thinking that's still allowed is about the How and Who. How can I best solve this task? Who would be best suited to do it? Who can help me? All other thoughts about the whys and wherefores have already been thoroughly considered beforehand. That is – hopefully – before the project was launched. Now it's too late, we're already in the thick of it. And it helps one's own motivation, and above all, to prevent doubts from arising, if one does not think about why and for what reason one is actually doing what one is doing after the project has started.

Being married to a project manager, we naturally had a proper project plan. To organise the tasks of the project, we used an online task management system where we had created a board for our "Immigrating to France" project. For each task, there was a card on this board. When you clicked on this card, a window opened with the task's details such as description, duration, deadline, possibly a checklist with subtasks, etc. Every Sunday, we sat together and decided who should take on which tasks in the following week. This was the moment our noses ended up on the card. We said "noses", meaning that we assigned the card to one of us, thereby displaying a small profile picture on the card. So, if my "nose" was on the card, then I had to get through it, whether I liked it or not.

Somehow, my nose had ended up on the task "call estate agents". I must have been distracted at a certain point in our weekly planning. Phone calls! And me of all people! I'm a very introverted person, and I only pick up a phone under threat of physical torture.

At such a point – when you have to do something you really don't like – what helps immensely is the consciousness that you're doing it for the bigger picture, for the big goal, for the dream of living in the South of France. Believe me, this goal is so big that you'll leap over your own shadow. I don't mean that you should think about the why and the whys and wherefores (as mentioned above, you shouldn't be doing that at this point), but simply focus on the result.

At this point, I'll reveal my secret of what I did – and what you can do too – to maintain motivation and counteract doubts (and doubters): Visualisation. The best, easiest and most relaxing way to visualise is to watch a film that plays in the future chosen home. For us, it was "A Good Year" by Ridley Scott. The light, the wine, the music, the Provencal villages… It was like dreaming with open eyes. We couldn't get enough of it. Don't tell anyone, but Russel Crowe wasn't too bad either, at least as far as I'm concerned. I suspect my husband was more into Marion Cotillard, but I never asked him about that.

Another possibility is to consciously run a film in front of your inner eye every evening before falling asleep, where you see yourself having achieved the goal. You need to go into great detail and experience with all your senses how the future life feels.

When all else failed, we resorted to the ultimate secret weapon. Refreshing memories on-site and in colour for a short week or just a weekend and refuelling your motivation reconnects your consciousness with the dream, and you can then restart with new energy and motivation.

So I had made it through the round of phone calls. I didn't set high hopes on it anyway. My previous experiences with calling estate agents had taught me that only luck, catching one directly, could help. They would certainly not call me back. This twist of fate had at least brought me one more viewing appointment. An estate agent in Aubagne had given me a *rendez-vous* in his *agence* and promised to show me what he had if I came (did he doubt whether I would come?). So now I had 3 appointments. What a yield!

I packed my suitcase, especially comfortable shoes were a must, and headed for Aubagne. On the one hand, I was looking forward to the trip. Heading south in January, where potentially spring-like temperatures awaited me, was not such a bad idea. On the other hand, as mentioned above, I was quite literally bricking it about this Mount Everest. Not only do I not get on with just going up to strangers out of the blue, that alone would have been bad enough, but I also had absolutely no hope that the mission could succeed.

The first night in the hotel was terrible. The neighbours had arrived in the middle of the night and taken an eternity to settle in. The lamp at my bed had kept on crackling, even though it had been turned off long ago. Sleep was out of the question, probably also due to the task ahead.

My mood was accordingly when I stepped out the door that morning. An icy wind hit me. Wakey, wakey! There was snow! My car was coated with a thick layer of ice. I had to scrape. Without gloves. I had left them at home. What was that about spring-like temperatures? I couldn't feel my fingers anymore. In the car, I turned on the seat heating. Ah, that felt good. Always tucking a frozen hand under my bottom, I drove towards La Ciotat. That was where my first appointment was. The closer I got to the coast, the higher the temperature rose, as indicated on the dashboard of my car. Not that it went very high, but anything was better than sub-zero temperatures. The morning fog lifted and at last even the sun came out. I headed straight for the sea front promenade. I needed to see the sea. A parking space was quickly found, entirely out of season. Just cross the road and…

There it was, gleaming flat like a mirror in the morning sunshine. It looked as if the horizon was steaming, so the sun was absorbing the fog. The sea immediately captivated me. It always does. I had to get to the water, just looking out from the promenade was not enough. A quick glance at the watch, yes I still had a few minutes. So off with shoes and socks. The feet had to be allowed to play in the sand. And then to the spot where beach and sea said a gently splashing good morning. The water was crystal clear. You could see every stone and every fish. The little baby sardines sparkled in the sunlight. I couldn't stop my big toe from dipping into this delight. Icy, but so wonderful! 'Ah, linger on, thou art so fair!', came this thought from somewhere. Yes, the bay of La Ciotat with its offshore island "*Ile verte*" and the primeval-shaped rocks at its right end is so beautiful that you never want to leave. Take a deep breath of salty air. Ah yes. 'How nice it would be if I could find an apartment here.'

The flat I was now viewing was in the hills, towards the railway station. It was on the ground floor of a villa, you would probably call it a granny annexe. You couldn't see the sea from here. But there was a piscine, right in front of the terrace. Well, that was something! But we wouldn't be allowed to splash about here, that was reserved for the owner. Blast! The flat was a dark hole. And stuffed with dark furniture. When I asked to what extent something could be changed to our needs, I was told we could clear out and store everything we didn't need. And when we moved out again, we just had to put all back in the way it was. That was a non-starter then. Things could only get better.

The plan for my next two weeks in the south involved visiting every estate agent on my list. All those who had hitherto amiably ignored me, believing me to be in far-off Germany, were about to deal with me in person. That's why I had brought the comfortable shoes, after all. The goal was to march into every estate agency and secure viewing appointments for this week and the next. If I hadn't found our project exciting enough up to now, surely this was exciting enough, right?

Since I was already in La Ciotat and had the entire afternoon free, I wanted to start right here. But first, lunch. Until two o'clock everything would be closed anyway. I found a small *Crêperie* by the harbour. The sun was shining, and the terrace was sheltered from the wind; I could sit outside. Hooray! While waiting for my *galette*, I lifted my nose to the sun and dreamed. About what? You get three guesses.

To be able to live in La Ciotat, that would really be the best. During our research tour last year, we fell in love with this little town. At second glance, so to speak. It has a manageable size, is located right on the sea, and practically offers no interesting tourist attractions. When I say it offers practically nothing for tourists, of course that's only partially true. It does offer the sea and a few small beaches. And it offers proximity to the utterly overpriced Cassis and the bustling Marseille. The advantage of few tourist attractions is that it makes it a much better place to live. It does get quite full in the summer, but nothing compared to the busloads of tourists that stream through Cassis.

The large shipyard that once existed in La Ciotat, for which the city was famous, went bankrupt decades ago, and the city has since endured a tough time, but has recovered well. On the former shipyard premises, many small businesses have been established, specialising in the maintenance and repair of luxury yachts. These huge yachts belonging to oligarchs and sheiks are quite interesting for people like us to look at. Most importantly, business seems to be going well for these companies and bringing income to the city. And – a crucial aspect for us – it ensures that the city is lively all year round.

La Ciotat was therefore our top favourite as a future place of residence. However, we had observed over the past few months that not much was happening here in the renting market. There weren't many rental apartments, which didn't bode well for our chances. That's why, as a backup plan, we had added the further inland Aubagne. There were noticeably more property advertisements there, and we therefore assumed it would likely be easier there. But Aubagne couldn't really generate any enthusiasm in us. More about that later.

My small midday break and grace period were over. Now it was time. There was no help for it; I had to get through it. Anyone who knows me knows how difficult it is for me to do what I was about to do. I had to approach complete strangers without them knowing that I was coming. I had to address them in a foreign language, which, although I mastered it well, was still a foreign language. I would face excuses and rejections. And I would have to insist on getting an appointment with the *agent* in charge of the rental, preferably tomorrow. And preferably with viewings as well… I would rather disappear into the nearest mousehole. I felt sick! I thought the harbour promenade was spinning. Or was it me spinning? The next bench was mine; I needed to sit down briefly and collect myself.

'Okay, don't make a fuss now, girl. You have no choice anyway. So go on. Deep breath. There's the first estate agent, so get in there!'

Said, done. I gathered all my courage, put on my most charming smile and… as quickly as I was in, I was out again. Didn't hurt at all. The friendly *Monsieur* didn't even let me finish. As soon as I reached the part of my spiel where it became clear to him that I wanted to rent something, he interrupted me.

"*On ne fait pas de la location.*" We don't do rentals. I was going to hear this line very often. After the second or third time, I got it. At the next estate agent, I started with this question:

"*Est-ce que vous faites de la location ?*" Do you do rentals? That was good, but not perfect. Because the immediate counter-question was:

"*Saisonnière ou à l'année ?*" which translates to holiday or all year round? Of course, I didn't want to rent a holiday home. As I am capable of learning, I modified my question as follows:

"*Est-ce que vous faites de la location à l'année ?*" Do you do year-round rentals?

Now it was perfect. This proved to be very efficient. With a single question, I could instantly separate the wheat from the chaff. Few estate agencies dealt with something as troublesome as year-round rentals. Most focused on sales, which offered a larger commission, and they didn't have to constantly deal with complaining tenants. And those types of estate agents that dealt with holiday rentals only did that and nothing else.

Over the past few weeks, I had noticed several rental listings at Century21. This was a place where I could be sure I wouldn't be turned down. Indeed, I was in luck as the lady in charge of rentals was there, I only had to wait a few minutes, and then she had time for me. Her name was Monique, and she was the spitting image of our idea of a Frenchwoman. Perfectly made up, scarf casually draped around her neck, suit, high heels. I explained what I was looking for. At some point, she looked at me thoughtfully and asked,

"This seems somewhat familiar to me. Is it possible that I have received a message or two from you?"

"*Oui*", I replied with the friendliest smile I could muster. I had to resist asking why she had never deemed it necessary to reply. So, she had received my messages. All of them. What could one say to that? Probably nothing. I was left waiting in vain for some sort of apology. She brushed it off as though nothing had happened. Since prospective tenants are regarded as second-class citizens in France, and I was more of a supplicant, I had to grin and bear it. It was hard, but I was to be rewarded for it.

Monique had several properties in her files that she hadn't yet managed to advertise on the agency's website or the property portals due to lack of time. She was pretty sure there was something suitable for me. She wanted to put together a little viewing programme for me. Yes, she had indeed understood that I was only here for two weeks.

"*Pas de souci* – no worries, I get it. *On va vous trouver quelque chose*, we will find something for you", she reassured me.

So, I got a *rendez-vous* for the following Thursday. I had to be on time at the agency and park my car at the harbour. Not to forget to get a parking ticket; the *flics* frequently checked there. And then, if it was alright with me, she wanted to take me in her car, which would be easier. And oh yes, was I alright with that.

The whole conversation went by so quickly, and Monique had spoken in such a rapid staccato that I felt dizzy as I stood outside the door again. I felt out of breath, even though I hadn't run or spoken much. She had done most of the talking. I had had my hands full trying to follow her. But hey! I was going to be shown several flats next week. What I felt now could be described as hope.

Right next to Century21, I noticed something that had escaped me during my internet research. It probably wasn't classified as *immobilier*, which is why I hadn't been able to find it. Across the door and shop window was a huge sign with the faded inscription "*Ciotat Gestion*". Those who know that the term *gestion* means something like administration, and is often used in connection with rental apartments, will understand that this sign attracted me like a magnet.

In France, it is customary for estate agencies to not only broker rental properties, but also to manage the rental after brokering, i.e., to take over the so-called *gestion*. This means that the tenant has to address all concerns to the agency, not the landlord. It is also the agency that collects the rent and issues the famous rent receipts.

Could this place actually deal with property? It wasn't clear from the name. There are also other things that can be managed. A look in the shop window confirmed it. These were definitely apartments, all for year-round rent. So, I went in and asked if, besides *gestion*, they also brokered the apartments.

"*Mais oui bien sûr !*" a placid looking matron replied. What was I looking for? A 2-bedroom apartment in La Ciotat? No problem. But the fact that we wanted to move in only in March, that was a *grand problème*.

"But I think I could show you 2 apartments anyways. Do you have a moment?"

"Of course."

She shuffled back into one of the offices. Files were shuffled around, drawers opened and closed, keys jingled. Was she about to show me the flats right now?

"My car is just around the corner. Will you come with me or follow me?" That seemed to answer the question of whether it was happening right now.

Of course, I wanted to go with her. Since she offered, I would have been crazy to decline. I just had to wait a bit; she was going to move her car. Where it was parked, getting in on the passenger side was out of the question. She had just driven it a bit into the alley next to the office, which was actually designated a pedestrian zone. Yes, parking in La Ciotat was a real problem. I should definitely aim to rent a flat with a parking spot if I wanted to be here in the summer too. I made a mental note: flat with parking.

We turned a hundred corners, winding through the narrow streets and alleys of the city. I had long lost any sense of where I was when we finally stopped outside a large residential building, a so-called *résidence*.

"*Nous y voilà*", she said, stepping out of the car.

The building had seen its best days decades ago. The facade was crumbling, and the shutters hung by their sheer will in their hinges. I quickly took a photo of the street sign so I could check later where I actually was. Then I followed her inside the *résidence*. We squeezed ourselves into a tiny lift, which despite its advanced age took us up to the sixth floor. The hallway smelt musty. Who puts carpet in such a corridor? Finally, she stopped in front of an apartment door, knocked briefly and began to work on the three door locks. Then the door opened, and a tracksuit with a young man inside greeted us with a "*Bonjour?*" with a large question mark at the end.

"Ah, *Monsieur* is present, I didn't expect that. May we come in anyway?"

He grumbled something unintelligible like "*Mwuai*", the mumbled version of '*Oui*', and stepped aside. The tracksuit man was the current tenant. He was just packing. But we shouldn't let his *bordel* (chaos) disturb us, it couldn't be avoided when moving. So, we stepped over boxes and piles, the matron always leading the way, me trailing behind. The flat was actually not so bad. The dark brown living room didn't have to stay that way. There were two balconies, one facing forward with a very small glimpse of the sea, *un petit aperçu mer*, as the matron said, and one at the back. And there was a storage room too. Not bad. Clearly, we'd need to renovate thoroughly. The kitchen probably needed to be disinfected from top to bottom. But otherwise… When would *Monsieur* be moving out, I asked him. Even before he could respond, the matron said:

"You needn't worry, the flat will be free by April 1st."

"That's not quite optimal for us as we need a flat by March 1st. Is there any chance *Monsieur* could clear out a bit earlier, he's already working on it", I asked.

The tracksuit shook his head vigorously. "*Non, impossible!*" No, impossible. What else did he want to occupy himself with for so long? Half the flat was already packed.

I said I would think it over.

The flat was not bad, after all. It was the first that could potentially, with a great willingness to compromise on our part, fit or be made to fit. I wanted to keep it on my radar. If necessary, we'd have to store our stuff for a few weeks. We'd figure that out.

"*Pas de soucis*", replied the matron, saying goodbye to the tracksuit.

Now we zigzagged through the alleys again. I had the feeling she was intentionally avoiding main roads to confuse me. In the end, we even ended up in a pedestrian zone. Could we really drive along here, I asked her. "*Oui oui, pas de soucis.*" That seemed to be one of her favourite phrases. It was the only access to the house after all. And she didn't want to walk endlessly just to show me the flat. Finally, she squeezed her car between parked mopeds into a small space. We were in the middle of the old town, behind us the pedestrian zone, in front of us a church. But it was no longer active, now used for exhibitions. And as I peeked around the corner past it, I could see the sea. Could this be a flat with a sea view? Gosh, that warmed my heart right away.

The crumbling facade, however, didn't offer much hope. It was an old townhouse with small, crooked windows. The entrance door was right on the ground floor behind the mopeds. She led us into a dark, narrow corridor. From here, it was first up a few steps. How were we supposed to get furniture in here? You could barely turn yourself. Halfway up, there was a micro toilet, the kind you'd better reverse into. A few steps further up, on the other side, was the kitchen. Oh dear, I was lost for words. I'd never seen anything like it. The room was so low, I almost bumped my head. There was an old sink, an even older gas stove, and around it, wooden furniture had been built to maximally utilise all void spaces. All of it must be as old as the house itself. The original colour of the wood was unrecognisable. Mould was thriving in every corner. No, I couldn't move in here. Absolutely not. But for fun, I wanted to see the rest of the flat. You had to climb a few more steps before you got to the living room. And it did indeed have – one might almost call it a large – window with a sea view. To the right, you saw the former church, straight ahead parked cars, beyond that the promenade and the sea.

Directly beneath the window was a street, and to the left of the house as well. So, one could have driven here without the detour through the pedestrian zone. But well. This was anything but a quiet location! And hadn't she mentioned something about a balcony? Where was that? Oh, that little thing with the railing in front of the window, that was supposed to be the balcony? Well, you could probably stand on it with one foot. What about parking here, and was that under the balcony a garage, I asked her. Yes, it was a garage, but it belonged to the other flat. And where should we park, on the small square in front of the house? Unlikely. Yes, one would have to see, in summer that was of course a problem. But you could rent a parking space from the city at the harbour. Of course. That couldn't shock me anymore, I had already decided this flat wouldn't be it. Just for completeness's sake, let me mention that to get to the bedroom you had to climb another flight of stairs, it was located under the roof, of course, all without air conditioning. And for this hole, they demanded a whopping 800 Euro rent, utilities not included, mind you.

Back in the *agence*, she handed me a piece of paper with the documents I would need to provide if I wanted to rent the flat. The first of the two flats, not the latter mind you. I tried not to show it, but at least inwardly my jaw dropped. Not only was the letter size sheet filled from top to bottom with the list of documents, but also because thanks to the letterhead, I realised that this *Ciotat Gestion* was an agency of the Foncia chain. That wouldn't work. But *madame* didn't have to know right here and now. There was always the possibility that her flat would be the only acceptable one left, and then I'd have to negotiate with her. And talk about her list. I asked her if they belonged to the Foncia group, just to make sure I wasn't mistaken. "*Oui*", she replied. That was it for me then.

Why could it never work out with Foncia? You'll likely remember our research trip last year to find suitable places to live. During this tour, we stopped by several estate agents to inquire under what exceptional circumstances they might be willing to rent us an apartment. There were several agents who handed us their more or less long list of required documents straight away. Others instantly noticed from our accent that we were foreigners and asked if we had a French income. Without this, they wouldn't even show us an apartment, let alone rent us one. And Foncia was one of the latter. And we had no French income.

I don't want to bore you with describing every single flat viewing. I've merely selected the highlights. The rest of the week flew by with alternating estate agent appointments and flat viewings, interspersed with walks along the sea. One must have a bit of balance after all.

The agent in Aubagne, who had promised me that he would show me everything he had if I came, kept his word. I met him at his agency. Without first showing me the dossiers of the flats, he immediately grabbed the keys and off we went. I was to follow him. He on his moped leading the way, me trailing behind in the car. I felt like I was on a racetrack. He was constantly disappearing around the next corner, and I had to watch out incredibly carefully to ensure I didn't lose him.

When we finally arrived at the first *residence*, my nerves were shot, sweat trickling down my back despite the winter chill. And he had mentioned several apartments. Indeed, this was how it would be for 3 more properties. On the way to the third apartment, I noticed that the seat heating in my car was still on. I must have forgotten to turn it off the day before. How silly. No wonder I was sweating so much. Anyone seeing me at that moment would have probably wondered why the *Madame,* sitting alone in her car, was slapping her forehead with her palm. Luckily, no one here knew me.

The more flats I viewed in Aubagne, the more frustrated I became. Not only did I not particularly like the town, there was not a single flat that I liked. I had the impression that the agents were only showing me their leftovers, i.e. the flats that no one else wanted and that they had had in their files forever without being able to get rid of them. At some point, I plucked up the courage and asked one of them if it was possible that he was only showing me things he couldn't get rid of. He avoided answering directly, but eventually admitted it. It was indeed the case. The reason was that I wanted to rent the flat in about three months' time only. Normally, flats do not remain vacant for that long. When a good property became available, it was usually gone a few days later. No landlord waited for several weeks, let alone months, without receiving rent. It would be quite a coincidence if I could find something good under those circumstances.

One could safely call this a learning experience. We had assumed that we could handle our flat search in a similar way to what we were used to in our home country. First, you look for a new flat. Once you've secured it and the rental contract is signed, with a rental start in three months, then you terminate the old contract. Well, wrong assumption. That's not how it works in France.

If you are looking for a flat here and find one that you like, you rent it, immediately. Usually, you can negotiate a delay of a week or two with the landlord. However, the rental start should be as soon as possible. This means that you might have to pay double rent for up to three months. The only way to avoid this is to take a full risk and terminate your old lease before you have found a new one. If you then don't immediately find a new one, it means you have to store your stuff and move into a hotel or holiday apartment to bridge the gap. Depending on the availability on the housing market, this can drag on.

If you then know that the new landlord wants to see the last three rent receipts from the previous flat, you also understand that it is rather ill-advised to leave the old flat prematurely. The longer you then live in a hotel or holiday apartment, the older the rent receipts become, and a potential new landlord may ask questions.

So, I had to change my strategy. From now on, I would not insist so strictly on my move-in date but would choose a somewhat more Solomonic formulation such as "as soon as possible". If necessary, I was prepared to pay double rent rather than leave here without a rental agreement.

There's Already a File on It

Another learning experience was waiting for me in Aubagne. But not just that.

The appointment with Henri, the friendly gentleman who had even sent me photos and the floor plan of the flat, was here. I had successfully navigated to the entrance of the residential area with my GPS. It was a so-called *lotissement*, which is a residential quarter. In contrast to a *résidence*, usually a large block of flats, a *lotissement* consists of several detached or semi-detached houses. This *lotissement* was fenced off and the entrance was secured with a gate or barrier. Henri had told me that the barrier would be open and that I could drive in. But it wasn't. So, I tried to find his name on the intercom system. In vain. I couldn't find it. I had assumed that he would live here too, but obviously, he didn't. As I rummaged for my documents to find a phone number, a large, black Land Rover approached from behind and flashed its lights at me. Was I in the way? Probably. I was parked right in front of the barrier. So, I moved a little to the side and let it pass. The window on the passenger side was lowered, the driver, a friendly older gentleman, leaned over and shouted at me:

"*Suivez moi !*"

I was to follow him. We hadn't even introduced ourselves yet. Well, it probably wasn't that difficult. He knew I was coming from Germany. There was a car with German number plates parked at the gate at the agreed time. Not exactly a tough guess.

He drove slowly in front of me, signalled to me where I should park, and after we had both parked our cars, he came up to me beaming with joy. I immediately liked this man. And he liked me.

"At last we get to know each other", he said. "I couldn't believe you'd come alone. In your emails, it was always 'I'm coming', but I thought that was *'une faute de frappe'* (a typo). And now here you are, indeed alone. My wife was right after all. She claimed, '*non, cette petite dame* writes so well, there's not a single mistake, she wouldn't have made one there either'. I should listen to my wife more. She was right."

This torrent of words washed over me so unexpectedly, and I didn't get a chance to say anything, even if I had thought of something to say. He did ask me if I'd found the place alright, but before I could answer, he answered the question himself:

"*Mais oui, puisque vous êtes là*", of course, as you are here.

What was I to say to that? I simply responded with a charming smile. I didn't get much of a word in for the next half hour. He showed me the *lotissement* and, of course, the flat. Both were beautiful, everything looked clean and relatively new. The flat had large, double-glazed windows, a rarity in this area, was freshly renovated, had an accompanying cellar, and two parking spaces. And all this was to cost only 800 euros in rent. By local standards, it was quite a bargain.

As he showed me everything, he talked non-stop. I could only give him an occasional keyword. So, I learned not only the many advantages of this flat but also half his life story. He was a native Swiss, married for the second time. They lived just around the corner, just a bit up the hill. You could see his fence from here, but to get there, you had to take a detour. All this terrain here belonged to him, but it was far too big to manage, so he had sectioned off a part and built these houses here.

"Built yourself or had built?" I ask him.

"Built myself. At least for the most part. I had the windows done, and the electrics. Anything to do with electricity, I respect, I don't touch. But the rest… I prefer to do things myself, then I know it's done properly. French artisans, you know… *oh lala*… they're all no good."

I nodded understandingly and showed appropriate admiration. I liked it here. This was a little *havre de paix* (peaceful haven) in the middle of Aubagne. Who would have thought that there was such a place in this town? Certainly not me. This put Aubagne in a whole different light. Here, I could actually imagine living. Even more so with such a likeable landlord. I was already beginning to distribute our furniture among the rooms in my mind when he said this fatal sentence:

"Oh, my dear, how much I would love to rent you this flat. You seem so nice and reliable. But as I already told you in my email, unfortunately, I already have *un dossier dessus*."

"Already a file on it? What does that mean?" I asked, as I truly had no clue what he was trying to say and how that could prevent him from renting me the flat. So, I received the following explanation.

Landlords in France often take advantage of rental default insurance, in French *Assurance loyers impayés*. The reason for this is that it can be very difficult to evict a tenant once they're in the property, even if they haven't paid their rent over a longer period of time. For landlords, such insurance isn't obligatory, but many wish to secure their assets. Now, when a landlord seeks a new tenant, they must, in order to be able to benefit from this insurance coverage later if needed, submit the prospective tenant's documents to the insurance company before signing the rental agreement. If they don't do this in advance, their insurance coverage remains, but when they report a rent default to the insurance company, they must then submit the tenant's documents, which are then checked by the insurance company and, of course, can also be rejected as inadequate. These numerous proofs that are required of us when we want to rent a flat are actually just for this insurance.

As soon as someone has viewed a flat and stated they wish to rent it, they must submit a whole package of documents to the estate agent or owner. This is the so-called *dossier locataire*. Depending on the insurance, the requirements for this dossier can vary. One may only accept proof of income from a French employer, another may be a bit more flexible. I've already extensively discussed what documents belong in such a dossier elsewhere and don't want to repeat myself here. This dossier is then submitted to the insurance company for review. They thoroughly examine the prospective tenant to be absolutely sure that they can pay the rent, preferably for the rest of their life, so the insurance company never has to find itself in the awkward position of possibly having to pay out to their client. If the insurance company gives its approval, the rental agreement signing can proceed. If not, then it can't.

The rule generally is – exceptions may confirm this rule – that the first person who comes and has submitted all their documents gets the flat if the insurance company accepts them. At this point, it no longer matters to the landlord whether they prefer people who view the flat later. *Premier venu premier servi*, first come first served. Of course, the estate agent or owner will continue to show the rental property to new interested people, as it's possible that the first candidate could be rejected by the insurance company. Then it's good to have other candidates on standby. Out of fairness to these subsequent interested parties, they must be told that a *dossier* from a potential tenant has already been submitted to the insurance company. So, when you hear this phrase "*Il y a déjà un dossier dessus*" (there's already a file on it), it's clear to everyone that their chances of getting this property have just dramatically decreased. Some may even forgo viewing the property. I've heard of candidates with such perfect tenant dossiers that they have a free choice of rental properties. Yes, such people really do exist!

Well, we were not such perfect candidates. And dear Henri had to inform me a few days later, much to his regret, that the first dossier had been accepted and he could therefore not rent me the flat. What he didn't know at that time was that his insurance would have certainly rejected our dossier. But he didn't need to know that. I didn't want to destroy the positive impression he had of me.

We said our heartfelt goodbyes and I had to promise him that I would definitely get in touch as soon as we'd arrived in the sunny south. We absolutely had to come for coffee, then we'd meet his wife. And of course, he was eager to meet *Monsieur*, the man who sent his wife ahead to rent a flat. And who also had such trust in his wife that he was sure she would choose something nice. He was already fond of this interesting couple, although he had only seen half of it so far.

"*Je suis sérieux là, c'est pas des paroles en l'air*", he said, reinforcing his invitation. It was not meant to be empty words, he was serious. I replied, "*Moi aussi*". And so, both of us felt that we would see each other again soon.

THE PARADOX OF MADAME PINEL

Once upon a time, there was a minister, Madame Cécile Duflot, who had the commendable idea to create housing for less well-off tenants by introducing a law that subsequently bore her name, as is customary in France, the "*loi Duflot*". This law aimed to reward property owners with tax benefits if, in return, they allowed the rents they could charge for their apartments to be capped. We owe it to this rental minister that in France, there was, and still is, intensive investment in affordable long-term rental accommodation. The law was later renamed the "*loi Pinel*", as the minister who succeeded Madame Duflot, Sylvia Pinel, also wanted to secure an entry in Wikipedia and thus found it fitting to revise and reintroduce the law. This newer version, with some adjustments, is still in effect today.

One thing I can tell you straight away: As soon as you see or hear the name Pinel in a property advertisement or from an estate agent, you can forget about that flat. You can just run away and try your luck elsewhere. Why? It is precisely the conditions of this law that make renting such a flat practically impossible for us immigrants.

The following conditions must be met:
- The property must be rented for a long time (6, 9, or 12 years), and it must be unfurnished.
- The income of the tenants must be below a certain cap. This depends on the zone in which the property is located, as well as the number of people in the household.
- The rent per square meter is capped, again depending on the zone.
- The rented flat must be in an apartment building, must be new, or must have been completely renovated.

The prospective tenant of such a flat must provide the following proof documents:
- Proof of identity (passport, ID card, driving licence)
- Proof of residence (electricity bill, rent receipts, certification from previous landlord)
- Proof of activity (employment contract, extract from the K or K bis, copy of the *carte professionnelle*)
- Proof of income (tax notice, balance sheet, payslips)

According to the law, foreigners can also rent if they meet the conditions. In this case, foreign and foreign-language proofs such as a foreign tax notice must actually be accepted. In theory. However, the law also states that the landlord must check the documents before signing the lease and then submit them with his tax return. And this is where it gets difficult for us as immigrants.

Before your emigration, you may have paid taxes in the UK, now perhaps you have a UK pension or may even be self-employed. Then you will have a large part of these proofs in English, issued at best by a British authority. Neither the estate agent nor the landlord can nor will check this. And even if they could, they wouldn't want to. I have found that you are immediately sent away as soon as the agent realises that you are not French. A British pension notice? No, thank you. Come back with something French.

I was able to view one flat, nonetheless. I assume the estate agent hadn't been paying proper attention or didn't herself know quite how things were supposed to proceed with this "*loi Pinel*", which was still quite new at the time. The rent was fairly cheap at just under 800 euros, and the flat looked freshly renovated in the advert's photos. It was located in an unattractive residential area well off the beaten track, which seemed to me sufficient explanation for the low price. With all the previous difficulties in finding accommodation, I was grateful for every viewing. There was no mention of this *Madame Pinel* in the advert.

During the viewing, I wasn't alone. It was a kind of collective appointment, all the interested parties at once. Each new arrival was handed a piece of paper with a list of the *justificatifs* (proof documents) that would have to be provided if one wanted to rent the flat. It included everything from proof of identity, electricity bill, the last three rent receipts, a certificate of good standing from the previous landlord, all proofs of activity, to the French tax assessments for the last three years and the last three payslips with a salary of at least three times the monthly rent. And the prospective tenant had to prove that he or she met the conditions of the "*loi Pinel*".

When I asked her if a foreign income might do it, she didn't seem wholly opposed to the idea; it would have to be checked, provided – it goes without saying – that it was at least three times the monthly rent. Only, the very moment that this income met the estate agent's condition, it was too high to also meet the conditions set by *Madame Pinel*. Faced with this paradox, the agent looked at me with wide eyes, allowed herself to be distracted by another interested party the very next moment, and from then on avoided even looking at me. On my way out, I handed the sheet back to the assistant, telling her that I was very sorry, but the paradox of *Madame Pinel* unfortunately did not allow me to rent this flat. I don't think she understood what I was talking about.

I Rent a Flat

Monique was waiting for me outside the Century21 agency. As I arrived, she looked at her watch. I was unaware of any wrongdoing, so I asked,

"Am I late?"

"No, not at all, we're waiting for a *Monsieur, un Parisien*, and he just called to say he's delayed; he's stuck in traffic. Now I'm wondering whether we should just go ahead and start with the first viewing. Bad luck for him if he can't be on time."

She seemed not to like unpunctuality. Good for me that I was punctual.

"*On y va?*" she asked.

"*On y va*", I replied.

Said and done. Monique's march through the narrow streets of the old town matched the tempo of her way of speaking. The staccato of her high heels clattered on the cobblestones. I would break my feet trying to do that. We went right, left, across a square, through an alley, and then left and right again. At every corner and in front of every shop, we ran into people she knew. Despite the rush, there was time for a quick "*Bonjour, ça va?*" in passing, or even a few cheek kisses here and there. Then her mobile rang; the Parisian was on the line. He'd arrived at the agency but didn't know where to go. She tried to explain the way to the flat we were about to view. In vain. He couldn't remember all the rights, lefts, and straight aheads. She quickly turned on her heel, called out "You wait here" to me, and she was gone.

There I was, amid the hustle and bustle of La Ciotat's old town. I should probably have paid more attention to the map earlier; then I might have known where I was. Perhaps. Probably not, though. Like the Parisian, I hadn't taken note of all the rights and lefts and hadn't really paid attention to my surroundings. Instead, I'd concentrated on keeping up with Madame Speedy Gonzales. I expected her to reappear with the Parisian in tow five minutes later. But a quarter of an hour had already passed, and there was no sign of her. We hadn't taken that long to get here. What was going on? Should I call her? No, I wanted to wait a little longer.

Finally, I saw her coming, with a lanky young man in tow. As they came closer, she rolled her eyes towards the Parisian. "*Monsieur* had to park his car; he couldn't just leave it outside the agency." She whispered, "*Les Parisiens…*" and winked at me. He hadn't made a good first impression.

Now the lost time had to be made up. Monique leading, us following, storming through the alleys until we finally arrived at the market square. Right next to the market hall, she headed towards the entrance of the *Résidence Lumière*, a building that almost looked modern among the others on the square. However, despite what its name seemed to promise, the building was not a highlight. Staircase, first floor. She led; we rushed after her through the flat. It wasn't bad, and there was even a fireplace, although it no longer worked. The balcony looked directly onto the marketplace. If that's your thing. I barely had time to photograph all the rooms before she closed the window shutters again. On to the next flat. Or rather, back to the agency first, where we continued by car. I got to sit in the front; the Parisian had to squeeze in next to the child seat in the back. I probably don't need to mention the pace at which we headed to the next flat, do I?

What we were shown next must have been an artist's dwelling. It was an old cottage in the *Saint Jean* neighbourhood. Every room, or rather each little space, was painted in a different colour. And by colour, I mean vibrant shades of pink, blue, green, and yellow. It had something of a doll's house about it. Somewhat cosy, but all rather small. Towards the back, a staircase led down from the first floor into a small garden. From there, one could enter another tiny space on the ground level, which could perhaps have been used as an office or something similar. But it was only accessible from outside. At least we were allowed to linger here a bit longer than in the previous apartment. Had she noticed that we didn't like the last one? And did she now sense more interest here? Maybe. Our friend from Paris, at least, inspected every corner and crawled into every nook. When she urged us to move on, as there was still another apartment to view, he declared that he didn't want to continue. For him, the matter was settled. He wanted this one or none at all. It was perfect for him and his partner.

I got a slight shock. What if the last apartment didn't appeal to me, and I had wanted to decide on this one? Monique must have seen my train of thought. Turning to him, she said:

"Ok, I'll make a note of that. But since *Madame* came to me first, you must wait to see how she decides." A wink at me, and that was it. Paris would have to wait.

We girls got back in the car, and five minutes later, we were at our destination. Then it occurred to me:

"How does the Parisian get back? We just left him standing there."

Monique hesitated for a moment, then shrugged her right shoulder and said:

"*Pff. C'est un grand garçon* (he's a big boy)."

Monique had, presumably intentionally, driven me along the seafront promenade before turning right into a smaller street. We had passed two cross streets, turned left into the third, and parked not far from the junction.

"*Nous y voilà*", she said, here we were.

The *Avenue du Dauphiné* had nothing of an avenue about it; it more resembled a bumpy track. The potholes had been patched year after year with blobs of asphalt, and there was no pavement. Rubbish bins stood in colourful disarray in front of the driveways. The building with the number 16 looked shabby, a windowpane at the top was shattered, and a shutter dangled dangerously in its hinge. The rolling gate to the driveway had to be shoved open with considerable muscle and did not look as though it could be locked at all. Grass was growing on some of the balconies. Scepticism was warranted. But the location!

We entered a dark stairwell. The stairs were made of those old speckled black-grey-white terrazzo tiles that are made to last for centuries. It was old, but clean. After three half floors, we stood before a dark brown apartment door. My excitement soared. Why had Monique looked at me so mischievously from the corner of her eye while searching for the right keys to unlock the three door locks? Finally, the door opened.

Inside, there were also terrazzo tiles, but lighter. Monique rushed ahead and opened all the shutters. To the right and left of the corridor were two rooms, *les chambres*, the bedrooms. The bathroom and toilet – as usual, separate – were newly tiled and renovated. There was even a new double-glazed window in the bathroom. It was the only one of its kind in the flat. The kitchen was also newly tiled. A kind of worktop had been installed, under which one could probably slide one's furniture or appliances. There was a small balcony in front of the kitchen, perfect for drying laundry. And then we came into the living room.

Monique struggled with the old wooden shutters, and when she finally opened them, the southern sun flooded the room through two large, full-height corner windows. Dust particles danced in the sunlight. At that moment, I knew this was my flat. I had made my decision. But I said nothing, I wanted to see everything first. Again, that sideways glance from Monique. Did she suspect something?

We would have to refurbish, the old wallpaper had to be removed. But it wasn't the first time we'd done something like this. And the rattling, single-glazed windows? Who cares, we would be living in the South, they could not deter me. The flat above us was rented, as was the one below. Only the ones beside us and the top one were empty, currently being renovated. That should fix the problem with the broken window. So, all good.

I stepped onto the balcony that ran around two sides of the living room. Somewhere out there had to be the sea. Yes, if you stood on tiptoe on the bottom rail of the balcony fence in the far corner and stretched as tall as you could, you could glimpse a little blue sliver. More important to me was that the balcony faced the backyard, and there was a lot of space up to the back of the next building. You could park down in the yard. There was also a cellar, but Monique couldn't show it to me as she didn't have the keys. I went through all the rooms again, taking as many photos as possible so I could remember all the details later. This time, she allowed me time to do so.

Monique came over, looked at me appraisingly, smiled and said,

"*Alors? On fait le contrat* (So? Shall we make the contract)?"

"*Oui*", I answered.

"*Je le savais* (I knew it)", she said.

I had expected that she would now give me an appointment for one of the coming days when I should come to her agency to sign the contract. But I was mistaken. When she said "Let's make the contract", she meant right then. So, we drove back to the agency. She slapped a standard rental agreement on her desk, and I had to unpack all my documents, which I had wisely been lugging around all day. She already knew from our first meeting to expect German documents. No problem for her. Numbers look the same in German as they do in French. So, I laid out copies of our passports, tax assessments, my husband's employment contract, and the last pay slips on the table. I felt a little uneasy. Would she accept all of this? She grabbed the stack, flicked through it, found the right numbers on the pay slips, and – was satisfied.

"*Tout a l'air bien*", she said – everything looked good. "Ah, the rent receipts are missing. Do you have them?"

In France, it's customary for the landlord to issue a receipt for the rent once it's received. Often, even today, the rent is paid by cheque, which must be mailed once a month. A few days later, the receipt is also sent by post. And you must keep these rent receipts carefully. They are the only proof that you've paid your rent properly. And if you want to move, you must produce the last three most recent rent receipts to be able to rent a new flat. That was the case here as well. I explained to Monique that we were currently living in our own appartment and therefore didn't pay rent at all. And that in Germany, it was common to pay rent by standing order, and the landlord didn't issue receipts. You had the transfers as proof that you had paid. She found this extraordinarily interesting. Different countries, different customs. The subject of rent receipts was off the table.

Without me asking for it, she offered that the landlady would waive one month's rent if we renovated the apartment ourselves. Nothing could please us more. We had to renovate anyway. And we knew that the result would likely be more satisfactory if we did it ourselves. This special arrangement was noted in the rental agreement. While she filled out the rest of the contract, she said:

"Fill out two cheques while I'm doing this. One for the agency's fee and one for the amount of one month's rent for the reservation."

I was taken aback. Cheques? I didn't have any cheques. At least not French ones. Was it going to fail because of this? I cleared my throat and said:

"*Désolée*, but I don't have any French cheques. We don't have a French account yet."

"Oh", she said and thought for a moment, left the office, and I heard her speaking with a man in the next room. The discussion went back and forth for a while. Then she returned with him, introduced him as her boss, and now he interrogated me. All the questions Monique had already asked me, I had to answer again. I was sweating. Monique chewed nervously on her lips. Finally, he turned to her:

"*T'as vérifié* (have you checked)?"

"*Oui*", she nodded

"Ok, then we'll make an exception and do this by transfer."

When he said those magic words, a huge weight had been lifted off my heart. Monique also seemed relieved. The rest was a breeze. I had to sign what felt like a hundred times, initial every single page. I received the agency's *RIB* and the order to make two transfers immediately when I got home. She emphasised precisely the amounts I had to transfer.

A *RIB*, or *relevé d'identité bancaire*, is a small slip of paper with the bank account details. These RIBs are often required in France, and they serve as proof that you are a respectable citizen and proud owner of a bank account.

"And do make sure to do it immediately, it's very important, or your *réservation* will be cancelled!" she hammered into me.

I promised her. At this point, I thought I had reached the goal of my dreams. The rental contract was signed. She had accepted my documents as they were. So, everything was perfect. I was just about to get up and say goodbye to her.

"Oh, and before I forget", she said, "I'll need a certification from your husband's employer that he will work from here. You'll send that to me by email as soon as possible, yes?"

Honestly, I have no idea how I managed to control my facial expressions at that point. A certification from the employer! From the same employer where my husband had handed in his resignation not quite six months ago, and which was due to expire at the end of this month. Bloody hell! I had come so smoothly this far. Monique never asked me about it, and I didn't volunteer anything. She simply assumed that since I had shown her this German employment contract and these German pay slips as proof of income, that this must be the job that would continue to support us. It was logical, wasn't it? I had let her believe that. That was our plan, our strategy to avoid that nasty *caution bancaire*. Those who don't ask questions shouldn't get any answers. (I refer again to the chapter on the flexible meaning of the word *produire*).

What now? My brain was working feverishly. What should I do? Until now, I hadn't really had to lie, just left out a few details. I had to decide in a split second. If I told her the truth now, she would know that I had left her under a false impression about this job. Turning to the *caution bancaire* at this point was no longer possible with her. Then I could forget about this *agence* and never have to come back again. I had no other property in sight. I would have to leave empty-handed and start looking for a new place another time, but without Century21. The seconds ticked away, I had to answer her. The questions pounded in my head 'What if they catch you? What if she got the idea to call and ask? How likely was she to do that without speaking German? What was the worst that could happen?' She would reject us, declare the rental agreement null and void, blacklist us at Century21. Could she report us? No idea! Did I have a choice? No, surrender was out of the question!

I would simply delay "producing" this certification as long as possible. If possible, I would just forget about it. Maybe she would forget it too. And if not, well, we would find a creative production solution. And if she later found out that my husband was no longer employed there, we could always claim that the employer had since terminated him, but I couldn't have known that at the time of signing the rental agreement. Or something like that…

"*Oui oui*, as soon as possible", I said, smiling, and hoping she didn't notice the quiver in my voice.

That was now truly and finally everything. As I gathered my belongings, she occupied herself with her papers, and I took the opportunity to breathe deeply and discreetly. Phew, that was close!

She reminded me once more of the transfers. Mentally, I was already bracing myself, expecting another nasty surprise at any moment. My nerves were as taut as steel cables. I just needed to get out of here with my contract and put some distance between us. Finally, she wished me a good journey home and "*À bientôt!*". With the very last of my energy, I managed a smiling "*Merci et au revoir*" and beat a hasty retreat.

Loaded with paper, my head pounding, my nerves frayed, but full of happiness, I left the *agence*. I stumbled across the street as if in a trance. To get out of the agency's line of sight, I staggered a few more meters towards the harbour. There, my so-called composure left me. I plumped down onto a low wall. Evening had come. I looked up at the sky, tinged pink by the setting sun, and – let the tears flow.

La Ciotat, here we come!

WE HAVE SOMETHING TO TELL YOU

It could no longer be concealed. In recent months, we had aroused suspicion in one or two of our friends through our dubious behaviour. They wanted to know what was going on. Up to now, we had avoided talking about our emigration plans. First of all, we wanted to be quite certain that it would work out. And that we wouldn't lose our nerve halfway through. It is rather embarrassing when you first trumpet grand plans and then have to backtrack, admitting that you have lost your nerve.

Now that I had brought the rental agreement from La Ciotat, there was no stopping us. Now we could and wanted to tell everyone, whether they wanted to know or not. In one of the many books and seminars we had attended during our decision-making phase, we had learned that within every person you meet, someone might be hiding who could help you realise your big dream, or who had done something similar themselves and from whose experience you could benefit. Even with the best of friends, you often wouldn't know this, it was said. Perhaps someone had the right contacts or was simply so thrilled with our plan that they would spontaneously lend us a hand. This clever guru called it finding your "WHOs". We thought that our enthusiasm for our grand plan would infect others, sparking a similar enthusiasm in them. If not for our plan, then at least for forging grand plans themselves.

So, we set out in search of our WHOs. Who can help us? Who has done it before? Who knows someone who knows someone? And so on and so forth.

Before they would find out from someone else, we had to inform our family. We knew that this would be the hardest task. Particularly, the thought of talking to my mother filled us with dread, me more than my husband. Quite logically so, since his relationship with her was not burdened by the past, and he could merely give her words the meaning that their literal sense conveyed. With me, it was different. I heard – and still hear – not just the words and their meaning as they would be in the dictionary. I also hear that undertone, which can vary depending on voice tone, ranging from sarcastic, offended, reproachful, or contemptuous, and which tells me more than the actual words do. My husband doesn't hear any of this and always wonders why I am getting so upset again. She, on the other hand, knows precisely that the subliminal messages are reaching me. And unfortunately, she knows that I know that she knows.

When I left home at 16, I discovered that I had a personality – and a will – of my own. From then on, I was allowed to be me. Physical distance has always helped me greatly in that regard. The more kilometres, the better. But every time I meet her in person, I am taken back into the past by Doctor Who. When she asks me at breakfast, "Have you already seen a comb today?", something clicks, and I'm 14 again. It takes all the self-control in the world not to blow a fuse. In recent years, we had found a form of peaceful coexistence based on a distance of 500 kilometres, carefully navigating around dangerous topics in conversations, just to avoid clashing.

The topic of emigrating was not one of those innocuous, harmless subjects. Quite the contrary.

This was not the first time we were moving to France. The last time, we had clashed terribly and shown little understanding on both sides. It even led to months of silence at one point. Several years had since passed. We had found jobs again in Germany and apparently settled down with the purchase of a flat near Stuttgart. Our relationship had normalised in recent years, and we spoke regularly and visited her as well.

Such a visit was scheduled for this weekend. Friday afternoon heading east with thousands of commuters, and Sunday evening back with the same commuters again. The many hours on the motorway were, as always, torture. But what wouldn't one do to ease one's guilty conscience? On Saturday, we took her out for lunch at a charming restaurant.

This was part of our strategy. We hoped that in public, the scene would be less dramatic. Yes, I think we were genuinely afraid of her reaction. During the meal, each of us waited for the other to begin. We should have coordinated better beforehand. When the empty dessert plates stood before us, Christian finally plucked up his courage.

"We have something to tell you", he began and paused, probably expecting me to take over. But I didn't intend to. In this mother-daughter relationship, my diplomatic skills regularly missed the mark. He was much better suited with his straightforward approach. So, I nodded encouragingly. He took a deep breath and continued.

"We're going to... um... move to the South of France..." The word 'emigrate' wouldn't pass his lips; it sounded too harsh, 'moving' was much milder.

"I thought as much!" was my mother's response. Our tension eased. We had not expected her to take it so lightly. She bombarded us with a thousand questions about the where and when and why, which we answered joyfully. Could it really be this simple? I began to doubt. I knew her better. And indeed, this was not the real reaction. That came later.

When Christian and I were alone for a moment, I whispered to him not to leave me alone with my mother for the rest of the weekend. He looked at me, surprised.

"Why? It's going great!" He really had no idea.

"Just promise me!" I demanded. He looked at me, bewildered, but promised.

However, nature is cruel. At some point in the evening, it required my husband to leave the living room where we had been sitting with my mother. I would have liked to have gone to the bathroom with him. But that would have been too noticeable. I held my breath... I didn't have to wait long. She knew that he would only be gone for a few minutes.

"Now you're doing this to me again, moving so far away!" she sobbed.

Ah, there it was, the real reaction. And why did she apply the second person singular "Du", which we have in German language to address the one person in front of us? It sounded as though I was solely responsible.

"No one is doing anything to anyone here", I tried to keep it calm. Where was Christian? What was he doing so long in the bathroom? "We're fulfilling our dream. Can't you be happy for us?" I added.

"But then I won't see you at all!" Her voice was dripping with reproach.

"Not less or more than now", I replied truthfully. Even now, we only visited her on her birthday and at Christmas. We believed that a fit retiree could occasionally get on a train to Stuttgart to visit us for a change. But she didn't. Because we didn't invite her, she had once said in her defence. She had never had to invite us; we came on our own. But let's leave that aside.

"Fine!" she concluded our short conversation as Christian – finally – came back. And this small, short "fine" was delivered with a whole wagonload of reproach, of which my unsuspecting husband once again noticed nothing. He looked at me, questioning. One look from me was enough. Lovingly, he put his arm around me and pulled me close. His way of showing that he understood. He grabbed the TV guide, hastily flipped to today's page, scanned the options, and found a harmless comedy to suggest. The evening was saved. I gratefully squeezed his hand.

I should mention here, for the sake of completeness, that the years following our emigration put a heavy strain on my relationship with my mother. I made an effort to call her regularly. But these efforts were fundamentally one-sided. The telephone line seemed to allow conversations in only one direction, from France to Germany, but not the other way around. The periods between my calls grew longer with each call, as I put off the unpleasant task until it was no longer defensible. We were in a downward spiral. My hesitation caused frustration in her, which she promptly took out on me when I did eventually get back in touch. At some point, I changed my strategy.

After another phone call, during which I felt miserable because I had once again been bombarded with accusations, I asked Christian to be present during future calls. He didn't have to say much, just give a sign that he was listening. That helped. In his presence, she controlled herself. And he provided distraction with flippant remarks as soon as there was a risk that she might lapse into complaining mode. That's how we handle it to this day. And it works.

Several years and moves later, our relationship is stably friendly. I suspect that a certain learning process has taken place. Just as all our friends and acquaintances have come to accept that we will probably never settle down, and if we should do one day, not in Germany, so she has eventually reduced her expectations to a minimum and now enjoys any sign of life from us. But perhaps I should delete this chapter from the book to keep it that way.

Some time later, we were invited to Christian's parents. His brother and his wife were also supposed to come. It was the perfect opportunity to distribute our news to a broad audience. We did not expect enthusiastic cheers. At best, indifferent shrugging of shoulders.

Our relationship with Christian's parents was not easy. Staying at home during his studies was certainly not his wisest decision. And falling in love with that girl from the east of the Republic on holiday surely didn't help either. Especially not that he then drove "over there" every free weekend – in the car that his father had bought him. And he spent his pocket money, paid monthly by his father, on petrol. Why couldn't he fall for a girl from the neighbourhood? Why did it have to be an "Ossine" (girl from East Germany)? But all the opposition, whether subtle or direct, helped nothing; he remained faithful to the girl.

After graduating, he sought distance. His first job took him to Northern France. So, distance seemed to do him good, too. As long as he had this job, even when the factory closed and he was brought back to the German headquarters, everything was mostly fine. He seemed to have a model engineering career ahead of him. The Ossine, who had since moved in with him, could be endured. She had to be accepted, whether they liked it or not. It would take decades for something like a friendly relationship to establish itself between my in-laws and me. Now we get along very well.

But before that happened, years went by in which we did quite a lot of nonsense. In their eyes. Well, admittedly, with the necessary distance, some of it we no longer count among our finest moments either. The first attempt at self-employment met with incomprehension. The word "childish nonsense", which his father used at the time, stuck with Christian for years. When he fell on his face, he harvested mockery and heard that un-word of the year frequently. Now married, we sought distance together.

Over the last few decades, we had remedied the mistake as best we could. Christian had one so-called decent job after another. He even made it to Managing Director. Only to ask himself, "I've come far, but what am I doing here?" But it had contributed to normalising the relationship with his parents. Until he told them that he would be going into business for himself again. The reaction was similar to before. But this time it didn't bother him as much. That was the starting situation for the evening of our announcement.

Again, we waited until the main course was over. If we were to be thrown out then, at least we would have something good in our stomachs. This time we had carefully coordinated beforehand who would say what when. Christian wanted to take it on himself.

"We have to tell you something", he began, just as his father stood up to carry something into the kitchen. As he stood, he stopped and replied:

"Why, do you need money?"

We hadn't counted on that. An embarrassing silence spread around the table. Some were silent expectantly, waiting for us to request financial support. Others were silent in embarrassment because they probably felt how inappropriate this reaction had been. And we were silent in astonishment because we simply didn't know what to say. We hadn't intended to ask for money. We didn't need any.

Helplessly, Christian looked at me. His eyes asked, 'What should I say now?' Our lovely preparation was completely ruined. Now improvisation was required. This was dangerous territory. Our next words would determine what our relationship with his parents would look like in the future. And whether there would be a relationship at all.

His father remembered that he had wanted to take something to the kitchen and did so now. Something else urgent to do must have occurred to him, for he did not return soon. Christian audibly exhaled. Had he been holding his breath until now? Possibly.

Finally, we were asked what it was we had wanted to announce. And so we told them. And we were not particularly surprised that the reactions were more than restrained. That was more like what we had expected. At least there was some understanding for the region we had chosen. They loved France, especially the south. That was a basis on which we could build in the future. We patiently answered all the questions. And left it to Christian's mother to inform her husband in detail later.

When we got into our car at the end of the evening, we took a deep breath and sat silently for a while before I started the engine. During the half-hour drive, we had plenty of time to evaluate the reactions. Except for the small incident, it had actually gone as we had expected. The sunny South would have to sort out the rest over time for us.

I wanted to break it to my best friend Anna as gently as possible. We had met at work, come to value and like each other. That was now 7 years ago. We knew everything about each other, confided everything to one another, comforted each other, and together grumbled about our jobs and bosses. But there was one thing I hadn't yet told her.

We regularly met after work at our favourite pizzeria. There, we could sit for hours, chatting away. Much to the chagrin of the owner, who would sigh softly when he saw us coming. But he liked us, somehow, since he always treated us to a deliciously sticky Amaretto. Sometimes we'd bring our colleague Mark along, to get him out of the house. He had the greatest pleasure in just listening to us talk. He was a silent guy, contributing only a word or two now and then to the conversation. We'd grown accustomed to having to coax every response from him, and he enjoyed it wonderfully. Most of the evening, he would just listen devoutly to our chatter, and we would ignore his presence.

It was the same today. I no longer worked at the company, and we didn't see each other as often as we used to. I had actually wanted to be alone with Anna, but she didn't know that. She had spontaneously invited Mark to come along as they were leaving the office. He never needed much convincing. He was always up for a good pizza. And he liked being with us. For a while, I even suspected that he was a little bit in love with me, but we never talked about that, of course. We had once teased out what kind of women he liked. We wanted to help the eternal bachelor find someone. What he described was my spitting image. Anna had noticed it and winked knowingly at me. But the description was such that it could have fit a thousand others. And he added, in the end, that the best ones were always already taken. Poor chap.

So, Mark was with us, too. That was alright. He'd find out at the same time then. This time I couldn't wait until dessert. We never made it after the hefty pizza. And the news was burning on my tongue so much that it had to come out quickly. So, I blurted it out as soon as we sat down and placed our orders.

"I have something to tell you", I began, as usual. Four eyes looked at me expectantly.

"Are you pregnant?" Mark asked, grinning cheekily.

"Are you mad?" Anna scolded Mark, not noticing his sly grin, taking his question seriously. She calmed down immediately when she saw his grin.

"Come on, spill it", she turned to me again.

"I would if you two chatterboxes would let me speak for a moment", I laughed.

And they both joined in, for Mark was anything but a chatterbox, and he knew it. And he knew that we knew.

Suddenly, I was nervous about how they would take it. Our friendship would have to continue at a distance. Would it endure? I stammered and hesitated, searching for the right words. But I found none. Not only did I not find the right words, but I found none at all.

"Um", I said and cleared my throat. Anna looked at me sideways.

"Spit it out! It can't be that bad", she said, nodding encouragingly.

"Alright." I took a deep breath. "We're moving to the South of France, near Marseille."

Bam! That hit home. Both looked at me with big eyes but said nothing. Were they still breathing? I wasn't sure. They were completely still. Now it was my turn to look at them expectantly. What would they say? Suddenly, they both took a deep breath simultaneously and let out a perfectly synchronized, bewildered "What?!".

I had to laugh. The two of them looked so comical.

"What's there to laugh at? That's not funny at all!" Mark burst out.

Anna had already started smiling some time ago, which had turned into suppressed giggling. After Mark's outburst, she couldn't hold it in any longer and laughed out loud. Mark and I looked at each other. What did that mean? Was I being laughed at? By Anna? No, there had to be another explanation.

"What's there to laugh at? That's not funny at all!" I repeated Mark's words with feigned horror.

And that made her laugh even more. We couldn't help but join in. When the pizza was brought by a bewildered-looking pizzaiolo, we could hardly stay in our chairs and had tears in our eyes. And we didn't quite know why we were laughing.

The pizza brought us back to earth. There was something right in front of our noses that demanded our attention. And we were hungry for pizza. A good remedy to help calm down after a laughing fit. With full mouths, Anna then explained why she had had to laugh so much. She had appeared tonight with a similar intention. She too had something to tell us. Something very similar, even. And she had worried so much beforehand about how to break it to us, how we would react. And now I had stolen her show, as it were. Before she could even start, I had blurted out my 'I have something to tell you'. So, she had had to wait. And I had tried her patience as I didn't know how to begin. When it finally came out, she first thought she had misheard. Or that I was playing a joke on her, because, against all odds, I had caught wind of something. Then she realised I was serious. And her worry about how – at least I – would take her news, was blown away.

"And what is it you wanted to tell us?" I couldn't contain my curiosity any longer. This long preamble was driving me crazy.

"We've bought a little house in Sardinia", she finally blurted out.

Now she looked at us expectantly. And now it was our turn to widen our eyes and open our mouths in amazement.

What can I tell you… Only with Anna and her husband could we exchange experiences, for they were going through something similar, encountering the same problems, only in Italian, and having to find some creative solutions like us. Among our friends, acquaintances, or people we met from then on, there was no one else like that.

Here are some examples of reactions that we were privileged to experience:

"You've gone mad!" (this was the most common)

"How will you live down there?" (and a thousand other questions that we had not even asked ourselves yet)

"Yeah right, one can always dream." (delivered with that condescending smile that means, you won't really do it)

"You can't have it all." (not fans of big dreams?)

"With the Frenchmen? How on earth did you come up with THAT idea?" (with great horror in their eyes)

"Wow, I'd never dare to do that." (this at least showed some admiration, and we therefore made it our favourite phrase)

"Well, YOU can do that, you don't have children." (little did they know, there are schools in France too)

"You're not serious!?" (yes, we are!)

"You can't do that, you'll be so far away!" (Yep!)

…

And so on and so forth.

In the beginning, expressions of disbelief prevailed. As it slowly became apparent that we were serious (e.g., when we sold our flat), the reactions then increasingly turned to doubts about our sanity and doubts in general.

Since our open communication at best garnered admiration and astonishment on the credit side, but a lot of doubt on the debit side, we would probably do things differently today. One has enough self-doubt about such an endeavour, without having to deal with the doubts of others. Not that we wouldn't tell anyone, but we would probably choose very carefully and only tell a very small number of people. Just those directly concerned (family), and good friends, from whom one can at least expect moral support.

Flat Handover

The past few weeks had been hectic. Our flat sale was entering its final stage. Removal companies had to be approached. We needed to decide which pieces of furniture were going to move with us. A substantial clear-out was in order. Time had flown by until this weekend in February – the date for the handover of our new flat in La Ciotat!

No, not the actual move-in, but simply the handover first. We had taken two days off to extend the weekend and planned to use this time for renovating so that all we would have to do on the actual moving day was putting the furniture in place, and we'd be done. One can dream, right…

We had loaded the boot of our car with work clothes and shoes, wallpapering table, paintbrushes and rollers, paint buckets – as they are much cheaper in Germany than in France – we even packed our small balcony table and two chairs, so we had something to sit on. After an overly long drive south, we fell completely exhausted into our beds at the Hotel Croix de Malte late in the evening. We hadn't noticed anything about the hotel, so weary were we. We had managed the check-in procedure almost half-asleep.

So, the surprise was all the greater when, the next morning, we went down for breakfast and were led into the courtyard by a cheerful young woman, to be seated at a table beneath a large plane tree. The air was pleasantly mild for a February morning. The morning sun played with the leaves and cast playful lights onto the tabletop. The aroma of coffee and fresh croissants filled the air, and they soon arrived at our table. We were alone. The other guests were probably still asleep. As we indulged in freshly squeezed orange juice and warm buttery croissants, the *patron* came by. These people must have a knack for appearing just when you have a mouthful of a big bite of croissant and crumbs of the same stuck around your mouth.

"*Tout va bien ?*", he asked.

"Hmmm!" we mumbled.

"*Allemands* ?" – Germans?

"Hmmm", we answered again. How had we given ourselves away?

"*Vous parlez Français ?*" he asked.

"Hmmm", we did for the third time, and nodded.

He introduced himself as Pierre, and if we needed anything, we should just tell him. Did we mind if he made himself comfortable at the table over there? He would surely not disturb us. We had no objections, of course. Why would we? He made a good impression. Had we not known better, we would have taken him for a sailor. He wore a faded, stretched, blue-and-white striped T-shirt and old jeans, cut just below the knee. Accompanied by the obligatory flip-flops, called *tongs* here. His age was hard to pin down; he was not old, but not young either. The sun and the sea – and perhaps a *petit rouge* or two had etched deep laugh lines into his face. His upper arms looked as though they could effortlessly row a fishing boat from Marseille to Algiers if need be. It was evident, he was in the mood for a chat. As soon as the first of us, which is always my husband, had finished his last croissant, he made a new attempt.

Were we here on holiday, he wanted to know. My husband then explained that we were moving to La Ciotat and had come to renovate our flat. At this, Pierre's eyes widened in astonishment. He could hardly believe it. Sceptically, he looked at each of us in turn.

"Why on Earth La Ciotat, and not something lovely like Cassis or Sanary or what do I know?" he wanted to know.

"Because we like La Ciotat better", I said.

"Really?" he asked, doubtingly, and continued, "But the foreigners always want to go to Cassis!"

"Not us! We're not pensioners; we still want to do something."

His features then brightened. He made an "Aaah!" and nodded. If that was the case, then it was a different matter. He wasn't fond of those foreign retirees, these Germans and even worse these English. They were just coming to take advantage of the French health insurance system. They hadn't paid in anything, but now they wanted everything reimbursed, *ces profiteurs*! They could do without them in La Ciotat.

I had apparently struck a nerve. He now told us about his hotel. It was a difficult business. One never knew whether a year would be good or bad. Planning was impossible. He wanted to do it for a few more years and then retire, then it would be only him, his boat and his dog. We looked at each other. A boatsman after all! We chatted until a glance at the watch told us that we had to hurry to make it on time for our appointment with Monique at Century21. Oh dear, and she couldn't stand unpunctuality one little bit. We leapt from the breakfast table. Without a detour to our room – we could brush our teeth later – we rushed to the *agence*. Luckily, it was not far from the hotel.

At precisely 10 a.m. and not a second later, we burst through the door of Century21 *agence*. The receptionist greeted us with a raised eyebrow. We were told to take a seat for a moment; Monique would be with us shortly. "Shortly" was very relative here. Monique was on the phone. We heard her speaking, initially patient, but the longer the conversation lasted, the more annoyed she seemed.

"Is that her?" Christian whispered to me.

I nodded in reply. His eyebrows twitched upwards, and his eyes twinkled mischievously. He had received a comprehensive description of Monique from me and was surely eager to meet her.

Finally, it seemed as if the conversation was nearing its end. We winked at each other and stared intently at the door to Monique's office, expecting it to be flung open at any second, with Monique storming out. But nothing happened. We looked at each other in surprise. The minutes passed. Christian cleared his throat to get the assistant's attention, reminding her that we were still waiting. She hesitated, stared at us uncomprehendingly for a moment, and we stared back. Then she jumped up and hurried into Monique's office.

Barely two seconds later, the door flew open, and Monique rushed towards us.

"*Oh mon Dieu! Monsieur et Madame Such !*" she exclaimed, once again mispronouncing our name, as all French people seem to love doing. The phone call had so consumed her that she had forgotten about us. She was embarrassed. She, who valued punctuality so highly, was late.

"Please excuse me… I don't know what to say… Have you been waiting long… surely you have been waiting long… *Oh mon Dieu!*" she gushed.

"No big deal", we laughed.

"Follow me", she said, once she had regained control.

We followed her into her office. Now that she had composed herself, the official greeting could take place.

"*Madame Such*, nice to see you again", she said, shaking my hand. Then she turned to Christian and seemed to notice him for the first time.

"*Monsieur Such !*" she continued, almost surprised. "How lovely to finally meet you! I was beginning to doubt that you even existed."

"I've heard a lot about you", he truthfully responded, with the same twinkle in his eye.

"He's rather nice!" she said to me, her voice and eyes filled with mischief.

"*Mais oui, je sais*", I answered. Yes, I knew.

We continued in this playful banter for a while. When she heard that we had come just for the weekend and wanted to start renovating right away, she said:

"Then let's not waste any time. Do you have the *attestation d'assurance*?"

"*Assurance*? Which insurance?" we asked in unison.

"Ohhhh!" she drew out. "Didn't I mention that? You must take out contents and liability insurance for the flat from today, the handover day."

We looked at each other. She hadn't told us that. She was clearly aware of this, so she made a concession:

"Actually, I'm not supposed to hand over the keys without the *attestation* from the insurance company. But you know what, there's an insurance broker next door. Go there, take out the insurance, and get the certificate. Then after lunch, we'll meet at the flat and do the handover."

This wasn't our usual way of taking out insurance. Normally, we would take time to compare. But here we had no choice. It's sink or swim. Or to put it another way, no insurance certificate, no flat keys. We therefore resigned ourselves to the inevitable.

That we would spend so much time on the flat handover, we had not anticipated. The appointment with Monique was at 10 o'clock. She had always been so hectic with everything else. So, we had thought we would be done with her by 11 at the latest. In the afternoon, we had already envisaged ourselves pulling down the wallpaper in youthful optimism. Now we were to go to the insurance broker and then have a leisurely lunch, before finally beginning the actual handover at 2 pm. How long would that take? We could probably write off the day. We wouldn't get to the renovations today. Oh well, things go a bit slower here in the South. Best to start getting used to it right away.

I was incredibly curious about what Christian would say about the flat. I had viewed it alone, made the decision immediately, and signed the rental contract right after the viewing. There had been no opportunity for even a brief consultation, as I had been with Monique the whole time. I had only been able to send him photos from the hotel in the evening. But by then, it would have been too late for any objections. So, he had had no choice but to confirm that he liked it. Anything else would have only brought him trouble; he knew that. So, I was accordingly nervous now, as he was finally going to see it in reality. Of course, he had repeatedly and continually asserted – even to others – that he trusted me and that I would have chosen something nice. But did he mean it? Now I would have to wait until the afternoon to find out.

We had some time until lunch, so we decided to go back to the hotel, catch up on brushing our teeth, and then park our car in front of our new flat. *16 Avenue du Dauphiné*. Woohoo, what a strange feeling! We would be doing this often from now on. Although, we would actually be parking in the courtyard then. We didn't dare do that yet, even if the courtyard gate didn't prevent us from driving in. There would be time for that later when we had the keys and had become official residents. At the very least, we wanted to carry all our renovation materials into the flat today. And maybe there would still be time to rip a few strips of wallpaper from the wall. Even if it was just to have started.

Christian looked around excitedly. He had not seen any of this before. I watched him. I knew that the building from the outside did not make a particularly good impression. Would he be alarmed? At least he didn't show it. I led him from our soon-to-be-new-home on the shortest path to the beach. I wanted to impress him with the short distance. It worked. He was blown away.

"Wow! We'll be on the beach in 5 minutes!" he said enthusiastically.

"And how about we now go and look for our new favourite restaurant?" I suggested. No sooner said than done. Studying the menus, we strolled along *Boulevard Beau Rivage*. We hadn't gone far when we saw *moules frites* chalked up on a board. Mussels! Oh yes, that's exactly what we needed now. And the tables were just a few metres from the water. There were free tables in the front row. Yes, we had to try this.

We got a table near one of those patio heaters and could imagine, with our eyes closed, that the sun's rays were warming us. It was February, and we were sitting on the terrace. The waves lapped right beside us; sometimes the water even splashed to our feet. The sun sparkled on the water. We breathed in the sea air deeply. We ate fresh mussels. And it wouldn't be long before we could do exactly this every day if we wanted to. Was this real? Or were we dreaming?

2 p.m. Finally, finally, finally! Monique was already waiting for us in front of the gate.

"Ready?" she asked, looking expectantly at my husband. She too was aware that he was seeing the flat for the first time today. How exciting! It almost felt to me as though I were seeing it for the first time myself, but this time through his eyes.

"What do we do if he doesn't like it?" Monique asked me with a twinkle in her eye.

"He'll like it", I replied. "He has no choice."

"You see, that's what always happens to me", Christian lamented.

We all laughed.

While Monique looked for the right key for the front door, it was flung open from the inside, and a lady with a stiffly teased-up hairdo and grey little suit virtually ran into us.

"*Pardon, excusez-moi*", she whispered, and was past us in the same instant.

"*Oh pardon*, may I introduce you to your new neighbours?" Monique called after her. She only glanced briefly over her shoulder before disappearing around the corner.

"Hm…", Monique said, "Your new neighbour from below."

"*D'accord*", we replied. Okay, that wasn't exactly the best first impression. It could only get better.

Inside, Monique was back to her old self. She put her form for the *état des lieux* – the handover of the flat – on her clipboard and dashed through the rooms, ticking boxes and making remarks. We barely kept up and had no idea what she was writing down. She switched on all the radiators to test if they were working. She operated all the light switches, to no avail. She looked for the main switch, found it finally outside in the corridor behind a locked cupboard door, opened it with a screwdriver, and switched it on. Nothing. We had no electricity. The landlady had let the electricity contract expire. Well, we just had to trust that everything worked. We were to inform her later if there were any problems.

Now, quickly down to the cellar. She hadn't been able to show it to me during the viewing because she didn't have the key. A steep staircase led down into a dark, dusty and cobwebbed dungeon. The individual cubicles were numbered, and in front of the only door, whose flimsy slats probably wouldn't have withstood a forceful kick, she stopped. Was this to be our cellar? Really? It looked as though a bomb had gone off. On two dented red barrels labelled "*Emballage Marine*", lay a roughly carpentered wooden plank that filled the right side of the room and might once have served as a worktop. On this – let's call it a tabletop – lay an indefinable wooden frame, torn-open boxes with leftover tiles that hadn't found a place in the bathroom and kitchen, remaining styrofoam panels from the bathroom ceiling, a torn-open package of plaster whose contents had distributed a fine powdered flour dust all over the cellar, and an old broom that had apparently never been used in this room.

Another wooden plank had been installed on the back side under the small window from one wall to the other. It rested on the right on the aforementioned plank and on the left on a wooden trestle. And on the left wall was another, slightly shorter wooden plank, resting on a similar wooden trestle.

Directly next to the entrance on our left stood a massive wardrobe, its mirror shattered, the wood scratched, and splattered with paint. It was locked. What secrets might it be hiding? Leaning against it was what must have once been our dining room door. From the ceiling dangled a mixture of cobwebs and strands of black, elastic adhesive that had loosened over time, convincing the insulation panels that had once clung to the ceiling to obey gravity. They were now scattered on the wardrobe, table-tops, and floor. Some of them had been leaned against the wall by someone in a desperate attempt to keep the cellar passable, and they now waited there, hoping for the tidying-up fairy to take pity on them.

"*D'accord!*" Monique groaned after several seconds of horrified silence.

"Okay!" we responded, audibly exhaling. At home, we had our own cellar full of tools and all those things that are usually stored in a cellar. We needed a solution.

"How about a different cellar? I saw an empty one back there", I suggested.

"*Non, pas possible*", Monique replied. Each cellar belonged to a specific apartment. Swapping was not an option. What to do?

"I'll keep the cellar key for now", she said after some thought. "The landlady should clear it out."

She promised to deposit the key in our letterbox so we would have it available on moving day, and we could have the removers take our things down to the cellar.

The meters were read, and the readings recorded on the form. The keys were counted, and since she didn't know which key fit which lock, she tried them all out.

Half an hour later, she was finished and presented us with the completed form. She went through each room with us again, explaining what she had noted. In the process, we learned a fascinating new word: *vétuste*. It means something like obsolete, battered, and appeared almost everywhere on the form. She explained to us that there were specific terms for the condition of rooms and fixtures. And *vétuste* was the lowest level; it doesn't get worse.

Well, it could actually be worse. A property could, of course, be *délabré* – dilapidated, ready for demolition. But then it would no longer be habitable, and by law, it couldn't be rented. A landlord or estate agent would probably be very careful not to describe a flat's condition as *délabré*, as they would have to laboriously restore it to a habitable state before renting it again. That might be why, as a tenant, I have never encountered a condition worse than *vétuste*. What mustn't be, can't be, if you understand what I mean.

The countless *vétustes* on our form might have been discouraging at first glance. Renting a flat where everything is described as outdated is not particularly encouraging. But this little word *vétuste* is, strictly speaking, the tenant's best friend. Yes, really! Because when one moves out of this flat one day and has to perform such an *état des lieux* again, the condition cannot have deteriorated. It was already at the lowest level. Whatever one has done, however much one has used up the flat, worse than *vétuste* is impossible. What one has to be wary of, conversely, are terms like *neuf* – new – or *peinture fraiche* – freshly painted. When moving out later, one must return these parts of the flat in precisely this condition. That creates work.

So, one day, when moving out, we would have nothing to do but sweep through once. Just as well.

Now, all we had to do was initial all the pages, write our "*lu et approuvé*" on the last page, and sign underneath. She handed us the keys.

"*Bienvenue !* – Welcome!", she said, bidding us farewell and rushing out the door.

Thus, we became the proud tenants of our new flat at *16 Avenue du Dauphiné*.

We stood in the empty living room. Was this really happening? It was so surreal. We looked at each other and grinned. We had a flat, we would live here! Now the celebration broke loose. We fell into each other's arms. Tightly embracing we jumped around the rooms like lunatics. Let the new neighbours think us mad. Weren't we, in a way? We finally came to our senses. Now I had to know.

"What do you say?" I asked, holding my breath.

"Hm… I don't really know… it will probably have to do", Christian replied, his voice hesitant. But his twinkling eyes and broad grin said something entirely different.

We fell into each other's arms again and stood that way for minutes. My eyes were already filling with tears. When I looked up at him, I saw that he was not faring much better. We had done it!

We brought our renovation materials into the flat. Should we really start today? Or would we rather celebrate? We opted for the latter. Instead, we wanted to start earlier and more energetically tomorrow. But we used the remaining daylight hours to measure all the rooms and draw plans. This flat was much smaller than our current one. Which of our furniture would we be able to place? Certainly not all of it.

A call to the EDF, the French electricity supplier, gave us hope that we could expect electricity this weekend.

The way back to the hotel was not very long. So, we decided to leave the car at our – yes, our! – flat and walk back. Like a newly in love couple, we strolled arm in arm along the promenade. We were on cloud nine. Passers-by smiled at us, an older woman turned to her even older husband, but so that we had to hear:

"*Regarde les amoureux* ! – Look at the lovers!"

We were almost startled by it. But the old couple laughed, and he patted his wife on the behind, saying:

"You were once so in love with me."

"Yes", she replied, laughing, "but today I would very much like to swap with the young lady."

We didn't hear what the two continued to say but hoped that they hadn't gotten into an argument because of us. A few weeks later, we were to learn that we had caused no harm.

Back at the hotel, we were already expected. Pierre, the owner of the hotel, wanted to know if everything had worked out and if he could now count us among the *Ciotadins*, as the inhabitants of La Ciotat are called.

"Ah, I don't even need to ask. One can see it from a mile away. You have *bananes* in your face!" he grinned.

"Bananas in our face? What does that mean?" we asked him, puzzled.

"Oh, you don't know that expression? *Avoir la banane*, you don't know? Well, look in the mirror, and you'll understand." With that, he made a sweeping motion from left to right in front of his mouth with his index finger, which could indeed have been a massive grinning banana. Now we understood him.

"I've been waiting for you… I've put together a little *dossier* for you", he continued, and handed us a folder with a theatrical bow, as if serving it to us on a silver platter. "You'll need this", he added, and disappeared into his office before we could even say thank you. The next morning, we found out that he had been doing business at the town hall. And since he was already there, he had asked if there was some sort of welcome information brochure for new residents of the town. They had then handed him everything that was of interest. And he had now presented this package to us with a puffed-up chest. We didn't know what to say. That was really nice. Of course, we had already gathered most of it ourselves, but we didn't have to tell him that. The fact that he had thought of us touched us.

This evening, we wanted to celebrate. We had overcome a massive hurdle. The search for an apartment had been nerve-wracking. Now, the joy of bringing it to such a successful conclusion was even greater. It had to be commemorated fittingly. We put on the best we could find in our small suitcase and made our way to the old town. Our destination was a small but fine restaurant on *Place Esquiros*. We had found the business card on the hotel's counter and then studied the menu online, our mouths watering in anticipation.

Place Esquiros was a tiny square, dominated by the *Chapelle Saint-Joseph*. Apart from this church, there wasn't much else here. Time-worn townhouses surrounded the square, cobbled streets, and the simple cast-iron tables and chairs of the small restaurant, still gathered against the wall; it was not the season yet for eating outside. We were early, typically German. But at least it secured us the best table in the restaurant. And the waitress didn't mind that we sat down and ordered an *apéro*. The rest would take a while. We were in no hurry. Quite the contrary! It gave us an opportunity to reflect on the day and begin decorating our new apartment – virtually, of course. The notes with the drawn room plans were still in my handbag. Time flew by until the waitress brought us the menus. Now, my notes had to disappear so we could focus entirely on dinner.

We quickly chose the meal, as we had already picked out what we wanted to eat while studying the online menu earlier. We were especially curious about the starter. Both the name and the creative composition had intrigued us. And finally, it arrived: *Foie gras façon crème brulée*! Combining France's most famous starter, *Foie gras* – duck liver pâté, with its most famous dessert, *Crème brulée*. *Eh voilà!* The result was heavenly bliss. *Foie gras* in a terracotta dish, coated with a layer of sugar, caramelised with a blow torch just before serving. Toasted bread, some salad, a few fruits scattered seemingly randomly on the plate – that was it. We couldn't get enough of it.

When we'd ordered the main course earlier, the waitress had asked whether we wanted our salmon well done or pink. That was new to us. We knew about cooking meat to different degrees, but fish was surely different. It had to be cooked through, didn't it? We asked, puzzled, and she explained willingly and with an indulgent smile that salmon could indeed be left glassy inside, making it more tender and juicy. People ate salmon tartare, where it was completely raw. We shouldn't worry, as long as it was fresh fish it would be fine. And her husband, the chef, knew what he was doing. We wanted to try. Now, as the first bite melted on our tongues, we knew we never wanted to eat salmon any other way. It was a revelation.

My husband has a habit of starting at the bottom part of the menu when selecting potential restaurants, always checking what desserts are on offer. He's a self-confessed chocoholic. If there's no chocolate dessert on the menu, we can't go there. He makes no compromises, no matter how tempting the rest of the menu may be. Well, as you might have guessed, we wouldn't be here now if he hadn't found something chocolatey on the menu. And he found not just something, but one of his favourite desserts: *cœur fondant au chocolat* – a warm chocolate fondant with a liquid core. The crowning glory to a life-changing day.

Full, happy, and content – and rather tipsy from the generous Rosé – we staggered back to the hotel. Life is so good!

Hard Work

Our future home office, adorned with pink floral wallpaper, was far from what one would envision as a workspace. Brown water stains around the window hinted at potential problems. The beige-brown marbled wallpaper in the living room bore the traces of every tenant from the past thirty years. Pale spots revealed where pictures had once hung. A large dark stain marked where a tube television had once stood, and delicious grease marks highlighted the places where heads had leaned against the wall while sitting on the sofa. Even the surfaces of the doors and windows were covered with colourful wallpapers, framed with golden painted wooden trims. Only our future bedroom was relatively neutrally decorated, with once-white wallpaper, jazzed up with a pink patterned border. So, the wallpaper in the office and living room had to come down before we moved in. We decided to warm up by starting with the smaller room, the office.

The floral wallpaper had once been soaked under the window. Not only had it received decorative brown water rings, but it had also detached itself from the wall so far that only goodwill had held it in place. That was a good starting point. Buckets of water, washing-up liquid, a sponge, and a scraper quickly laid bare large areas. The thin wallpaper was of the cheapest sort and barely put up a fight. The gold-framed pink fabric on the inside of the room door had to stay as it was for now, as did the royal lilies on the outside. There would be time for door painting later. By lunchtime, we were done in the office. This gave us hope. If things continued this way, we could strip down all the wallpaper today. We ordered takeaway pizza, our first lunch in the new flat. Yes, in the flat! It was raining today, and a cold, unpleasant wind was blowing. Our future balcony table was now standing in the living room, serving as a temporary dining table.

Now it was a matter of dividing our forces. While I repaired the damaged spots in the office walls, Christian attacked the wallpaper in the bedroom. This one was of a somewhat firmer variety and resisted somewhat. I had long finished my hole-patching work in the office when Christian began on wall number three. Together, it went better. A flying switch. I filled holes in the bedroom; he tackled the living room wallpaper. My task was quickly done, so we could work together again in the living room. Christian had just managed to remove the wooden decorative trim that had formed the top edge of the wallpaper, all around.

If we had hoped to continue at this pace and finish all wallpapers today, we were sorely mistaken. The beige-brown monstrosity in the living room was a different beast from the flimsy paper in the office. It was thick, and in places with the brownish pattern, even thicker. Soaking it took an eternity. And what on earth had they used to glue it? It seemed like the wallpaper was meant to hold the masonry together, not the other way around. If you tried to lift the wallpaper from the wall with a scraper, a brownish, papery layer would stick to the wall in places. This had to be soaked again, then scraped off millimetre by millimetre. Finally, we resorted to a hob scraper with a razor blade to peel this papier-mâché strip by strip from the wall.

We were sweating; the moisture from soaking the walls made the air inside feel as humid as a sauna. Outside, it was raining. The windows were steamed up. Why on earth was it so dreadfully warm in here? Could all this heat really have come from our physical exertion alone? Suddenly, the penny dropped. Christian had gone to the toilet and, on autopilot, switched on the light. That it was actually working hadn't even registered with him at the time. EDF had switched on our electricity without us even noticing. And yesterday, during the flat handover, Monique had turned on all the radiators to test if they were working. Without power, they naturally didn't. So, they had stayed on, and were now heating us up quite substantially. Proof that they were working was certainly provided. We rushed to turn them off and to open a few windows. Ah, much better!

Every metre of the living room wall that we painstakingly exposed brought new surprises from beneath the wallpaper. The walls here had holes, as if struck by a machine-gun salvo. There were wall plugs of every type and size. Even wooden wall plugs. Square wooden blocks hammered into the wall, with a small screw hole in the middle. We had never seen anything like it. Above the door, the plaster was crumbling from the wall. The absolute pinnacle, however, came when we stripped the wall facing the kitchen of its wallpaper. There, wonderfully centred in the middle of the wall, was a spot the size of a grown man's fist, filled rather poorly with a rubber-like, semi-transparent material. It didn't look very trustworthy. Its surface was sticky. As if to test whether it would fight back and attack us, Christian prodded it with his scraper. It gave way… fell out on the other side of the wall… and now granted us a view into the kitchen.

Well, at least we now knew that the walls here were made of decent bricks. At least, where there were no holes.

The living room wallpaper occupied us well into the night; we skipped dinner. We abandoned the hope of finishing painting all the rooms that weekend. Just before midnight, we returned to the hotel, dragged ourselves into the shower, and collapsed dead into our beds. The wallpaper had won; we were defeated.

The night had been too short. Our arms and hands ached from yesterday's unusual exertions. We only had today left; tomorrow we had to go back. All the moaning and groaning was of no help; we had to persevere. We had neither strength nor energy left, but we were highly motivated. We at least wanted to finish the office and the bedroom so that the furniture could be positioned correctly as soon as we moved in. We started again in the office.

While I was still masking the sockets, door and window frames, Christian had already begun painting the large surfaces. It was raining again today, so we couldn't open the windows, or else the rain would have come in. In no time, the panes were misted up. A tropical climate prevailed in the room. We worked in silence; we didn't have the energy for many words. And they weren't necessary. We each knew exactly what we had to do. Christian with the large paint roller for the broad surfaces, me with a small roller or brush for the corners and edges. That's how we had always handled it, and it worked well. My husband is more a man for rough work. The fine details are not his thing, and he can never do them well enough for me. We both know this and have come to terms with it.

Christian had just positioned his ladder in front of the room door and was working on the area above when there was a clatter at the flat door outside. We paused briefly. Was that at our door? No, it must have been next door. We carried on working. Now we heard a key being inserted into the lock. Apparently the wrong one, for the same noise repeated itself. This time with success, the bolt clicked. We looked at each other questioningly. Wasn't that at our door after all? No, that couldn't be. At that moment, the room door was thrust open with a vigorous swing. I let out a scream. Christian's ladder wobbled alarmingly. To save himself from falling, he quickly braced one hand against the door and the other against the freshly painted wall, more hanging than standing at a dizzying height in the corner of the room. I rushed over and held the ladder steady. It was a rescue in the nick of time, for the door was no longer offering support. It had closed again, and he had to let go if he didn't want to pinch his fingers.

Now that he had solid ground beneath his feet and the initial shock had passed, anger took over. He swore as I had rarely heard him swear before. And to maintain his good reputation, I will not repeat the words here. Armed with his paint roller, he stormed out of the room into the hallway, shouting:

"Who are you and what are you doing here?"

No answer. I hurried after him. In the kitchen, I finally found them. Christian was standing with a threateningly raised, dripping paint roller in front of a slight lady in her mature years, who was casting furtive glances towards the balcony door.

"I expect an answer", he barked at her.

She took two small steps backward. Did she really think she had to save herself with a daring jump from the balcony? I admit, my husband looked very dangerous at that moment with his paint roller. Perhaps she was just afraid he might splash her designer outfit. I had to suppress a laugh. This lady looked like my maths professor Miss Meier. A high-stacked concrete hairstyle, lipstick, eyeshadow, and nail polish a bit too bold for her age, a Chanel suit in mouse grey, accompanied by a silvery shimmering *foulard*, and matching grey shoes with a small heel, like those my grandmother used to wear. Several chunky jewels on her finger, thick round gold earrings, and a massive brooch on her scarf were probably intended to pep up her outfit.

"*Madame Bourgeois, enchantée*", she whispered, extending her hand to me, pointedly ignoring the barbarian with the paint roller.

Wait, I had seen that name somewhere before. Where had it been? Hesitatingly, I took the proffered hand and returned her greeting, still uncertain what to make of this person.

"Oh, our landlady!" I exclaimed, surprised, as it dawned on me. I had seen this name in our rental agreement. What a super start to our tenant-landlady relationship!

"Our landlady?" Christian asked. I nodded. Then he turned around, put on a hypocritical grin, and extended his hand in greeting. The hand with the fresh paint on it was taken, albeit hesitantly, and shaken. When *Madame* realised what she had touched, she let out a soft "Oh", fished a paper handkerchief from her handbag, and without a word about it, wiped off the paint.

The little revenge had succeeded. I could see it in his eyes, how much he delighted in it, even though he tried not to show it.

With icy politeness, *Madame* now explained the reason for her surprising visit. Monique from the *agence* had informed her that we wished for her to pick up a few things from the flat. Since she was in the area, she wanted to take the handful of items right away. We looked at each other and grinned.

"Well, then let me show you the handful of things you must take with you", I said. "Starting right here in the kitchen, you may take the non-functioning extractor hood. Then this old rusted clothes horse from the balcony. This metal frame over there in the corner, of course. The broken mirror standing in the bathtub, you may also take with you. The strange plastic box on the toilet can go as well. This table over here surely belongs to you. Now, only everything that's in the cellar. By when you think you can have all this removed?"

"I'll take it right now", she replied, unruffled.

"Oh really?" Christian asked. "Did you come here with a *camion*?"

"*Un camion ?*" she exclaimed. Why on earth would she need a lorry?

"Well, then let me show you the cellar", Christian suggested. "Follow me."

She followed.

I dared her to descend into the dark dungeon alone with the barbarian. A little punishment had to be meted out. Later, I learned that down there, she couldn't understand how those few *affaires* could bother us. Christian then made it clear that he expected to find an empty space when we moved in. He also provided her with his definition of the word "empty". She had promised to comply with his unusual request and clear out the cellar before we moved in.

Now, she actually gathered all the items I had mentioned around the flat and dragged them to her car. We let her proceed. We were even so mean as not to help her. We had walls to paint. She had held us up long enough. When she was finished, she knocked softly at the room door and opened it a crack. She wanted to say goodbye.

"*Les clés s'il vous plaît*", I said, holding my hand out ready to receive them. She could not keep the key to our flat. It was not acceptable for her to come and go as she pleased.

"*Quelles clés ?*" she asked.

"The keys to our flat", I answered.

"But I still need them", she replied, indignant.

"*Non*. You only need the cellar key. You don't need the keys to the flat anymore. You've taken everything with you. From now on, you may only enter the flat with our consent and in our presence", I explained to her.

"*Mais…*", she gasped. "That's outrageous! The flat belongs to me!"

She must have thought we were quite daft if she thought she'd get away with that. Well, you can always try it with these foreigners. Nice try!

"I'm not denying your ownership of the flat. But according to French rental law, you must hand over all existing keys to the tenant and may not enter the flat without their knowledge once the rental has begun. If you were to do so, it would be a *violation de domicile* – intrusion. Isn't that right, *Madame*?"

I said it as politely and kindly as possible. I admit, there might have been a slight ironic undertone.

She could hardly contain herself.

"*C'est une honte !*" she hissed. One could see how she wrestled with herself. Finally, she seemed to find a solution with which she could be satisfied.

"If that's the case, I will hand over the keys to the *agence*, so that it is properly noted in the protocol." Now she had shown us. She thought.

"*Bien*", I replied. "Then we'll see each other tomorrow morning at 9 a.m. at the *agence* for the key handover. I cannot grant you a longer period, as otherwise it is not ensured that unauthorized persons will not enter our flat in our absence."

I didn't really want to go to the *agence* again tomorrow morning. We wanted and needed to drive back home tomorrow. It was a long journey, and we wanted to leave early. But I didn't want to leave the keys with her. If I let her off the hook now, we could wait forever. And knowing that this lady could enter our flat at any time, even when we had moved in, was extremely unsettling to me. The rental agreement listed our landlady's address as Marseille. So, it was indeed associated with some effort for her to come to La Ciotat again tomorrow morning for the keys.

"*Eh bien... si vous y tenez tant* – if you insist so much", she finally said. "*Mais je veux une quittance* – I want a receipt!"

"*Evidemment, c'est normal*", I replied. Of course, she should have her receipt.

In icy silence, keys were exchanged for a receipt. How she must now regret having us as tenants. And how we regretted having such a frightful landlady. We were going to have some fun with her.

Now it was high time to continue with our renovation. The morning was drawing to a close and we hadn't yet finished our work in the office. Lunch would only be served once the office was done. At least the rain had stopped, and we could finally air out the place again. Does damp paint fumes make one feel high? We were in a peculiar mood. It might have been this combination of physical fatigue, the effect of this unique encounter, and triumph over our landlady that had put us in this state. We decided to take a short walk during our lunch break and eat "out". The takeaway pizza could be very well enjoyed on the wall of the beach promenade, with a view of the sea, of course.

To make a long story short, we also managed to finish the bedroom that day. No more and no less. We stowed our painting equipment in one of the built-in cupboards. The tools had to go back with us, as we would need them in our old flat until we moved out. We were not in a celebratory mood that day. We were far too worn out for that. Somehow, we managed to fill our bellies with something before we fell dead tired into our hotel beds again. The rest of the renovation would have to wait until after we moved in, and then it would fall on me alone. Well, I would manage it somehow.

Clearance Sale

The estate agent, with whom we had entrusted the sale of our old flat in Germany, had not given us much hope. The price we had paid for the flat at the time, plus the cost of refurbishment, would certainly not be recouped. However, we suspected that this was a standard strategy of all estate agents to prepare the seller not to be too persistent in negotiations if needed. We had little to no experience with property sales. With hindsight, we would never again entrust an estate agent with the sale of our property. But hindsight is always a wonderful thing.

The viewings had been going on for weeks now, and a reasonable offer was nowhere in sight. By reasonable, I mean an offer that came even close to our asking price. It seemed not to be a good time for sellers. That's how the estate agent had justified it, at least. Maybe he was just too inept to sell our flat? This thought had been crossing our minds more and more frequently of late. But since he was an acquaintance of an acquaintance, we wanted to give him one last chance. We had therefore set an ultimatum. If no acceptable offer was available by this deadline, we would try to handle it ourselves. We couldn't do worse on our own than he was doing.

The deadline was looming ominously closer, and we were becoming reconciled to the idea of placing a "private" ad ourselves. The last characters the estate agent had dragged in looked like people I wouldn't want to meet in the dark. All the less did I feel like showing them my flat, letting them look into all the cupboards, and touch everything. But I had no other choice. They had brought two children with them. The estate agent was dealing with the parents, and I had my hands full trying to keep the kids from getting up to any mischief. When the little one started pounding our glass shower cubicle with his saliva-covered Lego brick, I'd had enough and threw them out.

"You certainly won't get the flat sold like that", the estate agent complained.

"And will it sell better with a broken shower screen?" I replied.

That was the end of our estate agent-seller relationship. I fired him for incompetence. Yet it would not be the last time that we spoke to each other.

Time was pressing. We had to get rid of the flat. So, I placed an advert on this well-known property portal, emphasising "without estate agent!", of course. I'd spoken to the local notary by then, and it had turned out that there was absolutely no problem selling one's property oneself without the help of an estate agent. The notary wanted to send me a sample purchase contract to show to the buyer. Our particular agreements would be included in the contract, and then she would send it via email to both parties for review. The only thing that was important was to get a copy of the buyer's ID and to discuss all the details and put them in writing. She even offered to receive the purchase price from the buyer in trust and pass it on to us after deducting her fees after the confirmed handover of the flat. However, this would involve additional fees, and we should talk to our bank to see if we could get a cheaper offer for an escrow account.

No sooner said than done. We made an appointment with the branch manager of our bank, as we were planning to talk to him about dissolving the company anyway. And lo and behold, because we were such nice customers, he gave us the promise of a free escrow account. And that even though we'd told him in the same breath that he was losing us as customers because we would pay off all loans and close the accounts once we had dissolved the company and sold the flat. Very decent! And as a thank you, I'll make an exception and name names: it was a branch of Hypo-Vereinsbank. But it probably had more to do with our good relationship with the branch manager, and it's not to say that it is company policy.

My advert was hardly online when I started receiving the first calls. I had already learned from the so-called interested parties that the estate agent had brought us that it was sensible to ask a few qualifying questions on the phone beforehand. There's no point in wasting time on viewings that end up showing that the flat didn't match what they had in mind at all. Our estate agent had evidently neglected to do this. I'd prepared a list of questions for this purpose, which I added to with new questions after each caller and after each viewing. You wouldn't believe how little people read the text of the advert. It actually said in there that the flat was spread over two floors. And yet people came to view it and were utterly horrified to discover there was a staircase inside. The very staircase that was visible in the photos. Well, never mind. My tip to anyone in a similar situation is to sort things out on the phone beforehand. It saves time and nerves.

One visitor informed us during the viewing that he liked the flat very much and would like to buy it. Could we live with a moving-out date in a year's time? He was a bit tight for money at the moment. Really? My list of questions grew by another point.

The many flat viewings were getting on our nerves. Every time, the place had to be tidied and cleaned to show the flat at its best. And every time, you didn't know who was coming. The only disadvantage of selling privately is that the extra person – the estate agent – is missing during the viewings. I managed most of the viewings on my own, Christian had to work. So, every viewing was a bit of a challenge. I had to present the flat, answer curious questions, and keep an eye on all visitors to make sure no one took anything or touched anything they shouldn't. My list of questions eventually included the question "Are you coming with children?". Basically, those interested parties who come with a partner and children are the most promising candidates. With a flat of the size we were offering, one or two children's rooms were feasible. So, it was good if the kids were involved in the decision making straight away. But it was a nerve-wracking half hour for me all the same.

What I also learned is to actually decline preliminary viewings by just one of the partners along the lines of "I just want to get an idea". It doesn't get you anywhere. It just wastes my time. Because, honestly, what does the guy know about what kind of kitchen his wife wants? So please, both of you come together, even late in the evening if it can't be helped. Another point for the question list. You live and learn.

Then came the Reinhard family, with two well-behaved children, who shyly asked at the front door if they should take off their shoes. Point for the Reinhards. They seemed unenthusiastic, almost emotionless. However, they asked a lot of questions. So, the interest was there. Nevertheless, the viewing went so quickly that I thought as I said goodbye at the front door, I'll never see them again. A day later, I had an email with an offer. With a sum that didn't make us jump for joy, but at least it wasn't too far from our expectations. And time was pressing. What we didn't know at this point was that the Reinhards had been shown the dossier of our flat by our estate agent several weeks before. A fact that would cause us some trouble later.

They had told the agent back then that they wanted to think it over, whether a viewing even made sense, as the price was a bit high for them, and together with the agent's fees, it had been out of their budget. Now I had offered the flat myself, without agency fees. And suddenly, it was within reach again. They immediately recognised the photos. And they had fallen in love with our flat at first sight. Even though they had managed to hide it from me very well. We agreed on another appointment to dive deeper into the details.

Before the aforementioned deep-dive meeting with the Reinhards, a very energetic lady with a distinct Russian accent called me. Was the flat still available, she wanted to know. I hesitated briefly, as we had a half-decent offer on the table. But the Reinhards could still back out. So, before the ink was dry on the purchase agreement, the viewings had to continue. I told her we had an offer, but there was nothing in writing yet. If that was okay with her, I was available for a viewing.

And yes, she would bring her husband and son, as she generally made quick decisions. I pointed out that the sale should go through quickly. No problem, she said, she had the money immediately available. I felt a bit uneasy. They wanted to come that very evening. I was glad Christian could be there too.

Olga came. And Olga took over the entire conversation. Husband and child had nothing to say. And Olga was thrilled. Yes, even utterly enraptured. And Olga wanted our flat. Desperately. And our beautiful Provencal oak table, she wanted that too. Also desperately! She was ready to sign right here and now. We looked at each other. Did the good lady think we had a purchase agreement here? Didn't she know that this signature had to be made with a notary? What kind of business was this supposed to be? My uneasy feeling in the pit of my stomach grew stronger.

I told Olga that we already had an offer and that this interested party, since they were first, would get the opportunity from us to improve their bid. In our eyes, that was only fair. How much would we want to forget this other interested party? We swallowed and looked at each other. I would have liked to be better prepared for such a conversation now. But how can you prepare for something you don't see coming? I gathered all my courage and added €20,000 to Reinhard's offer. Olga said "Okay". And I thought, 'Damn, too low.'

Christian whispered to me, "You can't do that."

I whispered back, "Why not?" The evening would be long.

Olga willingly gave us her ID so we could make a copy. She lived on Olga Street. Really! And no, her husband would not be in the purchase agreement, she would buy the flat alone. And again, she had the money. She didn't have to apply for a loan. So, it could go as fast as we wanted. My stomach was audibly rumbling.

We said goodbye to Olga and her entourage and promised to get back to them as soon as possible. Of course, after we had spoken with the Reinhards. She reiterated how much she liked our flat and that she didn't want any other flat, this one or none!

The Reinhards could not and would not increase their offer. But they showed understanding, saying that if we had a significantly better offer, they would be very sad, but they would understand. We wanted to think about it. We were at a loss. The Russian Mafia or a fundamentally decent Swabian family? When I thought of Olga, my stomach rebelled. One should listen to one's gut feeling, right? I told Christian, I couldn't justify or even prove it, but I had a bad feeling about Olga. He felt the same way. Perhaps that's how business is done in Russia. She had frightened us. It may be that she was absolutely trustworthy and decent, but we didn't trust her.

The next day, I sent out two emails. The first to the Reinhards, stating that we had decided to accept their offer. The second to Olga, that despite her generous offer, we had decided to give preference to the others. Half an hour later, the phone rang. Olga was disappointed, upset, even outraged. It was only because she was Russian, she said. I tried to explain that it wasn't her accent that had frightened us, but her assertive manner and the frequent emphasis that she had the money immediately available without a loan.

"Ahhh that", she drawled. The money was already available because she had been close to buying an apartment recently and had already been granted the loan, which had then fallen through at the last minute. If she now found an apartment at a similar price, she could use this loan approval. She certainly did not have the money lying around in cash at home. That explained the matter. But it was too late. Olga had bluffed and lost our trust. Sorry, Olga.

Was this decision a mistake? Probably yes. Even guts can be wrong. Maybe we had just eaten something bad that night.

A few weeks after we moved out, while I was driving, I got a call from Germany. Without a greeting or introductory words, he started right away:

"Do you really think you can get away with that?"

I hadn't been able to look at the display and needed a second to remember the voice. It was our incompetent estate agent. I was completely clueless and couldn't make sense of what he was talking about. Since I didn't answer right away, he pressed on:

"You weren't expecting that, were you?"

"Getting away with what?" I asked, ignoring his last comment.

"You're withholding my fee", he said.

Slowly, it dawned on me what he was getting at. The Reinhards…

"You have no claim to a fee", I said. "We sold the flat without your help."

"You sold the flat to the Reinhard family, whom I presented the property to in my office. I have access to the database. Did you think I wouldn't find out?" he said.

"But the Reinhards obviously weren't interested, otherwise, they would have visited our flat with you. They didn't do that. And you didn't inform us about this prospective buyer. Just because the same people responded directly to my advertisement weeks later, it doesn't entitle you to a fee", I said.

"Oh yes!" he said. "I made them aware of the flat. That establishes my claim."

It went on like this for a while. He couldn't provide evidence that he had actually presented the flat to the Reinhards. Just because they had been in his estate agency did not mean he had actually shown them our flat's dossier. Of course, I knew it was true. The Reinhards had told me. But they also said that he had quickly shown them all sorts of flats on his computer during their appointment. They couldn't remember how many there had been. Most of them – including ours – they had dismissed without a closer look because the prices were above their budget and had kindly but firmly asked him to only show them flats that met their criteria, that is, were listed below their price limit. Only two flats were left, but they rejected both due to poor location. That ended the appointment. And the estate agent now referred to this quick run-through as a "presentation" of our flat. That was cheeky. If he did that with all the flats, it added up to a nice sum if he managed to collect his demands.

I wasn't sure if he had a legal claim, but it was clear to me that it would be very difficult for him to collect his demand abroad. But I wanted to close the matter and not leave too much scorched earth behind. He had lowered his fee considerably during his mandate because he couldn't achieve the initially estimated selling price.

"To close this matter, I offer you a one-time payment of 1000 Euros, provided that you waive any further demands against both us and the buyer", I said.

He let out an artificial laugh.

"Are you trying to take me for a fool?" he asked.

"No", I said. "Take the 1000 Euros or you get nothing."

"My fee is 5000 Euros!" he yelled.

"No", I said. "Your last offer was 2500 Euros for us and fee-free for the buyer. Since you didn't lift a finger for the sale contract, I don't see why you should be entitled to the full amount."

"Since you tried to cheat me, our agreements are void. The fee as per the schedule applies", he claimed.

"Don't even start with the cheating. You'll have a hard time enforcing your claim. It's on shaky ground anyway. And don't forget that I no longer live in Germany. Do you seriously think it will be easy to enforce your claim in France?" I said.

That hit home.

"Alright, I'll take the 1000 Euros. But I'm not retracting what I said about cheating", he said.

"Send me your fee invoice by email. And in the same email, please confirm that upon payment of this invoice, all claims against me and the buyer are settled", I said. "As soon as I have that, I'll transfer the amount."

He gasped.

"What business is it of yours whether I have a claim against the buyer or not?" he yelled at me.

I have found that the more the other party gets upset, and the calmer I remain, the more it makes them see red.

"I am referring to our last fee agreement, in which you granted the buyer exemption from the fee. You confirmed that in writing", I said.

There was a grinding noise on my phone. Had he just bitten into his mobile?

"Alright, you shall have your confirmation." With that, he hung up.

I was curious to see if the confirmation would actually be as I had demanded. When I arrived home that evening, I immediately checked my emails. And indeed, there it was. Fee invoice and confirmation as requested. In writing, he had not dared to talk of cheating or the like. On the contrary, he politely requested payment of his fee within the next 2 weeks.

We had to sort out our stuff, and quickly. Now that the sale was signed, sealed, and delivered and we had a moving-out date, we realised that we didn't have much time left to empty the flat. So far, we had put the topic off indefinitely. Always following the principle: no deadline, no stress. We didn't want to live in a half-empty flat for the rest of the yet-undefined time. Suddenly, it became urgent.

At this point, Christian's beloved Excel came into play again. This time it was to be a list of everything in our flat. We took an inventory. Every item, from the armchair to the Zester, was listed. And not just that! Each item was also measured, or its size at least roughly estimated. For furniture that could be disassembled, we gave the approximate size in its disassembled state. To complicate things a bit more, Christian had the idea that we should also include a column for the capacity of an item. When he first mentioned this idea to me, I just stared at him in bewilderment. What was that all about? But it actually made sense. A fridge, for example, can be put empty in the removal van, or it can be filled with small, lightweight items so as not to waste space. Moving volume costs money, every single cubic meter. And we had some items that could not be disassembled and thus could be filled.

After three days of inventory, we had a list of all our belongings. We could continue working with that.

It became a painful process. What was currently spread over 125 square meters was to fit into 60 square meters in the future. Our Excel table received an additional column in which we entered 'keep' (that was the easiest exercise), 'throw away' (not easy, but at least quick), and 'sell' (not at all easy and furthermore time-consuming). We had to go through the list several times and further thin out the 'keep' items. There was still too much left, and it was hard for us to part with some beloved pieces.

Selling was the most difficult. Furniture or electrical appliances that were still in good condition, we did not want to throw away or give away. We hoped to make a little money with them. We could use every penny. In France, it is common to sell used furniture or appliances. There are stores in every city like *"Troc"* or *"Dépot-vente"*. We like to browse around there. And we have often used them in the past to get rid of superfluous. You just drive your stuff there, negotiate a price that you get paid immediately, and that's it. More valuable things can also be put on consignment there. It is then displayed for a predefined period, and you receive the sales price minus commission as soon as the item has been sold. We bought our beautiful, Provencal oak table in this way in Carpentras. In addition to the negotiated purchase price, the 200kg gem also cost us a set of shock absorbers. But that is a story that does not belong in this book.

My impression was that the French are much more willing and accustomed than the Germans to buy used things. The people of Stuttgart, at least, did not want to buy any used furniture from us. We had photographed all the pieces from their best sides and posted them on the small ads portal. But nothing happened. In the end, we even offered like-new Ikea wardrobes and our insanely expensive giant sofa for free, just to get rid of them. I remember it as if it were yesterday... A young woman called and wanted the – free – sofa. But she didn't have a car. Could we bring it to her? I think I just hung up. Finally, we found a nice man who claimed he needed the items for a charitable cause and would pick up everything himself and also disassembly it himself. We didn't care who got the stuff. Just get rid of it. When he came, he showed me his ID and a confirmation from the Helping Hands association or something like that. He certainly had golden hands. He disassembled the cabinets alone and loaded everything into his van. At that point, I didn't even feel pain anymore as my beautiful sofa drove away. Just go!

It got uncomfortable in our flat. Everything that could be sold, we had sold. There wasn't much anyway. All the other large items that couldn't move with us were given away. A strange emptiness spread through the rooms. Where once a large corner sofa had stood, we had now hastily arranged air mattresses and blankets into a little cosy nook, which looked utterly meagre in the vast room. In the bedroom on the wall, where the wardrobe used to be, clothing boxes were now stacked. We had procured two of these large moving boxes with clothes rails, allowing clothes to be transported while hanging. They had a flap on one side, so you could open the box halfway. That's how they stood, open, in our bedroom, and we were living out of these boxes instead of the wardrobe. The closer we got to the moving date, the more things were packed into moving boxes. This made life feel like camping. Again and again, we wanted to use something that had either already been packed or disposed of. Often enough, we weren't even sure which was the case. And often enough, we told ourselves, well, we'll see if it reappears when we unpack in the new flat.

And all that despite having made a packing list. Yes, Excel again. You must be laughing by now. Every box was given a number. And in our packing list, we noted what was contained in that box. Brilliant idea, right? We always knew exactly where everything was. We just had to find the right box. And the right box, more often than not, was the one at the bottom of the pile. That would also be the case in our new flat. Only by then, unfortunately, we wouldn't remember what was in the boxes anymore.

So, as we packed the boxes, we wrote down on a piece of paper as much as possible of what we put in. In the evening, we would transfer what was on the paper to the Excel packing list on the computer. When we were looking for something, we just had to open the list, search for the term, and find out in a flash the number of the box containing the item. Additionally, we wrote on every box the room it belonged to, in addition to the number. Each room was assigned a different colour. The boxes with kitchen stuff now had *"Cuisine"* written in red; the office had green; the bedroom, black; and the cellar, blue. Why we had written the names of the rooms in French should remain our secret. The removal men certainly didn't understand French; it was a German company. Although they didn't really understand German either. So, in the end, it didn't matter anyway. The main thing was that we knew where each box belonged.

Time to say goodbye to our friends. As it slowly leaked out that we were going to emigrate, and as we started to put words into action, thus our credibility regarding this matter increased significantly, the invitations began to pile up. Everyone wanted to see us one last time before we disappeared forever. That's what these invitations sounded like. However, we were too stressed to accept them all. We didn't have time to visit each couple individually. So, we decided to throw a party – a proper farewell party. The date was quickly found. Not many Saturday evenings were left. The invitation was quickly cobbled together and emailed to everyone. The acceptances (and also the refusals) didn't take long to come in. Most managed to clear the evening for us. They all wanted to see these crazy emigrants one more time.

My friend Rosa offered to bring a pack of Rosé, which she would buy and chill in her fridge beforehand, so I didn't have to worry about it and had space in my fridge for food. We wanted to keep it simple. In that regard, we had no other choice; almost everything was already packed. However, it had to be something French. It goes without saying when you're moving to France. If only we could just quickly shop in France. But no, there was no time for that. We had to improvise. A large pot of *Taboulé* would be the base. We bought baguette and cheese. And lots of puff pastry, from which we baked sausage rolls. And since we had puff pastry, we baked a hundred *pains au chocolat* for dessert. How it smelled delicious!

My husband is usually no ace in the kitchen. Normally, he avoids anything remotely related to cooking. But that evening he helped me vigorously, rolling and wrapping sausages and chocolate in puff pastry. The shapes that resulted didn't always resemble what you might imagine a *pain au chocolat* to look like, but that didn't matter to anyone. They tasted good; that was the main thing.

My dear Rosa and her husband were the first guests. We were still baking when they arrived. But they brought the Rosé, and that couldn't be late. The two of them pitched in mightily to get the last preparations finished just in time before the other guests arrived.

The evening exceeded all our expectations. *CheriFM*, our favourite French radio station, blared from the mobile phone speakers. People who had never met before chatted animatedly with each other. All around, you could hear hearty laughter. Even we had time to talk to our guests. They took care of themselves. We'd simply laid food and wine on the kitchen counter, where everyone took what they liked.

We had specifically asked on the invitation not to bring us gifts, as we would then have to pack them, and we already had too much stuff to transport. Some couldn't resist, but all adhered to the stipulation that it could be eaten or drunk. We gave Württemberg wine to the French for months afterward when we were invited to an *apéro* or dinner. It was always received with a very mild smile. We were invited back anyway. Whether that spoke more for us or the wine, I dare not say.

As the evening progressed and the guests' blood alcohol level reached its zenith, we had everyone sit in a circle on the floor of the empty living room. The spin-the-bottle began. We spun the empty wine bottle in the middle of the circle. The person at whom the neck of the bottle pointed could –

or had to – take something out of a box and then take their turn to spin the bottle. We had filled a large moving box with everything we still wanted to get rid of but was too good to throw away. In this way, picture frames, paperweights, vases, whisks, and all sorts of dust traps changed owners. Some of our guests later went home with something they never wanted. This was the case with my colleague Mark, who was unlucky enough that the bottle pointed at him not just once but four times. He took it in stride.

Is saying goodbye supposed to be hard? Our friends didn't make it hard for us. Perhaps we were all too tipsy for sadness to arise. Each person who said goodbye wished us luck and promised to visit us down there soon. There was much laughter and hugging. Some were so filled with emotion that the hugging seemed to never end. The last to leave were – as expected – Rosa and her husband. They insisted on helping us clean up. We threw them out. We could clean up tomorrow. Now we just wanted to collapse into bed and sleep. At least the remaining 4 hours until the neighbours would wake us up again. As we lay in bed, we were still grinning. No, saying goodbye wasn't hard at all.

It's Always a Case of Some Losses

It was time. Today was moving day. Christian had to work and couldn't help me. With the help of our friends, I had prepared our flat for the move over the past few days. Everything that was unbreakable, we had packed ourselves in moving boxes. Anything that wasn't allowed in the new flat was gone. I had packed my suitcase and loaded it into the car to ensure it didn't accidentally end up on the lorry. Along with the suitcase, there were an air mattress, a sleeping bag, cleaning equipment, and plenty of things that I didn't want to entrust to the removers, so the car was already quite full. My accommodations for tonight, nearby, and tomorrow, halfway at friends', were organised.

This morning, I was up early to have time for the last-minute tasks. I had quickly run to the bakery and picked up fresh Pretzels. At 8 o'clock sharp, I was ready. The removal people could come.

But they didn't. I had found the moving company through an online moving auction. Do you know such a thing? On these platforms, you can enter the desired moving date, the volume of the move, and various special requests, and then receive offers from shipping companies. The offers were all significantly cheaper than any classic moving company in the area. An international move is never cheap. The special thing about these moving auctions is that the shipping companies use such orders to fill their loading space or empty return trips. It pays off for them. And it pays off for the customer. The latter may need to bring some flexibility regarding the date, so that the transport can be done with a planned empty trip.

I had found a company that had made a good offer and made a respectable impression to me. The boss himself, Mr. Eggermann, had made the offer. He was very pleasant on the phone and had accommodated all our requests. After some back and forth, we had managed to agree on the dates for moving out and in. As a special treat, he had offered that his people would bring packing material and pack everything. This isn't just a matter of convenience because you don't have to do it yourself. It's also a question of insurance. If something gets damaged in transit that they have packed, they are liable for it. If you've packed it yourself, they are not.

Just before our fixed moving date, Mr. Eggermann had called me. For a moment I thought, wow, he's really taking care of things. I was mistaken. He wanted to prepone our appointment.

"Can my people come on Monday to pack?" he asked.

"Monday?!?! ... No way!" I said. "Our move-out date isn't until Wednesday!"

At first, I assumed he'd just got confused and that the mistake would soon be cleared up. But he really meant what he said. They had finished a previous transport earlier than planned, and now the empty lorry was in Munich. If he could have it loaded at ours quickly, he could squeeze in an additional trip. But he couldn't, and I told him so. He said he wanted me to think it over and would call back in half an hour.

I couldn't see how I could do in just one day what I'd planned for three. No chance! Besides, that would mean I'd have to reorganize my overnight stays. My friend in Stuttgart was expecting me on Wednesday evening. Our friends in Lyon on Thursday evening. They had all cleared time for me. That wasn't easy to change. And then there was the handover of the flat to the buyers, planned for Thursday morning. Who would do that if I had to be in France by then? It remained a no-go.

When Mr. Eggermann called again, he seemed to expect that I would back down, and he was suitably angry when he found out that wasn't the case. All his friendliness was gone.

"As a user of a moving auction, you have to be flexible. Such date changes are normal."

"As you know, I was very flexible in finding a date and completely followed your planning", I reminded him. I stuck to my "no" and referred to his order confirmation, in which he had confirmed the date.

"I expect you to keep to your contract", I said.

"I will, of course", he replied before hanging up without saying goodbye.

He responded to my email, where I had asked for a reconfirmation of the date, with icy silence. So that was where things stood. I was not comfortable with all this. But I had no choice. You can't organize a Plan B in three days. But I had wondered more than once in these last three days if I shouldn't have acquiesced to his request. And now, on moving day at 11 am, with still no removers in sight, I was almost certain I had made a huge mistake.

By now, I had left several messages on the nice gentleman's voicemail. I was still waiting for a callback. Christian and I had already spoken several times during this period, considering what to do if they simply left us hanging. He would come right away, of course. We could ask friends for help. Which of our friends had time spontaneously during the week? We could try to rent a 3.5-tonne van and load it ourselves. That would take care of the move-out. And then? Then he would take time off. We could have moved three times over with the lost revenue. But it helped nothing. Okay, deep breath.

At 12 o'clock, Mr. Eggermann finally called me back.

"What are you getting so worked up about?" he asked. "You kept us waiting, and now we'll keep you waiting."

I gasped for air. I wanted to explode. But I couldn't. Now was the time to keep calm and swallow any nasty remarks. The important thing was that they will come at all.

"My people are on the way, they'll be there in half an hour", he said. I don't remember if I answered or what I might have said. If I did say something, it was evidently nothing that would have caused him to call his people back, for they did indeed show up an hour later, with broad grins on their faces. They had clearly been fully briefed by their boss. When I urged them to hurry, they replied:

"Why? We've still got time."

"Yes, exactly until this evening", I said. "Then everything must be packed and loaded on the truck."

"Why? Delivery isn't until Saturday; we can still pack tomorrow."

"No. Tomorrow you cannot pack. Tomorrow morning the flat must be empty for the handover."

"Don't get upset, Lady. We'll do it", they said.

They went about their work with a nonchalance that made me want to explode.

According to my original calculation – assuming a timely start – I had thought the lads would be finished by five at the latest. I would then have enough time to quickly vacuum everything and then spend a cosy evening with my friend. She had promised to cook us something delicious and really spoil me. I was completely wrong. When I called Ute to put her off until a later, still-to-be-determined time, she promptly jumped into her car and came to help me. At 8, the packers were still not finished. My cosy dinner had to wait. By 9, they were finally in the last stages. Half an hour later, we were finally rid of them and could let the vacuum cleaner whizz around. I made one last inspection. By chance, I took the stairs down instead of the lift. There, I almost stumbled over a large roll of carpet that someone had left on the stair landing. Upon closer inspection, I realized it was OUR carpet. The idiots from Eggermann had simply left it there.

I called them and ended up on their voicemail. "Drive back immediately and pick up the carpet", I said. There was no response. When the waiting became too long for us, we two girls heaved the heavy thing into the underground car park where my car was parked.

"It'll never fit in there", said Ute.

"It must", I said.

"I think you can dump that idea", she said.

"Would you rather I dumped the carpet right now?" I asked.

And so, a three-metre-long roll of sisal carpet was folded in half and heaved from diagonally rear to diagonally front into an already full car.

"It's always a case of some losses, someone once told me", said Ute.

I cried out inwardly. My stomach grumbled its discontent over the missed dinner. But I was too exhausted and tired to think about it any longer.

Shortly after 11 pm, I finally sat freshly showered at Ute's dining table. She insisted that I eat something. I really didn't feel like it anymore. But the appetite came with eating. My stomach quickly realised that it hadn't eaten anything all day, and now was the opportunity to make up for it. Fortunately, I had planned to sleep in a bit the next morning. The handover to the Reinhards wasn't until 10 o'clock. I wasn't expected by our friends in Lyon until the evening.

The Reinhards were, as always, overly punctual. I had prepared a handover protocol. The whole thing took half an hour.

"Everything is perfect", said Mr. Reinhard, signing the protocol.

At 11 o'clock, I was already *en route* to Lyon.

Jean Reno and the Apple

Finally, the French motorway! One might grumble about toll fees, but eventually, you get used to them, and then it's just the way it is. But I confess, I love driving on French motorways. The 130 km/h speed limit doesn't bother me; it's a comfortable cruising speed for long journeys, one that doesn't wear you out.

So here I was, finally in France. I had just left Belfort behind me. It was time for a break. I pulled into the next lay-by. I was all alone here. Not a soul in sight. I settled down at one of those picnic tables. The sun was shining, warming my face. As I was daydreaming, an old rickety transporter came rattling along and parked right next to my car. Of course, there were only about 100 other free parking spots. The driver got out and eyed my car. The passenger followed suit. Then two more men emerged from the van. Where had they found the room? They saw me sitting there and – naturally – made a beeline for the table next to mine. I felt a bit uneasy. You hear things about women travelling alone and motorway rest areas.

The men seemed to have come from a construction site, dressed in work clothes, and now they unpacked their sandwiches. One looked like Jean Reno – I mean, when he was still in his 30s. Tanned, huge, with close-cropped hair and a broken nose. There was also a much smaller, wiry guy, a bit older, presumably the one in charge for sanity and reason in the troop. And last but not least, two young lads, maybe in their early 20s, lanky, muscles plastered with tattoos, and unmistakably twins.

Their conversation revolved around the weather, the food, work, the architect they were slating, and finally – me. They appraised me unabashedly. They referred to me as "*La petite*", even though I'm not that small at 1.72m.

"*Quel châssis, la petite*… What a chassis, the little one. Drives a German car, where's she from, where's she going?… Go on, ask her if you dare…" and so on and so forth. I wasn't quite sure if they were referring to my chassis or that of my car. I tried to act as if I didn't notice. First and foremost, I tried to pretend that I didn't understand them. I admit, I never pull that off well. My face betrays every emotion. I can't put on a facade, no matter how much I might want to. I watched them out of the corner of my eye. At the very least, I wanted to notice right away if they decided to attack me.

Then Jean Reno stood up and came over to me with a broad grin. Did it have to be him?

"*Bonjour la fille*", he said, and with a kind of little bow, he placed an apple in front of me on the table. Then he said, "*bon appétit*", turned around, and rejoined his comrades.

I was so surprised that I couldn't find the words at first. My astonishment must have been apparent; they grinned at me. Or were they laughing about me? I had no choice but to join in. The ice was broken. I called out, "*Merci!*" In response, I received an invitation to their table.

"*Allez, viens, reste pas toute seule, on morde pas!*" The grammatically incorrect, but all the more efficient version of: don't sit there all alone, we won't bite. As I stood up and went over to them, they cheered. So, I had understood them; the proof was there. They had suspected it from the start.

My Jean Reno with the apple took the lead and introduced his mates:

"Little Fred over here is the grandpa of the gang, so we call him *patron*." In my opinion, he could hardly be 40, but okay.

"Those two are the brothers Patrick and Julien, the stars of EMBAR." At my puzzled look, he explained that EMBAR was the rugby club of Montbéliard and Belfort.

"And what's your name, *Monsieur Charmant*?" I asked.

"Jean", he replied. – No kidding?

"*Jean, comme Jean Reno ?*" I asked.

"*Eh oui, comme Jean Reno*", he answered, with a considerable amount of pride in his voice. I wonder if the real Jean Reno would have been as thrilled about this lookalike?

And then I had to answer a thousand questions. Where from? Stuttgart. Where to? Marseille. No idea why I said

Marseille instead of La Ciotat. Probably still a bit cautious. And why? I'm moving. Ah, hence the fully loaded car. You're moving to France? Permanently? To live here? "*Ça alors!*" And all alone? I explained to them that I was making the move alone because *Monsieur* had to work. They were wide-eyed. The *patron*, the wiry little one, tipped his imaginary hat. *Chapeau*, that was supposed to mean. Hats off. We chatted for a while longer, and then they had to go; work was calling. As a farewell, they wished me *bon courage* and even gave me a packet of biscuits, as I would need energy. Then they clambered back into their old Peugeot, and, honking and waving, they rattled away.

It was time for me to hit the road as well if I wanted to be on time for dinner with our friends.

PART 3: ARRIVED

A Stormy First Night

It was a cold welcome. If you expect spring-like temperatures at the beginning of March, you might be seriously mistaken. When I arrived in La Ciotat, the sky was grey, and a strong Mistral was blowing. Perhaps it was some other wind. I couldn't yet differentiate between the multitude of winds that all had names. It was cold, in any case. The flat was freezing cold. It had been unheated for months. And the insulation in the south is what it is: non-existent.

When I arrived in the evening, my first official act was to check the letterbox. I expected to find the cellar key there. You remember, the cellar had to be cleared out. Monique from the *agence* had promised to leave the key there. Unfortunately, no luck. No key. Only a lot of advertising flyers. I called the *agence*, but of course, no one answered at that time, so I left a message asking them to call me back first thing in the morning.

I was exhausted. Moving is draining. I cleared out the car. Except for the carpet. That had to wait for the removers. I piled everything in a corner in the kitchen where I knew it wouldn't be in the way. I had printed out floor plans with the furniture drawn on them. This was to prevent the removers from asking me where every single piece was to go. I planned to stick these papers to the doors with tape first thing tomorrow morning. Now it was time to inflate the air mattress, unroll the sleeping bag, and get into bed.

The cold stone floor of the bedroom did not look inviting at all. Grandma's old wool blanket would have a tough job as an insulating mat tonight. I was confident it would handle it. It had accompanied me to countless holiday camps and camping trips. That was a long time ago. Do wool blankets become weak with age? Since that night, I've been convinced of it. I had a blanket under the air mattress and one on top. I was in my down sleeping bag, had ice-cold feet, and shivered all night. Sleep was out of the question.

I need to pee when I'm cold. Is that the same for you? When I'm cold, I have to, and often. As I once again made my way to the toilet with the help of a dim torch, my foot stepped on something that didn't feel like a stone floor. It felt rubbery. It didn't sound like stone either; it crunched. What was that? When I shone the light on the spot, there was nothing to see. Had it fled? WHAT WAS THAT? Suddenly, I wasn't cold anymore. I made my way to the light switch. Thankfully, we had electricity and a light bulb on the ceiling in every room. Now that the room was properly illuminated, I saw what I had stepped on: a dried-up lizard carcass. I must have kicked it away with my foot so that it no longer lay in the same spot. Just to be sure, I nudged it again with my shoe. It was dead. Definitely dead. It was already mummified. How long had it been lying here? Well, it could lie here until tomorrow morning. At least, I had some company in the empty flat.

When I said that sleep was out of the question, it wasn't just due to the cold. That said, in the end, it somehow did have something to do with the cold. I'm talking about the wind. The *Mistral*, or one of its brothers, was blowing at a hundred miles an hour around the corner of the house, tugging at the dilapidated shutters. It made them rattle, and those not carefully secured squeaked in their hinges and slammed against the house wall. I could do nothing about it; all my shutters were properly closed. However, that didn't stop them from rattling either.

I wasn't quite sure, though, whether it was the shutters or the windows themselves that rattled louder. The windows shuddered alarmingly in their frames. Even the panes themselves clattered in the windows. It didn't take much imagination to weave this noise into a dream in which a horde of ecstatically drumming natives played the leading role.

I didn't enjoy this dream for long, however. I was woken up by a whistling noise. Perhaps it was also the cold. Who knows what came first. Once I lay awake on my improvisational bed, my brain could fully concentrate on the whistling. There was no blocking it out anymore. I could toss and turn for as long as I wanted, trying to ignore it. It was impossible. I had to find out where it was coming from. It was just as well, since I had to go to the toilet again anyway. So, it was all one process.

The whistling got stronger as I stepped into the hall. By the time I reached the toilet door, I had figured out that it was coming from the kitchen. One thing at a time, the most important first.

When in the kitchen, it sounded like a party of ghosts was having a bash. A strong draught whistled around my legs. It wasn't hard to find where it was coming from. There was a small balcony accessible only from the kitchen. The balcony door rattled and clattered as if someone was trying to gain access from outside.

Since there was a gas connection in the kitchen, a hole had been cut out of the bottom part of the balcony door, where there was wood instead of glass, and a ventilation wheel had been installed. A little wheel that you turn to adjust how much ventilation you want, from fully closed to very wide open. It should actually stay in the set position. But this one was spinning like the propeller of a small plane at full throttle just before takeoff.

A solution had to be found, and quickly. I looked for something to cover it. In my toilet bag, I found the brilliant solution: a shower cap. One of those you get in hotels. It had just the right diameter for my wind wheel. Quickly pulled over the frame and… Whoosh, it flew across the kitchen in a high arc.

Okay. I wasn't giving up that easily. I would simply tape it to the frame with packing tape. Easier said than done. I pulled the wind wheel's 'storm cap' over again. But I had to hold it with both hands, so it wouldn't get blown away again. I definitely needed two more hands to stick the tape on now. I tried with one hand on the 'storm cap' and the other on the tape. Whoosh, it was gone again. The battle lasted about half an hour. The *Mistral* emerged as the clear winner by knockout in the fourth round. The shower cap simply wasn't cut out to be a 'storm cap'.

Beaten, frustrated, and dead tired, the loser retreated to her mattress.

MOVING IN WITH OBSTACLES

The alarm clock jolted me from my air mattress at 6:30 am. I felt as though I had been run over. I'd hardly slept at all last night. The water from the tap was still cold. Something was off with the water heating. That went on the to-do list for later. Now, I needed to have a bit of breakfast first. If one wanted to take on these removal people, one needed to fortify oneself.

Just as I was about to sit down at my makeshift dining table, the doorbell rang. There was no intercom system. If one didn't want to keep the visitor waiting too long and risk them leaving, one had to hurry. So, I sprinted to the door, took several stairs in one leap, and... froze when I saw a lorry with the logo Eggermann parked in front of the house from the window of the first landing. Already?! Damn it, they were far too early! Instantly, I slowed my steps. They wouldn't drive away just like that. They were trying to reverse park in the yard.

Hang on, that wasn't MY lorry! This one was much smaller than mine. Had it shrunk on the way down here? And those weren't MY removal men! I'd never seen these people before. Not that I was particularly fond of my removal men, but in moments like this, it's not about affections. Even though I couldn't stand them, right now, I would have liked to see them again. What had happened? Had they mixed up the routes? Panic!

A small, grey-haired man with a cigarette in his mouth approached me. He must have been the one who had rang the doorbell.

"Mrs Sachs?" he asked, nearly tripping over his tongue.

"Yes", I said, and "Who are you? What happened to the others who loaded my stuff? And what happened to the lorry?"

He looked at me, uncomprehending, smiled awkwardly, shrugged, and said, "No understand."

"Ohhhhh!" I said. That was all I could think of at first. This was going to be fun. It turned out that he was the one of the two who could speak 'a bit' of German; the other one just smiled kindly in greeting, tapped his baseball cap with his forefinger, and turned back to his lorry. When he opened the tailgate, I held my breath. I didn't breathe again until I recognised the first familiar piece on the load area. So, it was at least our stuff. Phew!

They had apparently switched the lorry, and there was total chaos. I'd assumed that what had been loaded last would now be the first to be unloaded. There was no order anymore. The bed slats had mingled with parts of the worktable from the cellar and started a merry threesome with the floor lamp from the living room. I groaned. This move would go down in history. We had experienced quite a bit in our countless moves, but this one topped everything else.

I grabbed the little one with the cigarette, for I needed some answers. First, we had to figure out how we could communicate. I started with the basics, pointed to myself and said "Ines." He got it right away, laughed, pointed to himself and said "Jiri." He pronounced it like "Yearjy" with a very soft "j". Then he pointed to his colleague and said "Roman". I understood at the first name.

"Český?" I dredged from the deepest recesses of my memory.

"Ano!" he exclaimed, hopping with joy. I hurried to make clear to him that that was pretty much all I could say in Czech. Apart from "Pozor na vlak", which means "Beware of the train", something I had learned from the signs at railway crossings and hadn't forgotten over the last thirty years. The brain plays some strange tricks on you sometimes. It wouldn't be much use to me today.

Lacking the words, I grabbed Jiri's hand and dragged him up to the flat. No, not what you're thinking. He wasn't that cute. At least one of the two had to get an orientation. I showed him all the rooms. I quickly fumbled out the room plans and showed them to him. He was a bright spark and instantly understood what each room was supposed to be.

With his hands to his head and mimicking snoring, he confirmed that he knew we were in the bedroom. In the office opposite, he imitated typing and the sounds of a typewriter. In the living room, he sat on the floor where the future sofa would be, leaned against the wall, and crossed his legs comfortably. A quick thumbs up, and he was ready to leap away again.

"Stop!" I called after him. I still had to somehow teach him that he had things on the truck that needed to go into the cellar, but I had no key for it. But how? I asked him if he could speak English. He shook his head. I didn't dare ask about French.

I made it clear for him to follow me, and we went down the stairwell together. The door leading to the basement was locked. I emphatically pressed the door handle and then made the motion of unlocking with my hand.

"Ne mam", I said, because it suddenly came to my mind.

"Nemáš klíč?" he asked, nodding at the same time because he'd grasped what was going on. At the word "klíč" it clicked in my head, and I suddenly knew it meant key.

"Show", he said, perhaps meaning that I should show him the parts that belonged in the cellar. Or maybe he meant that I should show him where they should place the parts instead, since we obviously couldn't get them into the cellar. I was at a loss. I needed that blasted key. Oh man, I hope they had at least cleared out the cellar. But it wasn't even 8, no one would be working at the *agence* yet. Even though I knew better, I called the *agence* again and left another message on the answering machine. Maybe it would at least underline the urgency of the matter.

Now Jiri and Roman began unloading the lorry. Roman was a massive guy. When they stood next to each other, they looked like Asterix and Obelix from the famous French comic. The only missing piece was Obelix actually throwing his menhirs (or our furniture) off the truck. Roman the Great wielded on the loading area, placing piece after piece on the ramp and setting them in the yard. It didn't take long, and the entire yard was filled with our stuff. This also applied to the driveway. I prayed that none of my new neighbours would want to drive in or out right now. What was this supposed to be? Why were they spreading everything in the yard? Fortunately, the sun was shining today.

The neighbour with the tower hairstyle stepped out of the front door, looked around, raised an eyebrow, scrutinised me from top to bottom, raised her eyebrow a little higher, and staggered off. All I could do was hope that later, when I'd have transformed back into a human being, she wouldn't associate me with this dishevelled creature in scruffy work clothes. That hope would turn out to be unfulfilled, as I would later discover.

Now Jiri beckoned me over to him. "Show", he said again, pointing to the clutter spread around the courtyard. Oh, I see! They had emptied the lorry enough to get to everything, so I could now show them each item that was meant to go into the cellar. I finally understood. Each piece I pointed out, they grabbed and moved to the side of the house, where it would be somewhat protected and out of the way. There it seemed to be staying for the time being. I sincerely hoped that I could somehow get the cellar key that day. This stuff couldn't possibly stay there. Once the lorry and the removers gone, anyone could help themselves. It was all wonderfully visible from the street. And in France, items often just get placed on the street when they're not needed any more, and anyone can take what they can use. The stuff wasn't on the street but in the courtyard, but it was still stuff. Well, if people wanted to take it, all the better. Then I wouldn't need to find a solution for getting it into the cellar by myself once the removers were gone.

Now that the cellar stuff was sorted, the courtyard quickly emptied. Jiri had ushered me upstairs to the flat, making it clear that I was to stay near the entrance and direct them. He had stood there, flailing his arms like a policeman at an intersection where the traffic lights had failed. That had been easy enough to understand. Each time they came panting up the stairs, I pointed them in the direction they needed to take the item, like the policeman at the intersection. They simply filled the rooms, not thinking about the floor plans anymore. And I couldn't leave my post.

However, every now and then, when they were both downstairs, I snuck away to satisfy my curiosity. I tried in vain to estimate how much stuff was already upstairs and how much was still down in the courtyard. I found the rooms already bursting at the seams. Yet they kept on going, bringing up more and more items. Help! Where was all this supposed to go?

Around midday, Jiri came back up alone. With hand and mouth gestures, he made it unmistakably clear that they wanted to go and get something to eat.

"Break?" I asked, and he nodded.

This break was more than welcome. It was just before twelve. Just enough time to call the *agence* again, as they had still not got back to me. This time I was lucky; the assistant answered.

"*Oui, oui*, your key is ready here. You can pick it up."

I wanted to know why it wasn't in the letterbox as agreed. No, they would never do that, it wasn't allowed. I would have to sign a *quittance* for her to confirm that I had received the key. That wouldn't be possible if they left it in the letterbox… Damn it, couldn't they have told me that in the first place? And I said something to that effect to her.

"Can I come by now?" I asked.

"*Mais non!* Not right now, not until 2 pm."

I was boiling.

"*Mais non !*" I said, "I'll be there in five minutes, and you will wait for me. AFTER that, you can have lunch."

She audibly drew air into her nose. I was about to ruin her well-deserved lunch break.

"*Bon, d'accord*", she finally said.

I jumped into my car and raced to the *agence*. I didn't bother with a parking spot, but stopped right in front of the door, switching on the hazard lights. This was an emergency. I was still fuming. There was no room for polite greetings today.

"*La clé, s'il vous plaît*", the key, please, I said briefly. She handed it over to me, demonstratively bored, and pushed a piece of paper toward me. I scribbled something where the signature should go and was out the door.

I didn't take much more time for the return trip to the flat, for now, I wanted to know what the cellar looked like. Empty or not empty, that was the question. The tension rose immeasurably as I put the key in the door to the basement. I turned it over and over, but the door wouldn't open. What was this? Did I have the wrong key? It fitted into the keyhole and turned, but there was no sound of unlocking. I tried putting it in slightly less far, but then it jammed. Sweat broke out on my brow. Just when I was about to break down in despair, I heard footsteps on the stairs.

"*Puis-je vous être utile ?*", can I be of use to you, the man asked. I recognised the face, I thought. Where had I seen him before? Now was not the time to think about it.

"*Ah oui*, the lock always sticks, but there's a trick", he said, taking the key from me. With him, it worked the first time.

"*Eh voilà*", he said, smiling slyly at me.

"*Comment… ?*" How did you do that, was what I wanted to ask, but I didn't even get to finish my question. He began explaining and showing me how I had to do it.

I wanted to go straight down to the cellar to see our storage space, to get the question of empty or not empty answered. But I hadn't counted on the neighbour. He, of course, wanted to know who he had just unlocked the basement for.

"Are you our new neighbours moving in today? With the German lorry?" he asked. I nodded.

"Do you speak French?" he asked, probably because I had only nodded and said nothing. Then it occurred to him that the question was nonsense. He slapped his forehead and laughed: "*Mais oui*, you understood everything I've babbled. *Qu'est-ce que je suis con !*"

I wouldn't let the idea that he was stupid stand, and vehemently disagreed.

"How can you know I'm not stupid if we don't know each other?" he asked, bursting into hearty laughter, which I involuntarily joined.

"I won't keep you any longer, you must have a lot to do. We'll talk later", he said, and we said our goodbyes.

Now down to the cellar. The stairs were too steep and dark to move quickly. But I did take the last three steps in one jump. Damn, I'd forgotten to turn on the lights. Daylight reached down the stairs, but around the corner, it was pitch black. Where was the next light switch? I grope along the walls but found none. There had been one at the top of the stairs. Seriously? Did I really have to go back up? No choice. So back to the beginning. Not as punishment, just for practice. Finally, I stood before our cellar. Even through the slats, I could see that our landlady had indeed emptied it. Hallelujah! And the key fit too. Hallelujah, take two! When the lads came back from lunch, they could lug the junk into the cellar.

Speaking of lunch break, was that my stomach screaming? Oops, I had completely forgotten about that.

At the pizza stand on the beach promenade, I ran into two old acquaintances: Jiri and Roman, munching in the sun. When they saw me coming, they flinched, looking questioningly at the watch, probably thinking I wanted to drive them back to work. But I signalled them to relax. I'd come to eat, not to crack the whip. I ordered and sat down with them.

What followed could hardly be called a conversation. But somehow, we managed to communicate. It's always possible if you want it to be. A sweeping gesture with the arm, pointing to the bay of La Ciotat, followed by a thumbs up, indicated they were pleased with our choice of residence. I pulled the freshly acquired cellar key from my pocket and showed it to Jiri. "Aaaaah!" he said, grinning. Another thumbs up. His colleague looked at him quizzically, so he explained the story with the cellar key. At least that's what I assumed, as I couldn't understand him.

What I couldn't figure out was what had happened to the lorry and the colleagues. That subject was just too complex for international sign language. Well, it was quite irrelevant anyway. I liked these two here much better. And the most important thing was that our stuff was where it was supposed to be.

Well-fed after lunch, the two set about hefting the heavy workbench into the cellar. More precisely, strong Roman had to bear practically all the weight, as he went down the steep basement stairs first, and Jiri only had to ensure that nothing slipped from above. Using the same technique, they had also hefted our hundredweight oak table into the flat. Roman at the bottom with all the weight, and Jiri at the top. Here, however, he had to grab a little more as it went around the corners of the landings. Panting and dripping like wet dogs, they arrived at the top. But no word of curse or complaint passed their lips. At least none that I could hear. And now they had to manage such a load for the second time. I felt sorry for them.

The rest of the day should be somewhat easier for them. They now had to "only" reassemble the furniture. I asked them to start with the bed. I wanted to play it safe. If they managed nothing else today, I wanted that bed. Everything else was secondary. Said and done. In less than half an hour, the bed was in its place. Next, they tackled the office. When they were done, Jiri came to me and said:

"Finished."

That must be a word he had very gladly adopted into his vocabulary. I looked at him quizzically. Finished with what? He indicated that he thought they had done everything and now wanted to say goodbye. I shook my head.

They were far from finished. There were still two wardrobes to assemble in the bedroom. And then there was still the carpet in my car. I had shown it to them as soon as they had arrived, but they seemed to have forgotten it. When I pointed to my car from the window, he remembered. He smacked his forehead, grabbed Roman, and rushed down to the car. I didn't have to chase after them; I could open the car with the remote control from the balcony.

Now I was curious. The carpet was so large that it would almost fill the entire living room. And there was already the massive dining table in place. How would they manage to get the carpet under the table? There wasn't enough space in the flat to temporarily park the table elsewhere. They came with the carpet roll, still folded in the middle. Jiri pointed to the crease, made a face, and wagged his finger. Yes, I knew that it wasn't good for the carpet. I shrugged; I couldn't change it. So where to put it, they naturally wanted to know now. I pointed to the floor under and around the table. They nodded. A brief consultation in Czech. Then the carpet was uncreased, Roman had to lift one end of the table, and Jiri threaded the loose end of the roll under the table legs. Interesting technique, I thought, and I was curious how he would do it at the other end of the table. Roman could hardly be on both sides at once. Nor was he strong enough to lift the whole table alone.

But Jiri knew how to help himself. He crawled under the table, pressed against the tabletop with his back, lifted the table a bit, and tugged at the carpet. The latter made life increasingly difficult for him. The further the procedure progressed, the less the carpet wanted to move. Finally, he pulled and tugged it so far that the table legs all stood on the carpet. Jiri crawled out from under the table, looked at his work, and … was not yet satisfied. Nor was I, incidentally. The carpet needed to go further back. Another brief consultation. Then each positioned themselves at one corner of the carpet. And now they pulled, tugged, and shook the carpet until it moved to the correct position. Along with the table on top, of course. I was terrified for my beautiful sisal carpet, and I had to think of Ute's words: "It's always a case of some losses." It couldn't possibly survive this unscathed. But a sisal carpet is apparently more robust than one might think. After the crease had lain out for a few weeks, there was no sign of any of its treatments in the past.

Now they were finished, weren't they? I showed them the furniture that still needed to be assembled. Now it was Jiri's turn to shake his head. He pulled out a piece of paper. It was a list of all the boxes that Eggermann had packed, and all the pieces of furniture they had disassembled. He walked around the flat with me and put a tick next to each item that we could clearly identify. By the end of our tour, every item on his list had a tick. Of course. I had already started disassembling a few pieces myself that morning, while I was waiting for the people from Eggermann, as I had had nothing better to do, and had also hoped to save time later on. I groaned. This was my reward.

What wasn't on their list, they didn't have to reassemble. And I couldn't explain to them how this had come about, due to linguistic barriers. But they now wanted to unpack "their" boxes. According to their understanding, they had to unpack all the boxes on their list, i.e. all those that had been packed by Eggermann. Unfortunately, that was rather difficult because I didn't yet know where to put all the stuff. I knew well enough that Eggermann was now out of liability. Anything we didn't check right here and now, I could have broken later on.

I let them unpack the three boxes with the plates and glasses. We had provisionally placed one of the office cabinets in the kitchen until we could find a better solution. Temporary solutions can sometimes have a surprisingly long lifespan; when we moved out, the cabinet was still there. Into it, I had them place the plates and glasses. There was as yet no room for anything else. They understood that. They looked at each other, had a brief discussion, and disappeared into the bedroom. What's coming now, I wondered.

Because they had saved time and energy by not unpacking the boxes, I now got a bedroom wardrobe assembled. As a kind of compensation, I suppose. I thought it was very nice. Unfortunately, their generosity didn't extend to the second wardrobe. Perhaps it was also because I came up with my complaint too quickly.

While the two of them were busy in the bedroom, I had started unpacking the sideboard in the living room. It was a beautiful sideboard, styled antique and made to look like mahogany, with sliding doors. You could unhinge these sliding doors by reaching behind the door and unlocking something near the roller. That had worked quite well with three of the doors, but with the fourth, force had evidently been used, so the roller had been torn out. As if that wasn't enough, three out of four doors were scratched on the outside. The top of the furniture had also sustained some scuffs. It was ruined.

Jiri nodded when I showed him the damage, took out a claim form, had me fill it out and sign it, gave me the duplicate, and packed it away. For him, the matter was settled. For me, it was far from over.

When Jiri and Roman said their goodbyes, it was dark outside. But my working day was far from over. If I wanted to sleep in my bed tonight, I had to unpack the mattresses and bedding. And at least contain the chaos in the bedroom and corridor enough so I could get to the toilet safely. I toiled for roughly another two hours.

Just as I was about to retrieve the mirror standing in the bathtub so that I could shower, the doorbell rang. I hadn't yet had a chance to find out if there was a difference in the ringtone when someone rang at the house at the front door or at the door upstairs. I was already in the starting blocks for a sprint downstairs and nearly ran into my neighbour. It was the same who had helped me with the basement lock.

"*Tout va bien ?*" he asked. All good?

"*Oui*", I answered.

"*Venez prendre l'apéro !*" he said. Come for an aperitif!

"*Avec plaisir*", gladly, I answered, assuming that a time would now be arranged for it. However, he turned around and wanted to leave. That's when I realised he wanted me to come along right away.

"*Là maintenant ?*" I asked. Right now?

"*Oui, oui*", he replied.

"*Non, non!*" I countered. "I must first shower; I can't come to you like this."

Only then did he look at me properly. "*D'accord*, in half an hour then."

And I had so looked forward to a hot bath – yes, the water heater finally provided hot water. There was no shower curtain, so a bath wouldn't have been a bad idea. Well, that was out of the question now. I had to hurry to be ready, including washing and drying my hair, in half an hour. With still slightly damp hair, I was promptly at my neighbours' door.

There was no nameplate on the door. They lived half a floor diagonally below-next to us. We could look from our office window into their living room. Theoretically, I mean. I hadn't had a chance to do so yet. It would be days before I'd clear a path to the window. When we were here for the handover and renovation, the shutter had always been closed over there-below. We didn't even know if anyone lived there. That question was now answered. So here I was already making my introductory visit to the new neighbours. I hadn't expected it to happen so quickly.

I rang the doorbell. The neighbour opened it and invited me in. He directed me to the living room, where his wife was already busy at a small bar-counter with glasses and crackers.

"*Là voilà!*" he introduced me. There she is!

She looked up and smiled at me, came out from behind her counter, and pressed a kiss on each of my cheeks.

"*Bienvenue!*" she said. "I am Yvette, and you've already met my husband Marc."

Then it hit me. This was the couple we had encountered on the beach promenade after the handover, the ones who had joked about our happiness. What a coincidence that they were our neighbours.

"I've seen you before!" I said. "In February, on the beach promenade. Do you remember?" I described the encounter precisely, but they didn't remember. Nevertheless, I was delighted to meet them both. I took them to heart instantly. After the introductions were completed and drinks arranged,

I had to answer a thousand and one questions. They were quite astonished when they found out there was a *Monsieur*, but he would be coming later.

"And you did all this alone?" asked Yvette.

"Well, me and the removers, so I wasn't exactly alone."

"We saw the *bordel* in the yard", said Marc.

"Yes, that *bordel* is now in my apartment", I replied. We laughed.

You must know that the word "*bordel*" in French stands for chaos or mess, but it also literally means brothel, the world's oldest profession.

We laughed at many things. One glass of Muscat turned into two. I should have eaten something beforehand. Over these two hours, I learned half their life story. They were from Normandy and came down south every three months for three months. Marc was already over 80, though he didn't look it. And I told him so. Oh, what joy it was to receive such a compliment from such a young, pretty woman! He was beside himself with delight until Yvette brought him back to earth by saying:

"Ines is only saying that because she wants to be charming."

That wasn't true; I meant it. I thought he looked no more than 60. Yvette winked at me. Ah, I see, I shouldn't say anything more, or Marc would spend the rest of the night floating under the ceiling.

When I finally managed to say goodbye, it was nine o'clock. I had tried to prevent my glass from being refilled, but in the end, it had probably been a bit too much. Fortunately, the way home was not far. I staggered up the stairs and dragged myself into my kitchen. Here still stood the empty plate, the bag of toast, and the jar of Nutella that hadn't been used that morning. Quickly, I stuffed two or three slices of toast into myself. Man, I was starving! The alcohol clouded my brain. And my stomach made loud protest noises. It was not at all happy with this treatment. I promised to do better in the future.

The next days were spent unpacking, tidying, assembling furniture... and phoning. First, there was the tedious claim for our sideboard with Eggermann.

I don't want to bore you with this story. They claimed the sideboard was already in that condition. Fortunately, we had photographed all the furniture during our inventory. Thus, I was able to prove that the sideboard had been entirely fine before the move. While they acknowledged this, they were still unwilling to forward the matter to their insurance. After countless emails and phone calls, I cut the cord. I hadn't paid for the move in full yet. The last instalment had only been due after moving in, something I had insisted on. I kept that amount. The raging Eggermann could do nothing about it. He had an official complaint from me with proof photos. That's what insurance was for. Everything else was now his problem.

Then there were things like the bank (we urgently needed a bank account), the customer service of Darty (I desperately needed a fridge), and the customer service of Free (I urgently needed internet). I spent hours in hold queues, listened to automated messages, and pressed 1 to identify myself as a new customer, 3 to confirm I had already placed an order, and 5 to speak to a customer service representative. Only to be told, regrettably, that all the staff were currently in a conversation, and I should try again later. Why was I doing all this? Well, I'll get to that in the next chapter.

The moving boxes strewn throughout the flat posed a real challenge. The flat was too small. Boxes were everywhere. The lovely Excel list, showing what was in which box, was nowhere to be found. The computer must have eaten it. Or sent it to data-Nirvana, thinking I needed an additional challenge. I had no idea what was in the boxes. Only the labels "*cuisine*" or "*chambre*" gave me a slight hint. When I then dragged one of these heavy boxes into the bedroom to unpack it there, it turned out to contain lots of stuff I had no use for at that moment. It must have been in the bedroom in the old flat, but there was no space for dumbbells in this small bedroom now. So where to put them? In the office! They would be well placed on the floor of the built-in cupboard in the office. But that was filled with unpacked moving boxes. So, the dumbbells had to wait. Where? In the box, of course. And this half-unpacked box was in my way in the bedroom from then on.

And that's how it went with every second box I touched. Where was that damned packing list? I vowed that the next time I moved, I'd make roughly a hundred backup copies and store them in various places.

AFTER THE MOVE COMES THE NEXT MOVE

The next move comes inevitably. At least with us. Therefore, I would like to offer you a few tips at this point, as it fits so nicely here. This was not our first move to France. And it won't be the last either. And each of these moves held different disasters for us.

We later lived near Nice. Christian had a job in Monaco. We wanted to leave both the job and the Côte d'Azur. We no longer liked either. So, we had given notice on the flat. We wanted to take a break, travel the world, and figure out what we actually wanted and whether France was indeed the country where we wanted to live. We had no idea where we would end up.

Again, we had decluttered vigorously, sold furniture, and reduced our belongings. As the moving-out date drew nearer, we rented a box in a nearby storage. As we did with every move, we had calculated the volume we would need using our inventory list. Every square metre of space costs a lot of money with these boxes. And since we could now rightly call ourselves dropouts, we had to save money. So, we decided on a box with a floor area of 8 square metres. With a height of 2.50 metres, that was still 20 cubic metres of storage space we could fill.

What we overlooked was that you can't fill these 20 cubic metres right to the top. Try as you might, it doesn't work. And what we couldn't know was that the height of the box was wrongly indicated in the description. It was only 2 metres high in reality. And this missing half meter of height, even if it sounds little, makes a difference. It's still 4 cubic metres less.

We did our best to fill the box as efficiently as possible. We filled all the hollows of the fridge and cabinets and chests. We stacked as high as we could. It was damn tight. But we managed to squeeze our yucca in at the end. We didn't have much hope that it would survive this treatment. The leaves bent and weeks without light and water. Doubt was appropriate.

The lesson from this story was, firstly, that you should take a box 2 square metres larger than you've calculated in your wildest dreams. And secondly, that a yucca is tougher than you might think.

When we finally realised that we wanted to live in France after all, we returned penitently. The search for a flat began anew, and we found one in the Narbonne area. We rented a flat on a former vineyard, now owned by an Englishman. The flat was wonderfully quiet and had a fantastic view of the countryside. There was only one catch. Our massive oak table was too big for it. Although it would squeeze into the living room, it would then fill the room entirely. Besides, we had had enough of removers, and we also lacked the budget for it, so we had decided to do everything ourselves this time. And we would surely not get this ton-weight table top up the narrow wooden staircase ourselves. And why carry it up when it couldn't stand there?

We were briefly torn between two options. Option one was to sell the precious piece. But that meant a potential buyer had to be able to see it. In the box, where it was hidden under boxes and all sorts of stuff? And not exactly near Narbonne. Difficult. We opted for option two: sawing it in two.

On the day of the "move-out" from the box, I brought along a brand-new wood saw. We emptied the box as far as we could and packed everything into a rented lorry so that only the table was left in the box. While Christian stowed the things in the lorry and secured the load, I sat on the table and began… to saw. I should perhaps mention that the top was already loose on its frame, which of course I did not cut into. Have you ever sawed through a 7-centimetre-thick, well-seasoned oak top? Two hours later, I had cleanly cut the top into two parts. My arms felt like jelly. My back hurt. I couldn't feel my hands anymore. But the planks still had to be placed in the lorry. We started with the smaller part. That was easy.

But even that we had to carry together. The larger part, two-thirds of the original top, still awaited us. And despite being reduced by a third, the stupid thing still felt like it weighed a ton. With literally the very last of our strength, and thanks to the provided trolley, we managed to get the monster into the lorry. Christian had to sweep the box; I couldn't hold a broom anymore.

The lesson from this story? Firstly, a ton-weight oak top remains ton-weight even if you shorten it by a third. And secondly, you have to be young and foolish to do such nonsense. Or a bit less young but broke. That works too.

There were other moves that went off with fewer mishaps. I mention this just so you don't get the impression that we are cursed with bad luck. One of our moves from France to Germany was paid for by Christian's employer, as he had been transferred from the French headquarters to the German branch. The employer sent us their in-house shipping company, who handled all its transportation. We didn't have to do anything ourselves. Six of them came, disassembled all the furniture, and packed everything most meticulously. We were just in the way. What enthralled me most were their padded suitcases for the dishes. I'll never forget those. From the outside, they looked like blue Samsonite suitcases. Inside, they were completely lined with foam that somewhat resembled egg cartons. Open the suitcase, pop in a whole stack of plates, just as they stood on the shelf, add another stack or a few cups next to it. Close the lid. Done. Brilliant! No fussing with tissue paper and boxes. As quickly as they had packed them in the old flat, they were back on the shelf in the new one. And not a single piece was broken.

Ever since, whenever we have to pack dishes, we dream of these suitcases. We even considered getting some. With our many moves, they would have easily paid for themselves. But there are also those who claim that a motorhome would have long since paid for itself with us. Instead of setting up an apartment every time, renovating, buying furniture, and everything back in reverse when moving out, we might as well have just parked our motorhome somewhere and been done with it. A houseboat has also been suggested to us. Simply weigh anchor and off to new shores.

We don't like to hear this, but they were right. Only with each move we thought: this time it really is the last one. By the way, we've long since given up counting the moves or thinking about the profitability of a motorhome. And our friends have given up writing our new address in paper address books, after the layers of correction fluid next to our name became so thick that the little books wouldn't close anymore.

OF A THOUSAND AND ONE LITTLE THINGS

Long before the move, we had tried to open an online bank account. The friendly customer advisor on the hotline, *Monsieur Lecompte*, told us it wouldn't be a problem. All we would need were copies of our IDs and a copy of the rental agreement confirming our residence in France. We didn't want to arrive in France and be without a French bank account. We knew we'd need one. So, weeks before the move, once we had the rental contract in our hands, we started the procedure. Now I had moved in. And I still didn't have a bank account.

The process dragged on. I'd phoned *Monsieur Lecompte* a dozen times. After a long battle, I'd finally got his direct number. This made things considerably easier. He had received our IDs and rental contract ages ago. When we asked again, he demanded a utility bill. Naturally, at that point, we didn't have one as the ink on our rental contract was barely dry. We hadn't even moved in yet. We could only open an account once we were actually living in France, he explained. The fact that he had told us the exact opposite a few weeks earlier didn't faze him. Why would he care about yesterday's idle talk?

Now, I officially lived in France and had moved in. This surely should suffice for *Monsieur Lecompte* to open an account for us. He still wanted a utility bill as proof of residence, a "*justificatif de domicil*". I'd recently downloaded a bill from our EDF account (the national electricity provider; there are alternatives now). Because our landlady had let the electricity contract expire, we were now considered a new connection, incurring this activation fee. It was a bill from EDF. What they were charging for was irrelevant. Right?

Of course, it wasn't. This wasn't a consumption bill, the amiable bank man explained. He referred to it as "*consommation*". I'd consumed a bit of electricity by then, but there wasn't a bill for it yet. Digging deeper into our EDF account, I found out that the next meter reading would be in a year. Until then, there would be quarterly bills for the basic fee and EDF's estimated consumption for us. So, strictly speaking, these bills also didn't prove that and how much we were consuming. But the banker would be satisfied with them, he'd assured me. Thus, I eagerly awaited the first of these bills, checking EDF online almost daily. When the bill finally appeared, I downloaded it and sent it to the bank.

Now, surely, nothing stood in the way of our new bank account. Or so I thought. Well, everyone can be mistaken. The next day I called *Monsieur Lecompte* again to find out when I could expect the account details.

"Your application is currently under review", he said.

"And how long does that take?" I asked.

"Usually it's very quick, expect about three working days", he replied.

"Do you now have everything you need from us?" I wanted to know.

"I shall think so", he said.

After not hearing anything for a week – my patience was severely tested – I called him again. This time, he wanted proof of income.

"What? You said you had everything", I said.

"*C'est comme ça*", he replied. That's just how it is.

"Why do you want proof of income? It's a free online account!" I exclaimed.

"It's only free as long as a certain regular income goes into it", he said. I groaned inwardly.

I'd actually read something about this on the bank's website before. Quickly, I opened the website and right there on the front page was the button to open an account, with a link to the terms and conditions just below it. There it stated that an alternative was to make a one-time deposit of a certain amount. I suggested this to him.

"Yes, that's also an option", he said, sounding almost a touch disappointed. My neck relaxed. He would send me the number of a transfer account, to which we were supposed to deposit this sum. I was sceptical. Surely this amount should land in our account, not in some account of the bank where it would languish for weeks or months before we could access it again. I scrolled further down the page, found what I was looking for, and read aloud:

"You have 10 working days after opening the account to deposit this sum. If this time lapses without a deposit, the account will be deactivated."

Silence.

"*Non Monsieur*, not a transfer account!" I said. "Send me the account number and access data for OUR new account. As soon as I have that, I'll transfer the sum."

Silence.

It's really awkward when you're caught out trying to rip someone off.

"When can I expect the access details?" I pressed. Finally, he responded.

"*Dans une quatorzaine*", he said. When a French person mentions a "*quatorzaine*", they rarely mean exactly fourteen days. In essence, he was saying he had no idea. So, it could indeed take another fourteen days or significantly longer. I'd just have to be patient once more. I asked again if all the documents were in order, and once more he confirmed they were. We'll see.

Another week later, I called him again just to make sure everything was on track. I didn't really want to wait the full two weeks. It might turn out that yet another document was now missing. Everything was fine, the file was in progress, and we would soon receive the access details and credit cards.

"When exactly?" I needled him.

"*Dans une petite semaine*", he replied. So, in a 'short week' then. Another one of those imprecise timelines. I had no choice but to wait.

A generously counted week later, a whole four weeks after my move-in, I found a letter in the postbox. A plain envelope. No sender. That's how banks in France often send mail to their clients – so no unauthorised person can tell it's from a bank and might contain something of interest. The downside is, everyone knows this by now. So, they might as well write it on the envelope. In my hands, I held the access details for our brand spanking new French bank account. Mission accomplished!

Within the first few days of my arrival, I had gone shopping. Since the buyers of our former flat had taken over our entire kitchen, appliances like the refrigerator hadn't made the move. Our new kitchen equipment consisted of just a countertop and a sink. It was up to the tenant to put in the oven, dishwasher, and fridge.

We had a single, electric hotplate, from the days when Christian started his first job in Northern France. With it, I couldn't cook anything deserving of the term 'meal', but it sufficed for heating canned ravioli.

The issue of refrigeration was trickier. I'd banished the cooler box to the kitchen balcony because it was unbearably loud. But I was glad to have it. At least it could keep butter, milk, jam, and Christian's beloved *rillettes* cool. Not much more would fit inside.

There was a Darty in La Ciotat, as we'd found out on our initial exploration. I didn't want to spend much time looking for the perfect appliances. I needed them immediately. I wanted home delivery. I needed someone to install them. And a local store would be convenient in case of any complaints. That's what I expected from Darty.

So, on a fine day, I drove to Darty, looked around the shop, sought advice from a friendly saleswoman, and within half an hour, I'd bought an oven, dishwasher, and fridge. For each item the lady entered into her computer, I asked if it was truly in stock. Of course, everything was immediately available. She inquired if I had old appliances for them to collect. I said no, hence my urgency. She nodded understandingly and promised the earliest delivery slot.

The delivery was scheduled for the following Friday afternoon. I eagerly awaited that day because living without a fridge felt like camping. You couldn't really call it settled living. I impatiently waited for the doorbell that would announce my appliances' arrival.

Instead of the doorbell, my phone rang. The saleswoman from Darty informed me of a minor delivery issue. She regretfully told me to expect it by Monday. Monday would surely be the day.

Monday came and went with no action. Neither the doorbell rang nor did my phone. As evening approached, I dialled the number on my order slip. Thankfully, I had noted down the saleswoman's name when she'd called me on Friday.

To my surprise, I wasn't connected to the La Ciotat Darty shop but to the central office. After enduring endless minutes on hold and navigating through a maze of automated options, I finally got to speak to an actual human.

"*Tapez 1 … tapez 2 …* Press 1 if you're a new customer. Press 2 if you're an existing customer."

"2"

"Please enter your 6-digit customer number, followed by '*dièse*' to confirm."

What was a '*dièse*' again? The asterisk or the hash key? Damn it! Well, I'll go with the asterisk; it's a 50-50 shot.

"Your input wasn't recognised. Please try again." Click

Hey! I haven't even entered anything, you daft system!

Alright, so this '*dièse*' is the hash key. Let's try again.

…

"*Tapez 1 … tapez 2 … tapez 3 …* Press 1 to place an order. Press 2 to modify or cancel an order. Press 3 for inquiries about an order."

"3"

"*Tapez 1 … tapez 2 …* Press 1 to reschedule your delivery. Press 2 to speak to a customer service representative."

"2"

"Enter your 8-digit order number followed by '*dièse*'."

"594222"…Shit!

"Your input wasn't recognised. Please try again." Click

"Bloody Shit!"

Deep breath. Let's try again, this time with the correct order number.

…

"Currently, all our service representatives are busy. Please try again later. We regret the inconvenience."

WHAAAAAAT !?!?

A few years ago, we had attended a musical in Paris. Ali Baba stood before the Sesame and said, "*Sésame, ouvre-toi!*", which translates to "Open, Sesame!". In response, the Sesame answered with an automated voice, "*Tapez 1 pour…, tapez 2 pour…* and to open the Sesame, *tapez quelqu'un*" (hit somebody). The whole auditorium roared with laughter. Everyone instantly got the joke. Ali Baba gave his companion standing next to him a hearty slap on the head, and the Sesame opened. We always remember that moment whenever we're trapped in one of those automated menu loops. Right now, I also wanted to hit someone. And oh, how I wanted to hit someone. Ali Baba's slap would have barely sufficed.

When I finally got a real person on the phone, I demanded to speak to the lady whose name I had noted down. They couldn't connect me, but she would call me back. And she did, a day later. I was fuming. She got an earful.

Failing to keep a promise is a no-go for me. Absolutely not on. And coming at me with excuses only makes it worse.

"There were delivery issues with the fridge", she chirped.

"How can that be when you said it was in stock?"

"There was a minor problem…"

"I don't care", I said. "You promised me delivery yesterday."

"Yes, but I have no control over that."

"Perhaps, but you could've phoned to tell me I was going to be stood up."

"Yes, my colleagues should have done that. Something went wrong there. *Je suis désolée.*"

"And when will I get the appliances?"

"Friday this week has been set as the new delivery date."

I sighed and said, "Ok."

On Thursday, she called to tell me they wanted to reschedule again. The fridge still hadn't arrived.

"In that case I insist you deliver and install the appliances you have", I said.

"We normally don't do that. We only deliver complete orders", she replied.

"Well, you'll make an exception this time. Otherwise, I'm cancelling the entire order." That worked. On Friday, I got the stove and dishwasher.

By now, I had the direct line to the lady at Darty in La Ciotat. So I could call her daily to pester her with my question, "When will I get my fridge?" When she once again replied that she didn't know, I'd had enough. Weeks had passed since my order. Daytime temperatures were already soaring. Christian was around often, and now two people had to live out of the little cool box.

"How are we going to solve this? We've been living here for weeks without a fridge!" I said. The small print had stated that an order already partially delivered couldn't be cancelled. I would've loved to cancel. But I wanted her to do it so she couldn't charge me a cancellation fee.

"We could provide you with a used unit in the meantime", she said.

"*Ah bon ?*" I responded. "And you only think of this now?"

"*Eh bien*, I didn't realise the situation was so dire."

"Really? I told you in the store when I ordered, and every time we spoke on the phone, that I had no appliances. However. When will we get this old thing?"

"We can bring it to you tomorrow during the day."

"Great! Do it!"

And in fact, we got an ancient, germ-ridden thing the next day that must have once been a fridge. I bought a big bottle of *St Marc* and cleaning gloves and tackled the germs. No, it didn't look new again, but it was clean. We could turn it on.

Crackling and snapping followed by rising smoke from the plug then a distant click from the fuse box indicated that we wouldn't have a usable fridge that day. Exhausted, I slid down the door frame to the floor. I had spent two hours de-germing that damned thing and inhaling those delightful *St Marc* aromas. I was done.

This time it was Christian who called the lady from Darty and gave her a piece of his mind. I don't know why, but when a man does that, it seems to have a much more profound impact than when I do it. Is it just me? Two hours later, a Darty technician in boiler suit arrived, inspected the problem, nodded, and got his toolbox from the van. With big scissors, he simply cut the plug off, stripped the insulation, and attached a new one.

"*Voilà*", he said, plugging it in, and...

No click, no crackling or snapping, just a soft rumble followed by a steady hum. The fridge had started its duty.

Just for the sake of completeness, let me mention that we got our ordered fridge delivered two weeks later.

To have internet access, I had bought a USB data stick that I could plug into my laptop. Without it, I would have been utterly stuck. I couldn't even have sent an email.

My little lifesaver worked quite well... as long as it could pick up data. The only spot in the flat where it could scrape together a few dribbling bytes was right at the corner between the two balcony doors. The rest of the apartment was a dead zone for it. Its little blue bar indicator barely flickered. But right there in that corner, it would proudly display an astonishing two bars on its screen. The balcony would have been an even better spot, but there were times when I simply didn't fancy sitting outside, browsing the web or typing emails. Even in the South, the weather isn't always pleasant.

I had placed a small, 30cm-wide shelf in that corner between the balcony doors. Nothing larger would fit. Day in and day out, that's where I stood whenever I needed the internet. Not the most comfortable solution, admittedly. But it just had to bridge the time until we got a telephone connection including internet. Initially, we didn't imagine it would take long. However, to apply for a telephone connection, we needed a bank account. And as I've mentioned earlier, that took a bit longer than expected.

When I finally, finally got access to our new bank account, my very first act was to order a chequebook. Our friend Harald always called them "those French IOUs", because he didn't think these thin paper slips looked very trustworthy. They bore little resemblance to the chunkier German cheques of old. Moreover, hardly anyone in Germany used cheques anymore. So, he had every reason to poke fun at these tear-off notes.

In France, however, cheques have remained an integral part of daily life, even though their acceptance has dwindled somewhat. We were even asked to pay our rent by sending a cheque in an envelope to the *agence* every month. We didn't see the point in wasting an envelope and stamp for this purpose. Besides, the *agence* had grown accustomed to our bank transfers, which initially required special permission as we didn't have a French bank account. Well, more or less. From time to time, we'd receive a rent arrears notice from them because they would only check their received cheques to monitor payments. They seemingly forgot about their bank account. With each reminder we received, we would email them a screenshot of our latest transfer with a friendly suggestion that perhaps standing orders and bank transfers might have some future in this line of business. However, our efforts seemed to fall on deaf ears.

The company Free, the provider we had chosen for phone and internet, wanted a cheque too. Right after moving in, I had inquired at the Free boutique, hoping, of course, to be able to apply straight away. They then asked for my ID, my email address, my credit card… and my bank details. "Do you have a cheque with you?" they asked. And Mr. Free was quite surprised to hear that I didn't have a bank account. No, that wouldn't work at all. To open a phone line, I needed to provide a *'chèque nul'* and a *RIB*. The latter only if I wanted to pay by direct debit. But he insisted on the cheque. Nothing could proceed without it. I asked why I needed a cheque if I wanted to pay by credit card. The reply was, yet again, the one

143

they all fall back on when they don't have an explanation: "*C'est comme ça*". That's just the way it is. No need to justify it.

Since I had neither a *chèque*, whether *nul* or not *nul*, nor a *RIB*, I had to leave without accomplishing anything and wait until I had a functioning bank account. Once home, I first researched on the internet – with my little data stick friend – what a *'chèque nul'* even was. I understood the words, but I wasn't sure what it meant. Did it mean I had to write a zero for the amount?

It turned out that I had to draw a diagonal line across the cheque and write *'nul'* on that line to invalidate it. The cheque wasn't to be cashed; it simply served as proof that I had a bank account. It's crucial to draw the line across the entire cheque and not forget the little word *'nul'* to distinguish it from a crossed cheque, which is marked with two parallel diagonal lines above the text field.

And a RIB? You probably know it already. It's a *'relevé d'identité bancaire'*, essentially an identity proof of your bank account. It provides details like the account number, IBAN, BIC, and the bank's address. Usually, a few are included in your chequebook. You can also download them online from your bank account or get them at the bank counter. It's a good idea to always have one in your wallet, especially during your first months in France, as you'll need it everywhere. Why this double proof with the cheque and RIB was necessary remains a mystery to me.

Now that I finally had a bank account and could present both a cheque and RIB, I was allowed to apply for telephone and internet. Hooray! The very day I found the cheques in my letterbox, I went to the Free boutique. I laid out my passport, freshly minted credit card, newly printed RIBs, and the first cheque from my brand-new chequebook on the table, saying:

"I would like a telephone line and internet."

I then had to fill out what felt like dozens of forms. I knew my address by heart now. As I diligently filled in the forms and handed them to the lady across the desk, she began entering my details into her computer.

Sitting there, in this boutique to apply for a telephone line, and being asked for your phone number, felt odd. When I pointed this out to the lady, she looked at me blankly; my joke had clearly not landed.

"*Eh bien, votre mobile évidemment*", she said. Your mobile number, of course. I hadn't thought of that. Jokes seemed misplaced here. I scribbled my mobile number onto the form. But when she came to this very number, her computer rejected the format.

"I need a 10-digit phone number. This one is not correct", she said.

"But it is correct", I replied. I still had my German mobile number.

"Is it a foreign number?" she asked.

"*Oui*", I replied.

"That's not possible. The computer won't accept it. I need a French number", she stated.

"But I don't have one", I responded.

"*Eh bien…*", she said, looking at me inquisitively. When I showed no signs of offering a solution, she asked,

"Do you perhaps have a relative or friend whose number you can provide?"

"*Non*", I answered. "Why do you even need my mobile number?"

"It's for potential queries", she explained.

"But you can also contact me via email for this. Plus, I'll soon get a landline from you, then you can call me anytime with all the questions you want." I realised this wouldn't lead anywhere. Sarcasm wouldn't help. So, I said,

"One must be able to apply for a landline even if they don't have a mobile, right?" It was futile.

"*Non*, it's a mandatory field. I have to enter a mobile number."

I could have said that I had given her a mobile number and that one could indeed call me on it. But that wouldn't have helped. We were going in circles. So, I made a provocative suggestion:

"You sell prepaid cards here, right? Just give me one, then I can provide you with a French mobile number."

"*Ah oui !*" she exclaimed, seemingly relieved that she might soon be rid of this obstinate customer.

Again, forms had to be filled out and signed. Again, I had to produce my passport. And again, I had to present my credit card. Finally, she handed me a SIM card. I passed the enclosed slip back to her, saying,

"Here you go, my mobile phone number."

Having overcome that obstacle, she had another in store for me. But I was prepared for this one. Often, I'd inquired upfront which documents were required for a certain application, only to discover, upon arrival, that I was being asked for something previously unmentioned which I didn't have. Consequently, I adopted the habit of always carrying a folder containing copies of all possible documents. In it, there were copies of our passports, stacks of RIBs (bank identity certificates), a copy of our rental agreement, birth certificates, etc. Essentially, anything I'd ever been asked for in my expatriate journey. So, when she asked for a *justificatif de domicil* (proof of residence) – which had never been mentioned before – I could whip out the necessary document. "*Et voilà!*" No, *Madame*, you won't get the better of me that easily.

With the paperwork complete, I'd successfully applied for phone and internet services. However, I was advised to be patient. Without the previous tenant's phone number, the process would take a bit longer. They'd notify me. When I enquired how long this 'bit longer' might be, calculated in a unit of time in days, she said,

"*Une petite dizaine.*" So, I was none the wiser. Once again.

I only had one mobile phone. All our friends and relatives knew my old German number, which I wanted to keep. I swapped SIM cards daily to check for updates from Free. For two weeks, nothing. The SIM card edges became worn from constant switching. I grew so accustomed to the absence of notifications that when my phone finally buzzed after inserting the French card, I jumped so far back in my chair I hit the wall. I had to touch up the mark later with some leftover paint.

Free's text message contained our new number and informed me that the Freebox was en route to me. I was asked to ensure I was home on delivery day. The exact date would be communicated. They also mentioned giving me a *fourchette* (literally translated as 'fork'). In this context, it signifies a timeframe. I amusedly imagined the French using forks with just two prongs; one indicating the start time, the other the end. Three or four prongs would certainly create confusion.

From now on, I switched SIM cards twice a day, out of sheer fear of missing the next message with the delivery date and perhaps not being home when the parcel arrived. I expected at most a two-day delivery time, just as we were used to from Germany. There, I was sadly mistaken. Such a Freebox isn't dispatched that quickly. I even got the impression that it had been sent on foot. Perhaps it got lost along the way. Or maybe, just maybe, it kept stopping for a *petit rouge* and didn't stop at just one.

I jumped again, but not as much this time, when my phone buzzed as I inserted the French SIM card. The Freebox was to be delivered the next day. I had to be available from 8 am to 4 pm. So, this was the promised *fourchette*! Dear people from Free, that wasn't a fork; it was a full-blown rake that a professional gardener could use to clear a meter-wide strip of grass from leaves all at once! A reasonable time span deserving of the name *fourchette* would have been maybe two hours for me, but certainly not eight. By the way, ever since, whenever someone presents me with such a vast *fourchette*, I respond: "*C'est pas une fourchette, c'est un râteau!*" It's not a fork; it's a rake. Feel free to use that one.

The next day, by 8 am sharp, I was dressed and had had my breakfast. A real challenge for me. I'm not an early bird. I need my peace and quiet in the morning. My husband knows from painful experience that it's not a good idea to speak to me before 10 am. Any appointments before this time I consider a personal affront.

I had my phone loaded with the French SIM card, just in case the delivery service couldn't find my address. I dared not move away from my phone. Even the sadly necessary trips to the loo were done in the utmost haste since that could be the exact moment the doorbell rang. I gulped down my lunch, not even noticing what I was eating, eager to finish quickly. Afternoon turned into evening. There was no sign of the Freebox. Nothing had happened by 4 pm. I didn't want to be pedantic, so I gave it another hour. But even when I generously added another hour on top of that – something might have come up – nothing happened. No doorbell, no phone ring, no Freebox. During our usual evening phone call, I complained to Christian that the Freebox hadn't arrived.

"Did you check the letterbox?" he asked. "Maybe he was just too lazy to ring the bell and left a note saying he couldn't find you or something."

"No, I haven't", I said. It hadn't even crossed my mind.

My phone only had reception near the balcony door, so I couldn't simply pop across the flat and down the staircase to the letterbox while talking to him. However, curiosity ensured our conversation that evening was shorter than usual. Hanging up and grabbing the letterbox key became one fluid motion.

I unlocked the letterbox, expecting either an echoing void or a note inside. The door swung open and where there normally was a void, a brown cardboard surface stared back at me. The letterbox was packed to the last centimetre with a parcel. I stood in front of it, gaping at it as if it was a vision from another world. How did that thing get in there? I tiptoed to feel the top, crouched down to check the bottom to see if there was a secret flap for the postman. There wasn't. Magic must be at play here. Good no one was watching at that moment. My baffled face and search for secret entries would surely have gone viral on Facebook.

Later, I found out that every postman in France possesses a master key, and that the letterbox locks are standardised, thus any postman can open them. No magic needed.

Once I'd somewhat recovered from my confusion and began to accept the situation without needing to understand how it had happened, I attempted to remove the package from the letterbox. But it was impossible. I couldn't even fit a small finger between the box and the wall of the letterbox. The package was wedged in so tightly, as if it had been precisely fitted. There was a gap of only half a centimetre to the left, right, and above. No more. Clearly, some engineer at Free had meticulously ensured that the dimensions of the Freebox, including its packaging, matched the internal measurements of the standard French letterbox perfectly. How long had he spent refining it? Had he won an award for this?

For a while, I struggled, attempting to shift the box with my fingernail, hoping it might budge and come out. All I managed to do was push it in further until it was entirely jammed and would not move any more. My fingertips ached. I was frustrated. I had waited so long for this blasted internet, and now I was so close. That couldn't be true. I felt like the corpulent Obelix, who wasn't allowed to drink the magic potion that tasted oh so good to him.

I fiddled around for a bit longer when the downstairs neighbour arrived. The one with the concrete-like hairstyle who had, up to now, ignored me with polite indifference. She needed access to her letterbox, so I made room. Gathering all my courage, I addressed her:

"Do you have any idea how I can get this thing out?"

She first looked at me in surprise – it could talk – and then at the letterbox.

"Oh!" she remarked, shifting her gaze between me and the letterbox, giggling.

"*C'est un challange !*" she said, pronouncing the English word as "Shallansh". I couldn't help but giggle along. The situation was indeed absurd. She tried to use her key to pry the box out, but it wouldn't budge. We realised we couldn't gain enough leverage. And that had us giggling again.

"*J'ai une idee!*" she said after a while of fruitless effort. "*Attendez!*" she had a plan and I should wait. Naturally, I did, having nothing better to do. She dashed into her flat, returning shortly after, brandishing a spatula triumphantly. Together, with her fingers on the top of the package and the spatula below, we attempted to inch the parcel out. It might have moved a millimetre or two. But pulling it out was still a no-go. With a shrug, *Madame* Concrete-hair set the spatula aside. But she wasn't ready to give up. She was now fully engaged.

"*Attendez!*" she said again, disappearing into her flat once more. I was curious about her next choice of tool and whether she'd retain her confidence.

Returning with a roll of packing tape and scissors, she looked less confident but all the more determined.

"We'll fashion a handle", she declared, quickly sticking strips of the tape onto the visible surface of the box, ensuring a looped section protruded for gripping.

Gently and patiently, we pulled on this makeshift handle. The box shifted. But suddenly, snap! The tape peeled off the carton. It did not stick enough on the rough surface of the box. Although the tape didn't hold, the principle seemed promising. So, we tried again, using more tape at multiple points, and again employed the spatula for support. Slowly and delicately, to avoid pulling the tape off, we simultaneously pulled at different points with all four hands. And finally, we moved the package enough to grasp its side and pull it out.

"*Alléluia !*" she exclaimed when we finally got it out.

"*Accouchement difficile*", I added, it had indeed been a difficult birth, and we laughed.

"*Moi c'est Hélène*", she said, extending her hand. So, *Madame* Concrete-hair now had a name.

"*Moi, c'est Ines. Enchantée*", I replied.

"*De même*", she said. And with a "*Bonne soirée*" she turned to disappear into her flat. But on the landing, she changed her mind, turned back and said:

"You know, I really ought to apologise to you."

"Why?" I asked, unaware that she had done anything wrong.

"The other day, when you moved in, I mistook you for a removal woman, seeing you work with those two men in blue overalls. I was surprised that such a slender woman could do that job. That's why – if I remember correctly – I didn't even properly say *bonjour* to you. I'm embarrassed. I hope you can forgive me. It was a mistake", she said.

I had to laugh. She looked so miserable that laughing was probably inappropriate. But I couldn't help it.

"You thought I was a REMOVAL WOMAN?" I asked, striking a bodybuilder pose with a clenched fist and arm, flexing my non-existent biceps.

"Uhm… *oui*… I should have looked more closely", she said now, winking towards my biceps.

"I forgive you", I said with a theatrical bow.

"Well, that's settled then", she said. "Do drop by for a drink sometime."

"I'd love to", I replied.

"*Bonne soirée !*" she said and finally disappeared into her flat.

"*Bonne soirée !*" I replied to the closing flat door.

Our shared Freebox liberation adventure had broken the ice. I didn't take her casual invitation for a drink seriously. Without a set date, they were just empty words. But it was a start. The rest would follow.

More importantly, I had my Freebox. I spent the rest of the evening and all of the next day setting it up and getting it to work. With phone support from Christian. I admit, I usually leave such things to him and try to stay out of the immediate line of fire. But I had to face this battle alone, and I felt a certain pride when the internet connection was finally established, and I could send my success report via email to Christian and retire my little friend, the data stick. The little guy shouldn't be sad; it was just a temporary retirement.

APÉRO AT NOON...

The French *apéro* is a brilliant invention. Back when we moved to France for the first time over 20 years ago, we came to appreciate the merits of this *apéro*. We had rented a small, terraced house at the time. Behind the row of houses were towel-sized gardens. Calling them gardens might be a stretch; they were patches of lawn, more or less well-maintained, enclosed by wire mesh. The fence only came up to one's waist, so you could see right into all the little gardens in the row. Except for the very last one on the left next to us; that one was barricaded with towering wooden fences.

The rest of us had no privacy in our gardens. Every neighbour, and even any passerby, could see how long you'd been neglecting your lawn mowing duties, and that the snails had once again devoured the kitchen herbs. They could also see that my husband, upon returning from his pre-breakfast jogging round, would hang his sweaty running gear over the plastic chairs to air out and would do his stretching bare-chested.

A few weeks after we moved in, our neighbour caught up with him at the garden fence. He was a runner too and had finally found an opportunity to strike up a conversation. From then on, they'd often chat at the fence. During one of these chats, our neighbour learned that Christian didn't drink alcohol – no beer, no wine, nothing.

"*C'est pas possible!*" he exclaimed. That was utterly inconceivable! One couldn't live in France and not drink wine. It was unthinkable. We were invited for an *apéro* on Saturday evening.

"You'll drink wine after that!" he promised. He turned out to be right.

Saturday came. And we had a problem. The military doctor from next door hadn't specified what time we should come over. The invitation simply said "for *apéro*". He presumably assumed that any sensible person would know the timing of such an event. We didn't. Going over to ask felt too embarrassing. So, we turned to the internet...

The French *apéro* usually takes place at home, less often in a café or bistro if you've arranged to dine in the city. It can be before lunch or dinner. If you're "just" invited for an *apéro*, it typically means a glass of wine, Kir, Champagne, Pastis, or the like, depending on the region and preference. Sometimes, it might even be two glasses. Accompanying the drink, there might be nibbles like olives, nuts, crackers, tapenade, etc., again varying by region and taste.

And every person in France knows that after about an hour, you leave because *Madame* needs to prepare the family meal. So, if you work backwards and assume dinner is at 8 pm, then the *apéro* starts at 7 pm. One can only hope that the particular family you're visiting adheres to this rule.

What we didn't know back then, and thus got wrong, was that there's an unwritten rule. This rule states that an invitation to an *apéro* must be reciprocated. If you don't return the gesture, it's a way of saying, "We don't want anything more to do with you." The evening was pleasant, but that's it. If you wish to continue the acquaintance, at the very least, you should invite them for an *apéro*. If you want to deepen the relationship, you take it up a notch and invite them for dinner.

Just for completeness, I'd like to mention there's also the extended *apéro*, known as the *apéro dînatoire*. If you're invited to one of these, the host will have expressly mentioned it beforehand, so you don't make other plans for the evening and know not to prepare dinner at home. An *apéro dînatoire* is essentially an *apéro* that lasts the entire evening. It's essentially dinner, but instead of a typical French menu, there are hundreds of different small dishes, all served simultaneously and in no particular order.

I adore these *apéros dînatoires* because they're so wonderfully practical. When we invite friends over, I almost always do it this way. I prepare everything in advance and spread the filled plates and bowls on the table. Everyone eats what they like for as long as they wish. There's something for every palate. Latecomers aren't an issue. There's no roast in the oven that needs to be served at just the right moment. I don't have to keep popping into the kitchen and can fully enjoy the evening. The atmosphere is much more relaxed than with a three or four-course menu. Give it a try!

Promptly at seven, we stood at the Przybillas' door. They had been expecting us and wondered if we had forgotten the invitation.

"Why? Are we late?" Christian asked.

"No, no, you're actually right on time. We just expected you earlier because Germans tend to eat dinner much earlier than us French. We weren't sure if you knew the usual time for the *apéro*, so we've been prepared for the 'German invasion' since six", the Doc explained with a grin. Given he was military, one probably had to tolerate the 'German invasion' joke.

We were led into the living room. The three children were sitting around a kids' table, eating. The children always ate earlier when guests were expected, otherwise, they'd devour all the snacks, *Madame* explained. Quite sensible, we thought, eyeing the array of nibbles. We had also prudently eaten a little something beforehand. One could never be too safe.

Usually, during an *apéro*, guests are asked what they'd like to drink. Back then, Christian's answer would probably have been "*Coca*", but things have changed since. Today, we weren't asked. *Monsieur* Przybilla had a mission to accomplish. He had to convert a non-believer. He was somewhat relieved to learn he only had to convert Christian.

"*Ah, Madame sait apprécier le vin*", Madame appreciates the wine, he said, nodding at me approvingly.

With great ceremony, he took the bottle from the cooler, explaining that it was the perfect wine for beginners. Most novices, he said, made the mistake of starting with too dry a wine.

"This is a *Coteaux-du-Layon*, but not just any *Coteaux-du-Layon*. This one comes from my parents' vineyard", he declared solemnly as he uncorked and poured the wine.

"Somm Woll", he said, raising his glass. Where had he learned that? As we brought our glasses to our lips, his eyes were fixed intently on Christian's face. And when Christian's expression brightened and he smiled, the Doc nodded, already confident of his victory. When Christian let out a pleased "Hm!", he cheered.

"*Haha, je le savais!*" I knew it, he exclaimed, performing a little victory dance.

He had converted the non-believer. Dear *Monsieur* Przybilla, if only you knew…

That was more than twenty years ago. Let's return to the here and now, to the flat in La Ciotat. It was Sunday, but that didn't matter to me. All the days of the week were the same for me. And on all of them, I toiled away in the flat. I assembled furniture, unpacked boxes, rearranged things I'd already put away, shuffled furniture around…

I had risen early and had a quick breakfast. My goal for today: paint the living room. At least part of it. I couldn't reach all the walls. The room was too small, and it was crammed with furniture and boxes. Parts of our bookshelf, which I hadn't yet assembled, were leaning against one wall. I had to paint two walls first, wait for them to dry, rearrange things, and then paint the rest.

I'd spent the last few days filling in holes that we hadn't managed to fix during our renovation in February. There was even some wallpaper left in the living room. When I had torn down the strips above the door, plaster had crumbled down. A cautious tap on the remaining intact areas had dislodged more flakes of plaster. I had painstakingly filled these in. The walls were now as smooth as a baby's bottom. Ready for painting.

I'd spent half the morning taping off the floor, door frames, window frames, and sockets. Such things always take far too long. The first wall was painted along the edges, and

I could finally wield the large paint roller. At last, progress was visible.

There were definitely too many corners in this living room. Why couldn't they build straight walls? Because they had built a fitted wardrobe on the other side of the wall in the bedroom, that's why. Fine, fitted wardrobes were useful. But these corners were incredibly annoying. Once again, I was using the small brush to paint the edges. Once again, I was relieved to finally use the large roller.

I didn't pay attention to the time. After all, I was alone and could do what I wanted when I wanted. But it must have been past midday when the doorbell rang. I had just dipped the roller into the paint bucket and now stood there, helpless, not knowing where to put it. So, I decided, let whoever wants to ring the bell ring it; I'm not here. The doorbell rang again.

"*Je sais que vous êtes là, Ines!*" a voice called from outside the door. I know you're there, Ines! It was Marc's voice, our neighbour from diagonally-below-next-door. Damn, I cursed.

"*Une minute!*" I called out. With the dripping paint roller, I rushed to the kitchen to grab a rubbish bag to put it in.

Covered in paint from head to toe, I opened the door. Marc stared at me.

"*Mais, qu'est-ce qui vous arrive?*" he asked when he saw me like this. What happened to you?

"Well", I said, "I'm painting." Wasn't that obvious?

"*Ah bon?*" he said, and after a brief pause added, "*Venez prendre l'apéro!*" come for the *apéro*.

"What? ... Now? ... At noon?"

"*Oui, maintenant!*" he said. Yes, now! Oh no, I inwardly groaned, not now. This was the last thing I needed. But Marc was relentless. On Sundays, one had a proper lunch. So, beforehand, one must have a proper *apéro*. He took no prisoners. He had already turned away and was heading to his flat. Oh well, I thought, I can continue painting later. I was wrong about continuing to paint, but more on that shortly.

"*J'arrive!*" I called after him. I'm coming!

It must have been noon when he rang the doorbell. A quarter of an hour later, I stood at their door, somewhat cleaned of paint splatters.

By now, they knew from last time that I loved Muscat, so a generously filled glass awaited me as I entered the living room. Yvette playfully scolded me for working on a Sunday.

"Not even on Sunday does this girl take a break! But everyone needs a break now and then!" and so on and so forth.

"I'll take a break when the flat is finished", I countered. I was highly motivated. Christian was coming for the long Easter weekend. I wanted everything to be ready by then. There was still a lot of work to do and only a few days left. I had to get on with it. I explained this to them. They nodded.

"*Alors, ce fameux Monsieur*, he actually exists? We thought he didn't exist at all", Yvette said, winking at me.

"You'll see!" I replied, feigning a threatening tone.

We laughed, we chatted, one glass of Muscat became two, and two became three. There was so much to talk about. I learned that Marc had been a seaman as a young man. He brought out old photos. In one of these, he was doing a handstand on the bowsprit of a large merchant sailing ship, clad only in shorts and a shirt. You know, the bowsprit is the part that juts out at the front, beyond the railing, into empty space.

"*Ça, c'est moi!*" he said, puffing out his chest. Who else could it be?

"Wow!" I said, genuinely impressed.

He told me that he had once been left behind by his crew in New York because he had fallen ill, and the ship couldn't wait for him. It was expected in Buenos Aires. They planned to pick him up on the return journey. So, he had to kill some weeks in New York, which he managed splendidly. According to him, American girls were utterly helpless against the charms of a young Frenchman who spoke not a word of English. Well, I had seen the photos. I believed him.

"How did you communicate with the girls?" I wanted to know.

"*Mais, ma chère*, one doesn't need words for love", he replied, winking. Fair enough, no need to delve deeper into that. After all, his wife was present.

I wanted to steer the conversation into less risqué waters and asked:

"How long have you two been married?"

"Not that long, only for 10 years. Yvette is already my fourth", Marc said. Then they both laughingly told me how they had met.

Marc had been married to a woman thirty years his junior. They loved each other, but at some point, he felt he couldn't quite satisfy her anymore. Yes, that's how he actually put it. Yvette said the young woman had become too demanding for him. Well, the truth probably lay somewhere in between. They mutually and amicably decided to separate. However, she didn't want to leave him all alone. She worried about his well-being. So, she decided to find a new wife for him. She placed an ad on his behalf. The women who responded to the ad ended up with her. Some were too surprised and simply hung up. Those who got over the initial shock and stayed on the line were subjected to a thorough interview. Those who passed and were deemed good enough had to meet with the soon-to-be ex-wife. For orientation, as Yvette put it. Yvette was one of those who passed *Madame's* test and was still in the running when *Monsieur* finally got to meet a handpicked selection. And Yvette was ultimately his choice. Yvette was a better fit; for she was only twenty years younger than Marc. *Madame* packed her bags, moved out, and Yvette moved in. *Voilà!*

It was half-past two when I finally tore myself away from the couple. I couldn't go on. The laughter and the wine had done me in. The empty stomach might have played a small role as well. The hallway in their flat was moving. Luckily, it wasn't wide. I could hold on with both hands to the left and right. I applied the same technique in the stairwell, which also seemed to sway like a ship in a gale-force seven wind. I have no recollection of how I managed to get the key into the keyhole. But I must have succeeded somehow. Continuing with the tried-and-true hand-left-hand-right-against-the-wall technique, I fought my way through our hallway, took the first right, and collapsed onto the bed, where I fell into a coma.

When I woke up, it was dark outside. I probably wouldn't be painting anymore today. Oh well.

Some time after we had moved in, and Christian had also arrived in La Ciotat, we got new neighbours. The flat one landing above, so above Yvette and Marc, had finally been renovated. The roof above it had needed repairs; it had been leaking, and the water had found its way down to the living room ceiling of this flat. So, it had already been vacant when I had viewed our flat. Had it been ready back then, I wouldn't have hesitated for a second and would have taken it. Because from up there, you could see the sea. And I mean, really see it. The balcony and the large windows offered a magnificent view over the bay. We didn't know all this yet when the new neighbours moved in; we would find out later.

We met the new neighbour in the stairwell. He had just arrived and was lugging his stuff up the stairs when Christian was taking out the bin. We had no idea that we were getting new neighbours. So Christian was somewhat surprised when he introduced himself:

"*Bonjour*, I'm Frederic, your new neighbour from up there."

The two chatted animatedly as I joined them. We had an appointment in Marseille, and I had wondered where Christian had got to. Taking out the bin usually didn't take that long. And I knew that Marc and Yvette weren't around. So, there was really nothing that could have delayed him for so long.

I looked at Christian quizzically, and he eventually remembered to introduce him:

"This is our new neighbour, from up there."

We had no more time. We had to go. In the car, I asked Christian:

"And what's the name of our new neighbour?"

"I forgot", he confessed. That's why he had only introduced him as "our new neighbour." Fair enough. I would have to find out the name later. That wasn't so easy. Once someone has said their name, they assume you know it and don't keep repeating it. I had to be patient.

We crossed paths with him often in the stairwell. On one of these occasions, he told us that his wife Sylvie was still in Paris and would come later, once his probation period in Marseille was over. They wanted to make sure that his new job would work out before she applied for her transfer. She was an official. Once a transfer was requested, the wheels would be set in motion and couldn't be stopped. Whether it would work out immediately with the transfer, he didn't know. It could also take longer, depending on when a suitable position in Marseille would become available.

The next weekend, Sylvie came to La Ciotat. We met them both while walking on the beach and spontaneously invited them for an *apéro* that evening.

I had gotten into the habit of always having some nibbles and something tasty in the fridge for spontaneous *apéros* with Yvette and Marc. You never know. So, the spontaneous invitation to Sylvie and Fred – as we now knew thanks to Sylvie, because she had called him that – was no problem. When you live in France, you always need *apéro* supplies. Remember that!

Promptly at seven, Sylvie and Fred were at the door. They knew they were visiting Germans, so they had to be punctual. They had brought Cidre and apologised for not bringing anything better. They had nothing else at hand so spontaneously and didn't want to come empty-handed. Cidre was great, we said. We liked Cidre. But how did a Parisian come by Cidre? He was no Parisian at all. Oops. He was from Brittany. Hence the Cidre. Got it. We would have to be more careful with such statements in the future. Just because someone drives around in a car with a Parisian license plate doesn't mean there's a Parisian in it.

Do you have to bring something when you're invited for an *apéro*, we wanted to know. If so, we'd been doing it wrong all along.

You don't have to, but if it's the first time, it's generally customary. Oops, again!

But I think I was excused with Marc and Yvette. He had practically dragged me away from my work. They surely hadn't expected me to bring anything. The countless *apéros* we'd since shared with them amply proved that they either hadn't noticed the faux pas or hadn't taken it amiss.

We were delighted to have neighbours around our age in Sylvie and Fred. They might be a few years younger than us. We hit it off immediately. The conversation was lively, and the topics seemed endless. Time flew by.

As I've mentioned elsewhere, it's usually the norm for guests to leave after an hour, or an hour and a half at most, if they're only invited for a drink, or an *apéro*. Sylvie and Fred stayed. They had no intention of leaving. They were enjoying themselves, and the conversation was pleasant. And I was running out of nibbles. By nine, I asked if they were hungry and if I should pop a pizza in the oven. I'd been wrestling with myself for about an hour, wondering what to do.

What do you do when guests won't leave? You can't exactly kick them out. Especially not when they're as pleasant as these two. You just have to improvise. The frozen pizza was my last resort. It was enthusiastically received. Next time, I'd stock up more. Or just invite them for dinner.

By ten, Sylvie and Fred said their goodbyes. Sylvie had to get up early the next morning to go back to Paris. But the next time she came, we must definitely visit them. By then, Fred would surely have cleared up the worst of the chaos in their flat, she said, casting a mischievous glance at him.

"*Ok, je fais de mon mieux*", he said, laughing. He'd do his best. The way she looked at him, she probably knew not much would come of it.

A few weeks later, we were invited to Fred and Sylvie's. Not for an *apéro*, but for *dîner*, for dinner. They'd decided to take the next step. We were thrilled. And on this occasion, we also got to admire the magnificent view from their living room. We weren't envious at all. No, not one bit.

Waterfalls – and other Challenges

The long Easter weekend arrived, and it felt far too short. In the days leading up to it, I had worked like a horse to make the flat presentable before Christian arrived. I didn't want anyone to say that I'd just been lounging on the beach. Alright, I had done that once or twice, but it was still early in the year and the weather was a bit hit-or-miss.

Still, I couldn't shake the feeling that I hadn't done enough. There were so many unfinished tasks. I had revamped the built-in wardrobe in the bedroom by scrubbing it inside and lining the shelves with adhesive foil. Now it was clean and usable. The grubby built-in cupboard in the kitchen had also received a makeover. The old shelves had been thrown away, and I had new ones cut at the hardware store. I painted the interior walls white, making it look like new. I had even managed to finish painting the living room without Marc dragging me off for an *apéro*. I'd also managed to assemble the bedroom wardrobe by myself, so we could consider that room temporarily complete.

All of this had consumed a lot of time. I don't know why, but tasks like these always take twice as long as you initially think they will. So, it wasn't surprising that some things were left undone. Especially the tasks I didn't feel confident tackling alone, or simply didn't fancy doing by myself, like setting up the bookshelves. That eyesore in the living room bothered me immensely. So, that was our agenda for Easter weekend. Ideally, right at the start, so that when Yvette and Marc came to visit us for the first time, we could present a tidy living room.

The train station in La Ciotat is quite far from the city centre. I was as excited as a camel in the desert finally finding water, knowing that I would soon hold my darling in my arms again. I arrived at the station half an hour early. The train could arrive early, after all. It didn't. It was late. When it finally pulled in, my stomach was aflutter with excitement. Scanning the long line of carriages and finally seeing Christian disembark, my heart leapt. At last!

Although we had spoken on the phone as often and as long as possible over the past weeks, there was now so much to say. Yet neither of us could utter a word. We simply held each other tightly, not wanting to let go. Finally, we were together again. Now, into the car quickly; it had just started to drizzle. It would continue to rain throughout the entire Easter weekend. But that didn't matter; we had each other.

I had made a list of all the little tasks that were easier with four hands than two. Hanging ceiling lights by yourself is simply a pain; I'd tried. If the man thought he could laze around this weekend, he was sorely mistaken. When I showed him my list, he groaned at its sheer length.

"It doesn't all have to be done this weekend", I reassured him. "I can always ask Marc to help", I added with a grin. That did the trick. At nearly ninety, Marc wasn't exactly the most helpful. Nevertheless, he had offered to help me more than once. But I'd rather climb the ladder myself than risk him breaking his neck for my sake.

"Well then, let's not dilly-dally; let's get cracking", said Christian. It was going to be a working weekend. But not just that...

On Friday evening, the bookshelf was up. We placed a few decorative items in it so it wouldn't look so terribly empty. It looked odd. Nevertheless, it had to stay like that for now. Unpacking books wasn't on the list. We had more important things to do. On Saturday, we went to Ikea for a big shop. Big by our standards. We needed a new sofa. Our giant sofa hadn't made the move. I had provisionally filled the space where the sofa should go with an air mattress and cushions. When you sat on this makeshift sofa and leaned your back against the wall, the air mattress would slip out from under your bum. This had to stop.

I wanted a sofa. I had found one on Ikea's website that was small enough for our living room. We also wanted to upgrade the kitchen to have more storage space. We had already pushed the old drawer cabinet from the cellar into the gap under the worktop. It looked good there. Three new wall cabinets above it were meant to support its function.

I think you know well enough what it's like to shop at Ikea on a Saturday. It's no different in France than anywhere else. So, I'll spare you the details. We found what we were looking for, and a bit more. Luckily, everything fitted into our estate car. We could start the journey home. Somewhere between Marseille and Aubagne, the engine sputtered, and smoke rose from the cracks in the bonnet. We rolled onto the hard shoulder. Christian cautiously opened the bonnet. The radiator had run dry. We stood in the rain for half an hour until it had cooled down and Christian could refill the water. We listened intently to the clatter of the starter motor and breathed a sigh of relief when the engine started again. Phew, that was a close call! I still got my well-deserved telling-off. I could have refilled the water at some point in the last few weeks. Yes, I could have if I had thought of it.

On Saturday evening, just before seven, we sat completely exhausted but happy on our new sofa, awaiting Yvette and Marc for *apéro*. This invitation had been long overdue. They had invited me to their place several times. I had promised to invite them as well once the flat was ready. It wasn't ready yet, but it had to do. We didn't want to miss the opportunity for them to finally meet Christian.

Marc had been conspicuously busy in and around his garage for the last two days. The strategy was successful. He had caught Christian at the car and had a little chat with him. He also showed him his treasures in the garage and offered him the use of them anytime. No, not cars. Tools. The walls of his garage were lined with hooks, on which tools were neatly sorted. All shiny and polished, sorted by theme. Here was everything a craftsman's heart could desire. This was so typical of men. You show a man your tools. He hadn't shown them to me yet. I could have used one or two of them in the last few weeks. Just you wait, I'll give you a piece of my mind when you come over tonight, I thought!

"He's so sweet", Christian had said when he came up. I had to agree.

At seven o'clock sharp, the doorbell rang. Yvette and Marc stood in their Sunday best at our door, holding out an unwieldy, colourful paper-wrapped monstrosity.

"This is for your move-in. It's a bit late, but technically, you've only just really arrived", Yvette said. We hurried to relieve them of the monstrosity; it looked heavy. It was heavy. We heaved the thing into the living room. It turned out to be a Yucca in a colourful ceramic pot.

"It will look wonderful on our balcony", I said.

"*Exactement*", Yvette said. That's exactly what they had thought.

For now, it could stay where it was, standing in the way in our living room. The rain had intensified. In this weather, we didn't want to chase anyone out, not even a Yucca.

Just like me, Christian had immediately taken a liking to both of them. The feeling was mutual; you could sense it. When they said goodbye two hours later, we hadn't stopped talking for a second, and yet there was still so much left unsaid. This called for a repeat.

After we'd said goodbye to them, I headed to the kitchen to make us a quick dinner. Then I heard a "Oh, shit!" from the other end of the flat, followed by:

"Come quickly with a mop and bucket!"

I was already halfway there where the scream had come from. I ran back to the kitchen and arrived at the scene of the incident armed with a mop and bucket. I didn't even have to ask what had happened. The entire floor of the office was flooded. I took off my shoes and socks and waded in. Christian was busy hastily moving the computers, which were on the floor, onto the desks so they wouldn't get damaged, if they hadn't already. Under the – closed! – window, a waterfall was running down the wall. The rain was pelting against the panes. This wouldn't stop coming in until the rain stopped, I thought. I rushed to the window, flung it open, and got a splash of water and wind that soaked me in seconds. Dripping and blind, I fished for the window shutter locks. The wind ripped the shutters out of my hands again.

Christian, who had noticed my desperate attempts, joined me, and together we managed to catch a window shutter on each side and close them. Locking them and closing the window was one and the same. Now we stood dripping in front of the window and stared at the waterfall. It continued for a moment, then lessened and finally stopped altogether. For the moment, the danger was averted.

We could now turn our attention to the water on the floor. Thankfully, it was a stone floor and not carpet. We splashed, wiped, and wrung until everything was mostly dry again. We were still drenched, and my hair was dripping. We stepped into the bathtub and stripped off our wet clothes. As sexy as that may sound now, both of us wet and naked in the bathtub, it wasn't – don't get any wrong ideas. If we'd been exhausted before this waterfall incident, now we were dead on our feet.

On Easter Monday, it finally stopped raining. The sky was a radiant blue. That was hardly surprising, as the Mistral was blowing at a hundred miles an hour and had blown all the clouds away. One side of our balcony was sheltered from the wind and in the sun. We could sit outside. It was glorious. We let the sun shine on our bellies. Today we had the day off and were allowed to enjoy ourselves. You just had to not stick your nose around the corner and say hello to the Mistral, then everything was fine.

The Yucca from Yvette and Marc was still standing in the living room, right in the passage leading to the kitchen and hallway. After dancing around it one too many times, we'd had enough. It needed to fulfil its destiny and take its place on the balcony. It would have to get used to the wind if it was going to survive with us. It would have to endure far more than just the Mistral wind, but luckily it didn't know that yet. Otherwise, it might have quit during its probation period.

With combined effort, we lugged the pot onto the balcony. On the windy side, of course. We hoped it would act as a bit of a windbreak. The heavy pot stood firm and stable. It was cheerfully illuminated by the sun; it looked pretty. Satisfied with our work, we set off for a blustery Easter walk on the beach and let the Easter weekend wind down comfortably. Christian had to go back to Germany after the weekend, but it wouldn't be for long.

I later reported the leaky window to the *agence*. For weeks, I heard nothing. For weeks, I sat in the office with the shutters closed when rain was forecast. We had since elevated our computers onto small, homemade platforms to protect them from further water intrusion. Surprisingly, they had survived their first soaking. Our neighbours wondered why our shutters were so often closed even during the day. When I told them the story, Marc said I should threaten them with a *huissier* (bailiff); that would work wonders. And he was right. I sent a registered letter to the *agence*, demanding that the issue be resolved by a certain date. Usually, you give them two weeks. If these two weeks passed without any action, I would involve the *huissier*. Two days later, *Madame Bourgeois*, our landlady, was at the door wanting to inspect the window. The *agence* had called her yesterday, saying there was a minor issue with the window. Yesterday, eh? Well, if you say so. And the issue wasn't minor. I described what had happened. She didn't seem very impressed. I pointed out the rotten wood of the window frame. She just shrugged.

She would send someone over, she said, and took her leave. When would that happen? When nothing had happened two weeks later, I called the *huissier*. He listened to every detail, took notes, and finally said:

"*Je m'en occupe*", he would take care of it. And he did.

The next day, I received a call from the *agence*. They had commissioned a window builder; could he come over tomorrow to take measurements? He certainly could. The window builder came, inspected the window, and said:

"*Pas étonnant*", not surprising. He poked around with his screwdriver in various holes in the window frame. These holes were drainage holes, he explained, so that the water could flow away. They were blocked. The water had found another way. This should now actually solve the problem; I could safely open the shutters again. But he would still install a new window for me; this one was really beyond repair.

"*Totalement pourrie*", he called it, totally rotten.

Couldn't agree more, I thought.

Another two weeks later, I had a new window. And got to repaint the wall around it.

Spring had transitioned into summer faster than we'd planned. Christian's contract had ended, and he had finally become a true Southerner. By early May, it was already so hot that I dared to jump into the still very cold sea. I just had to get in. I always feel that way on days when the water is as clear as a mirror, without a single ripple, lying completely still. And if I'm lucky, I'm the only human far and wide, just me and the fish. Bliss!

Christian doesn't get it at all. When the water is that cold, not even ten horses could drag him in. He's more willing if there are big waves to jump into, but those are rare in the Mediterranean. And if they do occur, it's in winter when only the truly mad go swimming.

When we returned from the beach that day, our flat felt particularly stuffy. We flung open all the windows. The sun was allowed to flood the rooms, making the dust particles dance. This was exactly how we'd imagined life "down here". We were together, we were in the South. What more could you want?

I saw it coming. The balcony door started to move very slowly. Then it picked up speed. And before I could reach it, it slammed shut with a loud bang. There was a clatter and a crash. Glass shattered on the stone floor. One of the panes had completely fallen out of the frame and crashed onto the floor. The old, crumbling window putty couldn't hold it back.

Did I mention we had single-glazed windows?

The shards and glass splinters had spread throughout the living room. The impact had been so forceful that they'd been flung into every corner. Months later, we were still finding tiny glass splinters in the vacuum cleaner's dust container. Buying door stoppers shot to the top of our priority list.

We weren't quite sure how to proceed. Christian called the *agence* for advice. Normally, household insurance would cover this, he was told. They would send us the contact details of a glazier. No, not a window builder. What we needed was a glazier. He would give us a *devis*, a cost estimate, which we should submit to the insurance company. Once we had the go-ahead from the insurance, we could commission him. None of this sounded like a quick solution to the problem.

One side of the French door was now open. Moreover, this side of the balcony was visible from the street. "Feel free to break in!" seemed to be the message. "But please wipe your feet before letting yourself in." This was all well and good in nice weather, but what if it turned cold again?

I called the insurance company. They confirmed what we'd already learned from the *agence*. That's exactly how we should handle it. The glazier promised to drop by sometime this week to take measurements. Welcome to the South.

We found an old moving box and crafted a cover for the window opening. From then on, we not only closed the window shutters at night but also during the day when we left the flat. Not that the panes of the other balcony door would have offered any significant resistance to a determined burglar. That one was also single-glazed, and the putty was old and crumbling. A slight push against the glass would have sufficed. Oh, what am I saying? Probably even a slightly stronger push against the old wooden door frame would have done the trick. But we felt safer this way.

The next day, the glazier arrived. He happened to be in the area and thought he'd pop in. We had to tear down our lovely cardboard construction so he could take precise measurements.

"You could do this yourselves", he said. "Just get a pane cut at the hardware store and install it. Why do you need me?"

"Because we need a proper invoice for the insurance", Christian explained.

"And because we've never done this before", I added.

He smiled and said, "*D'accord.*" We should get in touch once we had the go-ahead from the insurance.

We did that three weeks later. Two days after that, the glazier arrived, followed by two lads gingerly manoeuvring a pane through the stairwell.

"*Ne cassez rien!*" he shouted over his shoulder. Don't break anything! And to us, he said, "*Ça va les Allemands?*"

Ah, so we were already filed under "the Germans".

We had pre-emptively removed our cardboard construction so the glaziers could get straight to work. The master took out his tape measure, checked the height and width, and frowned. He pulled an old piece of paper from his shirt pocket – the same paper where he'd scribbled the measurements of our window nearly four weeks ago. I recognised it because it had come from my desk and had a promotional print in the corner. He measured again, and frowned again.

"*Mais, qu'est-ce que j'ai fait?*" he muttered. What have I done? This didn't sound good.

The lads had already brought the pane into the living room. They were growing tired of standing there holding it and began to set it down on the floor. That snapped the master out of his reverie.

"*Mais vous êtes cons!*" he shouted. Are you mad!

They paused halfway and looked confused.

"Not on the stone floor!" the master yelled.

"Ah, ok", they nodded and carefully set the pane down on their shoes. Just don't make a wrong move now, I thought.

Master Glazier had mismeasured. Or misnoted. Either way, the pane was too small. A centimetre was missing at the top – or bottom, depending on how you looked at it. He didn't tell us this; he didn't want to lose face. But we could see for ourselves.

From his jacket pocket, he fumbled out some nails, which he pressed into the window frame. No hammer was needed for the rotten wood. The nails were obviously meant to lift the pane a few millimetres. If it doesn't fit, make it fit.

Carefully, very carefully, the two lads now lifted the pane into the window frame. It crunched a bit as it came to rest on the nails at the bottom. One of the apprentices – I assume they were apprentices – jumped out to hold it from the outside, so it wouldn't suddenly fall out. Once it was in place, you could see there was still a half-centimetre gap at the top. We were curious to see what Master Glazier would do next. I never thought installing a simple windowpane could be as exciting as the best Saturday night crime drama.

Master Glazier saw the gap and raised an eyebrow. More nails were inserted at the bottom. The gap barely narrowed. Now he also stuck nails into the wood at the top to hold the pane. A few more nails on the sides, and it was done. Would this withstand a strong Mistral? Now he took a large portion of something that looked like grey play dough from a plastic bucket. And as you do with play dough, he kneaded it into long sausages. Another large portion was handed to one of the apprentices, who did the same. They pressed these sausages into the edges. The bucket emptied. Apprentice number two was sent to the car for more. You'd think this kneading and pressing must somehow give them inner satisfaction, as they spent an eternity on it. In the end, we had a very nice, thick, and even window putty joint that looked a little thicker at the top than on the sides and bottom. It needed to dry now, so please be careful.

We promised to be oh-so-careful. But would the Mistral be?

"Don't worry", he said. Once the putty had dried, it would withstand even the strongest Mistral. Until then, we should just close the window shutter when the Mistral was blowing. We were used to that.

Before Master Glazier left, he gave us some good advice:

"You need new windows", he said, gesturing dismissively at what were supposed to be our windows. "Otherwise, you'll freeze your arses off here next winter."

We nodded and thought, come on, we're in the South; it can't get that cold in winter. He would turn out to be right.

This window, with its thick putty sausages, really did withstand every Mistral. We, of course, ignored the glazier's advice to install new windows. That wasn't in the budget.

And our landlady felt the old windows were still up to snuff. Financial contribution from her side was out of the question. So, we quickly put the topic to bed.

The litmus test for the new pane came one evening when the Mistral was unusually fierce, gusting at 180 km/h around the corners of the buildings. The windows rattled in their frames. The pane held. Still, we didn't entirely trust the situation, so we closed the shutters for the night.

When we woke up the next morning and opened the shutters, we saw just how ferociously the wind had raged the previous night. The neighbour's shutter had been ripped from its hinges and had sailed into the courtyard. Good thing our car was parked far enough away. The pine trees in the yard had lost some branches, all of which had been blown into the far corner against the hedge.

And on our balcony, the Mistral had knocked over the Yucca. We were impressed. The pot was heavy; it had taken both of us to carry it. We set it upright again, gathered the soil, straightened the bent fronds, and tied the trunk to the lower balcony railing. *Monsieur Mistral* wasn't going to pull that stunt on us again. The pot now had a small chip on the edge, but we could turn that to the back. The Yucca had survived its first stress test, albeit with a few bent leaves.

THE NEVER-ENDING STORY OF THE CAR REGISTRATION

We had put it off for a long time. Normally, we're quite conscientious about such matters. But this task loomed before us like Mount Everest just before the storm of the century. Then one day, a letter arrived from our German car insurance company, essentially saying they were kicking us out. It wasn't phrased quite so harshly, of course. They regretted that they could no longer insure us, as our residence now appeared to be permanently abroad. They gave us a grace period of six weeks. After that, the insurance would automatically expire. We had to re-register our car at our new place of residence.

Months ago, we had looked into what documents we would need for this. There had been talk of a European Certificate of Conformity. These days, you probably download something like that from the internet. We couldn't find one. We scoured all our paperwork from when we had bought the car. We had carefully kept the vehicle registration document and the purchase contract. But nothing in these documents was called anything like 'conformity'. So, one afternoon, we happened to pass by an Opel dealer and spontaneously popped in to ask if he had ever heard of such a certificate. He hadn't. But he called the boss, who did know what we were talking about. This certificate confirmed that the vehicle, built in Europe, met European standards, and could therefore be driven in France, a European country. Why a car built in one European country needed a European Certificate of Conformity to be registered in another European country, he couldn't tell.

"*Eh bah, c'est la bureaucratie*", he said, shrugging his shoulders. That's just how bureaucracy is.

"Can you issue us one?" we asked.

"Haha", he laughed, shaking his head. "Do I look like a civil servant?"

"No", we said. "Not really. But like someone who knows about this stuff."

"Haha", he laughed again. "I'd love to help you, but I can't. You have to contact the manufacturer for that."

So we did. We wrote to Opel Germany and asked them to send us such a certificate. Other than an automatically generated email thanking us for our message, we heard and saw nothing from Opel. After several weeks of waiting in vain, we sent our email again. Maybe it had got lost in data nirvana. Again, we received the automatic words of thanks. And then nothing more. That's where it had stayed until this letter from the insurance company arrived. I'll admit, we hadn't exactly put this issue at the top of our priority list. Until now.

I rummaged through the old sent emails to find the two messages to Opel. I wanted to have ammunition when I called Opel now. But calling wasn't that simple. Sure, I found a phone number for some central office, but the friendly lady there couldn't help me, and unfortunately, she also didn't know who in their corporation could. After battling my way through customer service, sales, and the export department, I ended up with a gentleman from the legal department who told me he couldn't help me; such requests had to be made in writing. And no, an email was not a proper written form. I had to send a letter and include a copy of the vehicle registration document. Then, and only then, could it be properly processed. Groan!

Just as I was resigning myself to waiting a few weeks for a response from Mr. Opel, Christian came up with a creative idea. We could make one last attempt and call the dealer where we had once bought the car. Maybe he could expedite the process. I didn't hold out much hope but let him try. What did we have to lose? Ten minutes later, he reappeared, beaming, and said,

"I've got it!"

"What have you got?" I said.

"The certificate!" he said.

"Which certificate?" I was clueless. I couldn't even begin to think he was talking about THAT certificate. Impossible. He laughed at my bewildered expression.

"Let me spell it out for you: I have the European Certificate of Conformity for our car", he said slowly.

"How is that even possible?" I said.

"I called the dealer and asked how to get such a thing as quickly as possible. He said, 'No problem, just give me the chassis number, and I'll send it to you.' And he just did. The email is already here."

I was speechless.

So, there it was, the Certificate of Conformity, or CoC for short, mocking us from our inbox as if to say, what took you so long? It was so simple.

Once again, we went through our notes and found that we now had everything we needed to register our car. I would have gladly left this task to my husband, but the car was registered in my name, so I had to go. We took our folder of documents and headed to the *Préfecture*. There, we took a number and sat in the waiting room. When our number was finally called, we laid out our forms and documents on the lady's desk and said,

"We'd like to register our car."

She looked through the documents. With each new paper she picked up, a new grey cloud seemed to form on her forehead. When she put down the last document, she said,

"*Une voiture étrangère!*" a foreign car! And it sounded like an accusation, as if we dared to bother her with something so outrageous. We nodded guiltily.

Without another word, she got up and disappeared. We looked at each other, puzzled. Was that it? Had she fled from us? Should we wait here, or should we go?

We agreed that leaving was not an option. The car had to be registered in France, whether the lady liked it or not. We breathed a sigh of relief when we saw her reappear at the other end of the office.

"These are the documents you need to bring", she said, handing us a printout. Then she turned away and immersed herself in her computer. For her, the conversation was over. Not for us.

She probably expected us to vacate the space for the next visitors. But we had no intention of doing so. We were fully convinced that we had all the necessary documents. After all, we had already been here once to inquire what we would need to present. And we had all of that with us. So we stayed put and went through the new list point by point:

- *Certificat d'immatriculation d'origine* – original registration certificate – we had that.
- *Certificat de conformité européen (COC)* – European Certificate of Conformity (COC) – oh yes, we had that!
- *Facture* – Invoice – of course, we had that.
- The application form was filled out.
- Passport copy of the vehicle owner – no problem.
- *Justificatif de domicile de moins de 6 mois* – Proof of residence less than 6 months old – we had that.
- Copy of my driving licence – we had that.
- *Contrôle technique FRANCAIS de moins de 6 mois* – French technical inspection less than 6 months old – well, we had done the major inspection but only had a provisional certificate since we had driven the car there with German plates. As soon as we had the new French plates, we would have to take it back. But that was the only way it could be done, so she had to accept that. A bored nod of the head at the computer signalled to us that this was okay.
- *Attestation d'assurance* – Insurance certificate – We had the German insurance certificate. Logically, we didn't have French insurance yet. The face at the computer raised an eyebrow. Maybe two, but we couldn't see the second one. We needed

French insurance? Really? How, when the car was still... Another shrug of the shoulders taught us that further questions were pointless.

- *Quitus fiscal* – What was THAT?

Did a small, triumphant smile flit across the face at the computer? I would almost say yes.

"Nobody ever mentioned such a fiscal receipt", I said. We had never heard of it. She just shrugged her shoulders. Where would we get that, we asked. Without turning her face away from the computer, she said,

"*Centre des finances*" – Tax Office.

We realized that we couldn't achieve anything here today and left, frustrated. That was car registration Act One. More were to follow.

I should perhaps mention at this point that the events described took place some years ago. Nowadays, you don't go to the *Préfecture* anymore. Well, of course, you can still walk there, but not to register a car. That's done online via the ANTS portal, the *Agence nationale des titres sécurisés*. From what I hear from friends, it hasn't made things easier or faster. The documents required are still the same.

I should also mention that the deadline for registering the car after moving to France is just one month. I find that extremely short, but no one asks for my opinion. We didn't stick to it. And I don't know anyone who has. But in the unlikely event that you get caught and the *gendarme* just had a row with his wife, you can expect a hefty fine.

Why do I say "unlikely event"? Because the car is indistinguishable from that of a tourist from abroad. Why should a *gendarme* stop such a car? And if he does, he's shown foreign papers and a foreign driving licence. Nothing indicates that the car should have been registered in France long ago. Only if you speed and get a ticket sent to you, and there's no longer a deliverable address in your home country, only then it becomes noticeable. But you can avoid that, can't you?

As we left the *Préfecture*, we asked our way to the *Centre des finances*. Every man and woman in France know where this building is located in the town. And everyone we asked had that sympathetic look for us when explaining the way. It said as much as "You poor things, you have to go there."

In our youthful naivety, we thought it couldn't be far and set off on foot. At some point, we wondered if we shouldn't have taken the car. And at some point, we were sure we should have taken the car. But now we had come so far, it really couldn't be much further. We just slipped through the entrance door as the porter was about to close it for lunch. That was not a good omen. Never prevent an official from taking his well-deserved lunch break. But that's exactly what we did.

The lady at the counter didn't make a fuss. She looked at the purchase contract and glanced at it briefly. We had no idea what this *Quittance fiscale* was all about. We just wanted to get it over with and paid the amount she requested. She issued this receipt, and five minutes later she could have lunch, and we could walk our way back. The *Préfecture* was now closed, so there was no question of continuing with the *Quittance fiscale* today. Anyway, we had to solve the insurance issue too.

When we got home, we caught up on the missed information about this *Quittance fiscale*. We learned that it was a certificate stating that we had no tax debts to the French state and that our "*situation*" could be described as "*régulière*".

In addition to the pure registration costs, you also have to pay taxes in France when importing a car. There's the *taxe régionale*, which varies from region to region and depends on the level of motorisation, the *chevaux fiscaux* (CV) of the vehicle.

Then there's the *taxe écologique*, also known as "*écotaxe*", to be paid. This also depends on the level of motorisation, but also on how much environmental pollution the vehicle causes.

If you import a used vehicle from the EU, you are exempt from paying VAT in France. Our car clearly met the criteria.

It was older than six months, and the mileage was more than 6,000 km. We had already paid the VAT when we had bought it in Germany. And it was listed on the invoice. Fortunately, we had met all the conditions for exemption from VAT.

All in all, we ended up with a sum of around 600 euros, but as I said, it depends on the vehicle how much you will have to pay.

You only pay these taxes in France once, either when buying or – as in our case – when importing from abroad. It matters little how many annual taxes you have already paid for the car in your home country.

Now, "just" the insurance left to sort... We were supposed to insure a car in France that wasn't even registered there yet. We didn't think it would be straightforward. But in the end, it was much easier and quicker than we'd expected.

Using an insurance comparison site, we quickly found a handful of candidates. On each of their websites, you could calculate the insurance premium and have an offer sent to you. But when we wanted to accept the offer and conclude an insurance contract, we hit a snag with all of them: they required the vehicle's registration number, and anything other than a French one wasn't accepted. So, we made three attempts and aborted each time. And that's where it stayed. Except for one.

A few days after our last unsuccessful attempt, a friendly lady from one of the insurance companies called. I won't name names here to avoid being accused of surreptitious advertising. She'd noticed that we'd tried to take out insurance with them but had aborted the process. She profusely apologised for bothering us and kindly asked why we'd aborted.

We explained the issue. She listened patiently and then said,

"*Pas de problème, Madame.* I can temporarily enter the German registration number into the insurance certificate until the car is registered in France."

She could draw up the contract and an insurance certificate right away. We could sort it all out over the phone. She asked a lot of questions, such as where the car would be parked overnight, who the drivers would be, when our driving licences were issued, and so on and so forth.

Then she wanted to know what our *bonus-malus* was. We were already familiar with this system from before. It's kind of a no-claims classes discount. I told her that we had a similar system in Germany. She then wanted to know what percentage discount my class offered. I was at something around 50% at the time. This seemed to impress her. She asked for a moment to do some calculations. After a while, she said,

"Ok, I'll send you the revised offer by email right away. If you could just confirm it by reply, I'll prepare the contract for you."

When the offer came, we were surprised at how cheep it was. They had already been very competitive in the insurance comparison. Now she had even undercut her own automatically calculated offer. We were pleased and confirmed it. And it didn't take long before we received the insurance certificate and the confirmation we needed for the registration.

A few words on the *bonus-malus* system, as I think you might find it interesting. This bonus or malus reflects the driver's behaviour. The starting point is a coefficient of 1. For each year without an at-fault accident, you get a 5% discount on this coefficient, so one year without an accident results in a coefficient of 0.95. This coefficient is then multiplied by the insurance premium. For example: an insurance premium of €1,000 multiplied by the coefficient of 0.95 results in an insurance premium of €950.

The maximum possible discount is 50%, corresponding to a coefficient of 0.50. You reach this after roughly 13 accident-free years. Anything less than 0.50 is not possible. So, when I told her I had about a 50% discount, she was so impressed because, for her, that was the smallest possible coefficient possible. She couldn't know that in Germany, I was far from being in the best no-claims category. So far for the 'bonus' part of *bonus-malus*.

You've probably guessed it; there's also the opposite case, the malus. For each at-fault accident, you get a 25% surcharge added to your coefficient. Yes, the surcharge is significantly higher. You can do the maths yourself to see what an at-fault accident does to your coefficient. And what it would do if you had another accident the following year. Your coefficient could even exceed 1, although it's capped at a maximum of 3.5.

In the event of partial fault in an accident, you only get half, or 12.5%, added. And the fact that the nice lady from the insurance company had classified me with a coefficient of 0.50 would have meant that my first at-fault accident would not have been counted.

To benefit from the bonus when moving from an EU country to France, you'll need an international certificate of no-claims years from your previous insurer in your home country which you'll have to present to your new French car insurance. Unless you're as lucky as I was and encounter such a nice lady who waives it. There aren't many of those left; they seem to be a dying breed. So, it's better to get this certificate from your insurer right away. Some insurers seem a bit reluctant to issue it, either refusing or delaying. In this case, you can kindly point out that they are obliged to issue this certificate under EU law. They will courteously inform you that this will nullify your classification in your home country no-claims category, and you'll have no more claim to it. Don't let that shock you. You're transferring this claim to France now. And if you ever have to return one day – which we neither expect nor hope for – you'll do the same thing in reverse. You'll request an international certificate of your *bonus-malus* from your French insurer and transfer it to the country you are moving to, where it will be converted into the no-claims category by your then-new insurer. *Et voilà, pas de problème.*

The next visit to the *Préfecture* was upon us. We now had all the documents together. At least we hoped so. But we couldn't be entirely sure. Something new could have been added in the meantime. Again, we had to take a number, wait, and once more we ended up with the same lady as last time. What luck we had. She must have felt the same way. As soon as she saw us approaching, she stood up and left the open-plan office through a door at the other end. What were we to do? She had called our number. The same number would certainly not be called again. So we sat down for the time being and waited. Just as we had decided to take another number to be on the safe side, she returned, towing a colleague behind her. She whispered something to her colleague and disappeared.

The new one took her seat at the desk, shuffled the documents lying on the table from left to right and back again, then turned to the computer and typed away, raised an eyebrow, stood up and vanished.

Again? She hadn't even spoken a word to us yet. In that regard, she had outdone her predecessor; she had fled much faster. Would she ever come back? She did. And she spoke:

"*Désolée*, I couldn't log in. What can I do for you?"

So, once again, everything from the beginning. We told her that we wanted to register our car, currently still registered in Germany, in France because we now lived permanently in the beautiful La Ciotat. A bit of flattery sometimes helps. We laid all our documents on the table. She looked through them and seemed almost a bit disappointed when she saw that everything was indeed there.

"*Très bien*", she said, and it sounded like "Traaaaaih biaing.".

She clattered endlessly on her keyboard, requested this document, asked for that document. In the end, I felt like I had to sign about a hundred times, and then that was it.

"It may take a while for you to receive the *Carte Grise*", she said. But with this *Certificat provisoire d'Immatriculation*, a provisional registration certificate, we could now get number plates made, go for the *Contrôle technique*, and drive around just like any French person. *"Bonne journée!"*

But above all, we could now deregister the car in Germany. We wanted to do that anyway, so we wouldn't have to continue paying the annual vehicle tax in Germany. We had new number plates made with our French registration number, unscrewed the old ones and attached the new French ones.

Attaching the new ones was not that a quick thing. Did you know that number plates in France must be rivetted to the car? Never attached in any other way! But we were lucky to have a neighbour like Marc who had, of course he did, a riveter in his garage. And as he trusted nobody but himself handling it right, he volunteered to do the job for us.

I called the registration office in Esslingen, which was responsible for our former German residence, to find out how to go about this deregistration. At first, they couldn't understand why I didn't just pop in instead of bothering them on the phone. But when I explained that "popping in" for me meant a journey of nearly 1000 kilometres one way, they were willing to consider alternative solutions. I was to render the old number plates invalid and send them along with a written confirmation from the French registration authority, stating that the vehicle was now registered in France, but please in German. And I should include a brief informal letter requesting the deregistration of the vehicle. I asked if a copy of the provisional registration certificate wouldn't suffice. Unfortunately, I had to confirm that it was only in French, and that was absolutely not acceptable. They wanted something in German; otherwise, it could say anything. I suggested having the French certificate translated, stamped by a sworn translator. No, they absolutely needed an official confirmation from an authority. That's precisely what this *Certificat provisoire d'Immatriculation* was; it said exactly what was required and was issued by an authority, complete with stamp and all the trimmings. It was in vain. They wanted a letter specifically addressed to them from an authority. They didn't want to hear any of my objections that this could be difficult. Why should they? It wasn't their problem. It was my problem, and I was allowed to keep it.

So how were we to get a document written in German that confirmed the car's registration in France? We had the *Certificat provisoire d'Immatriculation*, which did precisely that, but they didn't want it in Esslingen.

Have you ever tried to get anything in German from a French authority deep in the south of the country? It was like trying to order ice cubes for red wine in a restaurant. Not happening! We didn't even bother to ask. It would have been hopeless anyway. English might have been possible, but even there, I have my doubts. So, I called the *Préfecture* and asked for a letter. They didn't do that at the *Préfecture*; for that, I had to contact the *Mairie*. Don't ask me why the *Mairie* should be responsible for that.

So, I called the *Mairie*, explained what I needed, and they were actually willing to help me. They didn't really understand why I needed it, after all, I had the *Certificat provisoire d'Immatriculation* for that very purpose. Yes, I said, I know, but they want it like this so that I can deregister the car in Germany. Well, they were happy to issue such a letter for me. I should come by tomorrow with the original *Certificat provisoire d'Immatriculation*, as they needed proof of what they were confirming was true. I made a daring move and asked if it was perhaps, by any chance, possible to get this letter in German if I provided them with the text in German. Hahaha, good joke. I surely didn't mean it. No, of course not.

The next day, I took our provisional certificate and headed to the *Mairie* (town hall). They had already been expecting me. The letter was already prepared; they just needed to insert the details. Wisely anticipating this, I had written down the address of the registration authority on a piece of paper so they could type it out character by character. That helped. The letter was printed and… No, I didn't get it right away; that would have been too easy. It went into a folder for signatures. *Monsieur le Maire* had yet to sign it. And of course, that couldn't possibly happen right then and there.

A mayor is a very busy man, after all. It would be ready tomorrow.

I explained to the ladies that I wanted to pick up the letter myself. Under no circumstances should they send it by post; I would come in person. The last thing I needed was for them to send it directly to Esslingen. Yes, they understood; I should come back tomorrow afternoon to collect it.

When I returned the next day, there was a new set of faces at the reception. I asked for the letter that was supposed to be waiting for me. The ladies knew nothing about it. I explained what it was about. They looked puzzled. They asked for the address of the receiver and began searching. It was nowhere to be found. I asked them to look again. I had seen with my own eyes how their colleague had placed it in the folder for *Monsieur le Maire's* signature. They searched all the compartments of the folder. They even looked on the mayor's desk. Nothing. A suspicion began to form in my mind.

They assured me not to worry; it would turn up eventually. I had a hunch where it might turn up, if at all. I should call tomorrow when their colleagues would be back. And so I did.

She recognised me immediately. Before I could even explain why I was calling, she interrupted me, apologising a thousand times. *Monsieur le Maire* had returned so late that they had already left the office. He had simply left the folder on her colleague's desk, who had put all the letters in the post. She was truly, truly sorry. She knew I had wanted to have the letter translated first. That was at least what I had told her. Would that be a problem now? I explained that they would probably just throw it away in Esslingen. She was horrified. How could they dare! I tried to calm her; I wasn't certain they would commit such a heinous act, but it wasn't impossible. How could she make it right, she wanted to know. I said I still needed the letter, so could we please start from scratch. Print it out again, have *Monsieur le Maire* sign it again, but this time don't send it away. I'll pick it up. She promised to guard the letter as if it were the apple of her eye. I should come this very afternoon to collect it; then nothing could go wrong. Would *Monsieur le Maire* sign it that quickly, I asked.

"Count on me", she replied.

Right after lunch, I made my way to the *Mairie*. They were already waiting for me. Yes, the mayor had signed it.

"*Voilà!*" she said, holding the letter up to my nose. I thanked her and was about to leave when the mayor stepped out of his office.

"Ah, the *Madame* with this peculiar letter that I've had to sign twice now, and today even on express!" he said. He approached me and shook my hand. He was a tanned, grey-haired, slightly portly man with bushy eyebrows, beneath which a pair of friendly eyes twinkled. I took an immediate liking to him.

"*Eh oui*", I replied, as nothing better came to mind.

"*Alors*, if I understand correctly, you've recently settled in our beautiful La Ciotat", he said. "How did that come about?"

I briefly summarised how we had conducted our research and how we had ultimately chosen La Ciotat. He was thrilled.

"Of all the beautiful places on the Côte, you chose La Ciotat! *Mais c'est ma-gni-fique!*" he exclaimed.

As the conversation progressed, I realised that the word *magnifique* was one of his favourites; he used it repeatedly. In the end, he said he hoped to see me again soon and to meet my husband as well. I told him that would be delightful. And so we parted as the best of friends.

A week later, we bumped into him in town. He remembered having seen me before and returned my greeting warmly. Later, we saw him at a soirée welcoming new residents to the town, and he exchanged a few pleasant, non-committal words with us, as he probably did with everyone that evening. We saw him around town several more times, but he no longer recognised us. As a new resident, you're something of a pass-through item. And the mayor is only human, after all.

Now, the beautiful French word *produire* finally came into its own. I scanned the letter from the *Mairie*, copied a poor translation over the text, printed it out, added a few creases to the sheet for good measure, and packed it into a large envelope along with the cut-up number plates and a cover letter. Four weeks later, I received a letter from Esslingen stating that my request to deregister the vehicle with the registration number blablabla had been granted.

I should point out, just to be on the safe side, that I'll deny everything and invoke poetic license if you now want to report me for forgery. But perhaps you'll think to yourself that a person can be poor; they just need to know how to help themselves. To ease my conscience, I always told myself that it wasn't really forgery, as I had an original that said exactly what my "copy" said; it was just in a different language.

Weeks passed. Our lovely provisional registration certificate was valid for 30 days from the date of issue. As this deadline approached, we grew anxious. How long could one actually drive around with such a provisional document? Well, certainly not once it had expired. Or so we thought, in typical German fashion. Christian once again made his way to the *Préfecture*, took another number, waited patiently, and eventually presented the provisional slip to the lady, asking when we could finally count on receiving the definite *Certificat d'Immatriculation*.

"What do I know?" was the response.

"Well, perhaps you could check your clever computer to see if there's any issue", said Christian.

No, there was no issue; he simply needed to be patient.

"Can we continue to drive with this slip? It's expired since yesterday", he asked.

A shrug and a "*Bof*" were the answer. It seemed as though no one really cared. But we're Germans, after all.

"Could you issue me a new one or extend this one?" he asked.

"*Mwuai*, if you insist", she said.

"*Oui*, I do insist", said Christian.

Her face said, "You're a pain in the ass!" but she managed to muster the energy to stamp the sheet and scribble "*Prolongé*" on it. Once this Herculean task was completed, she slid the sheet across the desk.

"*Merci beaucoup*", said Christian, taking the sheet.

We had just repeated the same procedure for the second time when, a few days later, we found a registered letter in our letterbox. It requested – specifically me – to report to the police. My initial shock subsided as I read on and learned that my new *Carte Grise* was ready for collection.

A few months later, we would leave La Ciotat and return to Germany. Fortunately, we didn't know that at the time.

Since I've already hinted at our return, let me tell you about an incident we experienced during our next move to France. Having returned to Germany, we registered the car there again. The French number plates and documents were confiscated at the registration office with the statement that they would be sent to France for the vehicle to be deregistered there. I didn't need to worry about anything.

Almost two years later, we returned to France with the same car. And again, we faced the issue of registration. This time, however, we had kept copies of the old French documents. Armed with these, we went to the *Préfecture*. We hoped that with the old documents, the process could be significantly shortened and perhaps even made cheaper, as we could prove that we had already paid the taxes for this vehicle in France.

The lady at the reception listened attentively to our story. The more we told her, the rounder her eyes became, until they seemed about to pop out of their sockets.

"You seriously moved from Germany to France, then back to Germany, and now back to France again, every time with the same car?" she said, utterly bewildered. "And each time you registered it?" she added, as if that were the cherry on top.

We nodded guiltily.

"I've never come across anything like this", she said, laughing, once she had recovered from her shock.

"Are you sure you want to stay this time?" she asked, unknowingly touching a very sore point for us. We had been sure every time. Unfortunately, life had had other plans each time.

"*Oui!*" we said. We'd love to be sure.

"*Allons voir*", she said, let's see, and turned to her computer. She had grabbed the copy of our old *Carte Grise*, now entered the registration number into her computer, raised her eyebrows, shook her head, and asked:

"And you say the Germans took your *Carte Grise* and the number plates?"

"*Oui*", I said. "To send them to France."

"You know... For me, your car never left France", she said.

"What do you mean?" I said.

"The *immatriculation* is active; there's no mention of deregistration or anything like that."

"How come?" I said.

"I don't know", she said. "It seems the German authorities never forwarded it to France. No deregistration was made."

"But they told me that. And they took everything from me", I said.

"I believe you", she said.

All three of us looked at each other, bewildered. No, she had certainly never encountered a case like this before.

"What do we do now?" Christian said in his usual solution-oriented manner.

"*Eh bien...*" she said, hesitating a bit, wondering whether she should really voice what she had just thought.

"You could file a loss report and apply for a duplicate of your *Carte Grise*. It costs 20 Euros and is quite quick. Then you can get new number plates made with it."

That was an interesting suggestion. We hadn't expected anything like that.

"I had to hand in the *Carte Grise*, so I didn't actually lose it", I objected in German correctness.

"Well, in a way, it did get lost from you, didn't it?" she said, winking.

"Well, if you put it that way", I said.

With her help, we filled out the application for the duplicate and paid the 20 Euros.

Two weeks later, I received a registered letter and was asked to collect my *Duplicata de Certificat d'Immatriculation*. The duty officer kindly pointed out that my *contrôle technique* was overdue and that I should get it sorted as soon as possible. I promised him I would and made my exit with my new old *Carte Grise*. I bet no one has ever registered a car in France that quickly.

COFFEE PARTY

Do you remember the flat viewing in Aubagne with Henri, who unfortunately already had a dossier on the flat? We had such a nice chat, and he repeatedly said we should definitely come over for coffee once we were settled in.

I had completely let that slide. Initially, Christian wasn't there yet, and the invitation had been to both of us. I had done the viewing alone, and Henri was keen to meet my better half. So going alone was out of the question. Then Christian was there, but we had so much to do that we completely forgot about the invitation. I admit, initially, we weren't too keen on going out. We were enjoying our regained togetherness. And then there was also the issue that our flat had to be set up to a point where we could receive guests. We already felt bad about Yvette and Marc, who kept inviting us and whom we had to put off for weeks with a counter-invitation. I know, all lame excuses. Approaching strangers is hard for me. And I wasn't sure if Henri had been serious about the invitation or if it was just polite chit-chat.

So much time had passed that I thought, well, there's no point bringing it up now. He's long forgotten it. Or so I thought.

One day, we found an email in our inbox. Henri was asking if we had arrived in the sunny South, if we were doing well and had settled in nicely. And by the way, the invitation for coffee was still open. He hadn't forgotten. I must have made quite an impression.

I wrote back, claiming that we would be in the area next Saturday, and asked if we could come over for coffee. We could. He was looking forward to it and sent directions, noting that all navigation systems either couldn't find their address or had it listed incorrectly. With these perfect directions, nothing could go wrong; we found the property right away. Then we stood in front of the gate. There were four doorbell labels. Two bore the correct surname Antonin, but none had the matching first name Henri. Which bell should we ring?

In my desperation, I pressed the first Antonin button. Nothing. No response. So, the second Antonin button. Again, nothing. Had they not heard us? Or had they forgotten us? Then I remembered that I had a mobile phone and Henri's number. So, I called him.

"*Allô*", he answered.

"Henri?" I asked.

"*Oui*", he said.

"We're standing at the gate. Can you let us in?" I said.

"I can't do that. You have to ring the bell; only then can I activate the buzzer", he said.

"Yes, but which name should we ring?" I asked.

"*Chez Julliot*", he said and hung up.

That name also existed twice. Which button should I press this time? In my desperation, I pressed both. I didn't want to call again. And lo and behold, the gate opened.

We drove along a long, bumpy driveway and parked, as he had said, in front of *Madame's* gleaming black Audi, next to which our old, dirty Opel looked rather shabby. Next time, we should at least give it a wash beforehand. We got out and looked around. We were on a huge property. Apart from the driveway, everything looked very well-kept. Not like English lawn, no, but by southern French standards, it was very tidy. The trees were neatly pruned, the lawn was almost green and mowed. And the house! It was one of those stone cottages that glow so invitingly in the sun and into which we always want to move immediately. A wisteria vine stretched across the glass conservatory along the entire front of the house. The wooden shutters on the first-floor windows had apparently been freshly painted in lavender blue not too long ago. The stones of the terrace shone in the sun. The "Kärcher" pressure washer was still standing in the corner in front of the garage.

As welcoming as the house looked, so too were its inhabitants. The first to burst out when the glass door of the conservatory slid open were two little Yorkshire Terriers, a third followed at a more leisurely pace. The dogs danced around our legs and jumped up at us – I was glad I was wearing shorts. At least my trousers wouldn't get dirty. One of them could jump like a spring, reaching hip height. They squeaked in a friendly manner; you couldn't call these noises barking. Then they were called back by their mistress and soundly scolded before she turned to us, laughing.

"The dogs already love you, so a warm welcome!" she called to us from the door.

I had estimated Henri to be over 70. His wife must have been significantly younger. I guessed her to be at most in her late 50s. We still don't know for sure. She wore her hair in a cheeky short cut and dyed black, which perfectly suited her round, sun-tanned face. Her bright red mouth smiled cheerfully. Behind the large sunglasses, lively dark eyes sparkled. She wore shorts and a T-shirt, both of which probably came in her size, but she must have been convinced she could still wear a size 40. Despite the love handles emphasised by the tight T-shirt, she looked exceedingly elegant. This was probably because she tottered towards us in sandals with high heels as if she had spent her entire life walking in stilettos.

Henri shuffled out behind her in old flip-flops. With his sun-tanned, wrinkled skin and grey hair, he looked more like her father than her husband. He wore crumpled linen trousers and a once-white, stretched-out T-shirt. Both trousers and T-shirt clearly showed that they had actively helped with painting the window shutters. Madame glanced back at him, raised an eyebrow, and said:

"Weren't you going to change?"

Henri shrugged his shoulders as if to apologise and replied,

"*Oui mais…*" pointing at us, meaning he probably hadn't had time because we were already there.

"But you do know that Germans are always punctual, right?" she said to him. And turning to us, she said, "*Comme un petit garçon*", and shook her head, laughing. Like a little boy.

"*Désolé*", he said to us, gesturing at his outfit. "We are in the countryside here."

His wife wouldn't let this last remark stand. Yes, they were in the countryside. *Décontracté*, relaxed, was allowed, but not like this. She gestured at his outfit. He promised to go and change as soon as he had greeted his guests.

"*TES invités? Mais non, NOS invités!*" YOUR guests? No, OUR guests, she said, correcting him.

"*NOS invités*", he corrected himself.

While the two were thus occupied with each other, they had lost sight of the dogs. Seizing the opportunity, the dogs had come back to us. We had petted them when they stood still. I had caught the springy dog and now had him in my arms.

"*Oh, Thaïs!*" *Madame* exclaimed when she saw this. "He's incorrigible", she apologised.

The dog had briefly turned his head towards his mistress, and it seemed to me as if he had grinned at her. I could be mistaken, though.

"Now let's give you a proper welcome", Henri finally said. "*Voici ma femme Christiane*", this is my wife Christiane.

Since Henri and I already knew each other, it was now my turn to introduce my husband:

"*Et voici mon mari Christian*", I said, deliberately pronouncing his name in German, making it sound just like the French Christiane.

"And what's the name?" she asked.

She had fallen into my trap. This was precisely what I had been aiming for, and why I hadn't said "Christjong" as usual. I found it a funny coincidence that the two had almost the same first name. A single letter made the difference. And if you pronounced the names as they should be pronounced in their respective homelands, there was no difference to be heard.

Christian relieved Christiane of her confusion and said,

"Christjong, if you say it in French. In Germany, we say Christian (pronounced Kriztian)."

"Aaaaah!" The penny had dropped. "*Quelle coïncidence!*" she said, what a coincidence.

Only now did she take the time to look at us closely.

"You didn't tell me they were so young!" she said to Henri. He just shrugged his shoulders. It didn't matter to him. He found us nice; that was enough for him.

"*Mais, venez, venez!*" Christiane called. We shouldn't just stand around here like this.

There was coffee and cake. Completely untypical for the French. But we were only dealing with half-French here. Henri was Swiss. Proudly, he told us he had instructed his wife to bake a cake for the Germans. We'd appreciate it. We did, very much so.

"Your wish is always my command, Benoît", she cheekily said to him.

Ah, there it was again. All afternoon she had been calling him Benoît. The first time, I thought I had misheard. Now there was no doubt. I plucked up the courage and said,

"This whole thing is confusing me; it has to stop. Who on earth is Benoît? And if he's Benoît, where is Henri? And who among you is Antonin and who is Julliot? And why are there two of each name on the gate?"

They laughed as if I'd told the joke of the year. Gasping, Christiane began to explain,

"Yes, you're right. It's confusing. So, Henri and Benoît are one and the same person. His real name is Henri, but I never liked that name. I told him that from the start, at every *rendez-vous*."

"On the third *rendez-vous*, I told her if my name bothers her so much, she should give me a different one", he interjected.

"So, I baptised him Benoît", she said. "As for the surnames, mine is Julliot; I kept my name when we got married. And *Monsieur* is Antonin."

"And the other two nameplates on the gate?" I probed.

"One is my mother. She lives over there", she said, pointing to a small house on the other side of the property, a miniature replica of the main house. "And the other is my daughter Emma, who officially still lives here and even shows up now and then. You might see her later."

Now we could more or less navigate through the name maze. Why she disliked the name Henri so much was something she couldn't explain. It was just the way it was.

"And Benoît is better?"

"Much, much better!"

After the coffee and cake, we were given a tour. Until then, we had only seen the terrace outside. Now we were allowed to enter the inner sanctum. Besides the three dogs, there was also a cat, who jostled with the dogs for our attention. Or rather, she made it clear to the dogs that it was her turn, and they preferred to give her precedence. She was a grey, shimmering beauty who knew how to wrap us around her velvety paws.

On our tour of the house, she was our constant companion. As curious as we were, she peeked into every room whose door was opened to us, circled the room as if to say, "Look, I present to you the guest room, isn't it lovely?" The same happened in every room. It was clear who was the mistress of the house. Or at least felt like she was.

Henri – sorry, Benoît – took over the tour of the yard and garden. We learned that you shouldn't plant bamboo near the terrace. It overgrows everything and is unstoppable.

"*C'est noté*", duely noted, I said, winking at him.

He proudly showed us the swimming pool he had built himself, extra deep so the water stayed nice and cold. Next time, we should bring swimsuits so we could make a *plouf* if we felt like it.

"*C'est noté*", I said again.

At the far end of the property, he asked us to look over the fence.

"*Tu reconnais?*" Do you recognise it, he asked me, switching to the French informal "*tu*". Oups, how come?

"Ah yes", I said, "that's the residence where I viewed the flat. I hadn't realised it was right behind the fence."

"Yes, exactly", he said. "The last house on the right", he explained to my husband, who hadn't been there at the time.

It was a shame that there had already been a dossier on it back then. He would have loved to have us as tenants. It was available again, by the way. The *petit connard* hadn't paid his rent, and he'd lied to him as well, moving in with his in-laws and four children, although only two had been mentioned before. So, he'd kicked him out, him and his whole entourage. It had to be quick so he could get rid of him before winter. In winter, you can't evict a tenant, whether they pay or not, it's against the law. Just last week, he had repainted all the walls, *au pistolet*, he said, meaning with a spray gun. A fine thing, he said. We wouldn't believe the mess they'd left behind. After every tenant, he had to clean the flats completely and repaint them. Tenants were really the worst. So, if we weren't happy with our flat, we could move in here anytime, he offered. Now that he knew us better, he would save himself the insurance premium and rely on us to pay the rent properly.

"*C'est noté*", I said for the third time. He laughed and nodded.

"*Oui, oui*, we can't compete with La Ciotat here. *Ici, c'est la campagne. La Ciotat, c'est la mer*", he said. He was right; here we were in the countryside, the sea was in La Ciotat. Who would want to leave La Ciotat?

The tour had taken a long time. At every piece of wall, every tree, every bush, Benoît, formerly Henri, had stopped to explain that he had built or planted it himself, what the challenges had been, and what to consider for its care. The driveway was in a sorry state; he absolutely had to redo it. The last rain had washed away the gravel and caused a small landslide. After the tour, we were sure we didn't want a house. Unless we could hire Benoît as a pool boy, gardener, and caretaker. When we returned to the terrace, Christiane winked at us:

"Well, did you take good notes? He'll quiz you next time."

"Oh!" said Christian. "No, we didn't. Guess we'll have to start the tour all over again."

"*Ah non!*" she protested. "*On va passer à l'apéro là*", we're moving on to the aperitif now. "You're staying, aren't you?" she asked, already disappearing into the kitchen without waiting for an answer.

Good thing we hadn't planned anything else for the rest of the day. So, now Benoît had casually switched to the informal French "*tu*", but apparently hadn't informed his wife, so she stayed with the formal "*vous*". It would be months before she offered us the "*tu*". Until then, we had to get used to constantly switching between "*tu*" and "*vous*".

"What will you have?" asked Benoît. We still had to get used to the new name.

"What do you have?" we asked back.

"*De la bière!*" he exclaimed, nodding proudly. "Any proper German drinks beer, right?" he said to Christian.

"Uh... *non*... then I guess I'm not a proper German", said Christian.

"*Quoi!?* You don't drink beer?" he exclaimed, outraged. It couldn't and shouldn't be true. A German who didn't like beer, where had you ever seen such a thing. It was unheard of. And so it went on for a while until Christiane came out of the kitchen to see if all the glasses were filled and she could serve the *apéro* snacks. She was surprised that we hadn't made any progress.

"*Mais, qu'est-ce que c'est que ça?*" what's going on here, she exclaimed. This reignited Benoît's outrage about the German who didn't drink beer, only now she had to listen to his astonished exclamations.

"*Eh bah*", she said. "*Chacun à son goût*", to each their own. Exactly. And now he should finally pour something into the glasses. Anything! The snacks were ready."

Obviously, he was more at ease with my not wanting beer. So, he asked me first,

"*Alors, Inès*, what would you like?" He had a lovely little Muscat de Lunel; did I fancy that? Oh yes! Bullseye!

Then he looked at Christian, pondered for a moment, and said,

199

"*Et toi, un pastaga?*" A Pastis? Around Marseille, a man drinks Pastis, affectionately called *pastaga* here. If this German didn't like beer, he was still a man. In the South. So, Pastis it was.

"*Oui*, very much so", Christian replied. Benoît's facial features relaxed.

Finally, the glasses were filled. Christiane brought out a sizzling pan of deliciously smelling dates wrapped in ham. Our mouths watered.

"*Chin-chin!*" The glasses clinked. "To new friends!" said Benoît.

"To new friends!" we echoed.

Just as we took our first sips and were savouring the first nibbles, each with a dog or a cat on our laps, we heard a car coming up the driveway. Another shiny black Audi, albeit a slightly smaller version. Emma's coming!

No, no, stay seated, don't disturb yourself. That applied to us, not to *Maman*, who couldn't stay in her chair and leapt up to rush towards her daughter.

"*Emma, ma cherie!*" she exclaimed.

Behind the tinted windows, we'd only vaguely made out a long-haired woman with dark sunglasses. Now the beauty stepped out. We were transfixed by endlessly long, brown legs in high heels, the first thing we saw. The legs were followed by the rest: a short black skirt, more of a belt than a skirt, a light beige blouse, slender brown arms, a chunky watch on one wrist, jingling silver bangles on the other. Long, shiny hair and massive sunglasses. This creature seemed to have descended directly from a film premiere in Cannes onto our humble patch of earth. Wow! So, this was Emma, or rather, Emmanuelle.

The beauty made little fuss about her beauty, grabbed the nearest folding chair, and joined us. From now on, we were off Madame Cat's radar. Emma was clearly her favourite. But we had our hands full with three dogs. They would've loved the fragrant ham-wrapped dates, but they weren't allowed any. Try having such a cute little creature with black beady eyes on your lap and try not to give it any nibbles while it hypnotises you as you pop a piece into your mouth. Alright, they could have a tiny piece of date, but no more. Ha, now they were really onto something. Where there's a tiny piece of date that also smells and tastes of ham, there must be more, right? *Maman* could scold all she wanted. *Maman* wasn't always attentive. Sometimes *Maman* even had to go to the kitchen. Ha!

Emma naturally took the lead in the ongoing conversation. Her parents seemed to have no objections. We'd chatted all afternoon. Now it was Emma's turn.

The conversation was lively. It turned out we could have a wonderful exchange about marketing and social media. On the topic of marketing, we'd lost *papa*. On social media, we'd also lost *maman*. They held back and were pleased that we were getting along so well. We could tell they were hoping that the "young" people would get along well. But she was too bubbly for us, too much of a party girl, too engrossed in topics like fashion and beauty. We were probably too old for her. But we made the best of it. On both sides. The will was there. Just not the spark.

We'd been wondering for some time whether we should stay for dinner. They'd so naturally assumed we'd stay for the *apéro* that we were slowly starting to doubt whether we'd ever leave. But dinner is a different kettle of fish compared to coffee or *apéro*. Both of those can be easily thrown together. The *apéro* nibbles had probably been waiting in the freezer in the garage for just such an occasion. But dinner?

We secretly signalled to each other that it was time to make a move. When Benoît wanted to refill the glasses, I broached the subject of driving.

"Who's driving, you or me?"

"You", Christian replied instantly, letting himself be poured another Pastis.

"*Comme toujours*", I said, declining another Muscat.

This was also a veiled signal to *Madame*. She got the message. From then on, she restrained Benoît whenever he tried again and again to refill our glasses. So it slowly dawned on him that we wanted to leave.

"You really want to go already?" he asked. "But you've only just arrived!"

Christiane rolled her eyes. This man could really put her in a tight spot as a hostess if he insisted we stay for dinner now.

"Next time", I assured Benoît.

"Absolutely!" he exclaimed. And Christiane agreed with that.

"When you come next time, we'll fire up the BBQ and I'll make you my *Magret de Canard*", said Benoît.

We love grilled duck breast and told him so.

"He makes the best *Magret* you've ever eaten", said Christiane. That sounded promising. And we promised to come back.

"But first, you must come and visit us in La Ciotat", I said, and Christian nodded in agreement.

"We'd be delighted", they both said in unison.

Our car was trapped between the family's two "Odies". Over the course of the evening, we'd also touched on the subject of cars. The ladies loved Audi. Only Benoît needed something more rugged. They'd pronounced the brand like "Odie". We hadn't understood at first. They loved Odie. Ok. Who was Odie? Well, the German car brand Odie, you must know it. Ah, Audi! We'd laughed. The same happened when we talked about actors. Who on earth was Rishaar Share? Don't you know? Impossible. Haven't you seen Prottie Woman? It was a long time ago, but you must know him. Of course, we knew him.

So now only the little "Odie" had to be re-parked. I tried not to scrape their beloved vehicles while reversing, which required a lot of concentration. One Muscat too many had probably been had.

For our next invitation, we took the next step (you live and learn) and invited them for dinner. We'd toasted to friendship. Again and again. And we'd found real friends here. We're still in touch with them today. Benoît still looks 70, and Christiane still looks late 50s. It's nice that some things never change. I hope it stays that way for a long time.

AMONGST IMMIGRANTS

When emigrating, you're not just leaving the country; you're also leaving the people. Of course, you'll promise each other to stay in close contact. Some people even manage to do that. But those are more the exceptions than the rule. So, the task at hand in your new country is to find new friends. How does that work in France?

I've already given you a few tips in the preceding chapters. Inviting the neighbours over for an *apéro* is an almost foolproof method. If you get an invitation for coffee, like I did, then you really must kick yourself in the ass and accept it. But such invitations are like winning the lottery. If you wait for them, you'll be drinking your *petit rouge* alone for many years.

We often find it quite difficult to connect with locals. But that wasn't just the case in France. No, it was the same back in our home country as well. People have been living there since time immemorial, have their regular pubs, have their circle of friends. Any newcomer is eyed sceptically and, depending on the region, has to prove over years that their intentions are long-term. For us frequent movers, that's sometimes simply not feasible. By the time they started taking an interest in us, we were about leaving again. And sadly, we didn't have children or dogs to facilitate making contacts.

It's easier for us to connect with other newcomers (or in the case of France, other immigrants). If you feel the same, then look for groups in your region on Facebook & Co. There are groups like "Expats in France" or "Expat Women in France" or "Everything French" or "Moving to France" or "Living in France" just to name a few.

In Marseille, for example, we stumbled upon a German-French regulars' table where a colourful mix of Germans and a few brave French people met once a month. Similar things existed in Germany – and I guess in your home country too – if you want to practice your French a bit in preparation for your emigration.

And as you speak English (as you are reading this in English), the possibilities are countless as there are so many Americans, Australians, or British around here, and you can even connect with people of other nationalities speaking English.

In La Ciotat, we received an invitation from the mayor one day, inviting all new residents of the town to a soirée. The event took place in a charming *château* nearby. The mayor greeted every male guest with a firm handshake and every lady with a kiss on each cheek. It took a while for all the guests to get inside. We were handed a glass of champagne – what else? – and welcomed to the town with a few warm words from the mayor. The town's most important wineries had set up little tasting stalls in the courtyard. The butcher offered freshly sliced ham. The local clubs had information stands, ready to welcome us with open arms if we were interested. They were also responsible for the evening's entertainment. The local dance group showcased their skills in traditional costumes. One of the clubs called itself "*Jumelage La Ciotat*" and had four large national flags draped behind them, including the German one. As we passed this stand, Christian said,

"Oh, look, La Ciotat has a twin town in Germany."

As softly as he had said it, it hadn't gone unnoticed. A man – Jochen, as we later found out – had strategically positioned himself next to the stand. He was also German and had been living here for a year with his French wife. They had previously lived together in Germany. When they retired, she wanted to return to her homeland. So, he had to come along. Struggling to adapt and not quite fluent in French, she advised him to connect with other Germans in the area. That's how he started a regular meet-up, and he was looking for new members that evening. We chatted for a bit, he got our business card, and two weeks later, we received our first invitation to the meet-up.

Contrary to what he had told us, the meet-up this time was not going to be in a restaurant in town as usual. Instead, a couple from the group had invited everyone to their home in the hills of Gemenos. They had just been to Germany and brought back tonnes of Leberkäse (a type of meatloaf from southern Germany). We hesitated to accept the invitation. It felt awkward to go to the home of complete strangers as newcomers to the group. We were also a bit worried that this would set a precedent, and everyone else would expect a similar gesture. That's not what we wanted, and our small flat wouldn't allow for it anyway. Or so we thought. Jochen put our minds at ease. No, it was an absolute exception and should not become the norm. Anne and Willi were informed that two new people were coming, and they were looking forward to meeting us. There was no turning back now.

On the evening of the meet-up, we set off for Gemenos. The sat-nav directed us further and further up into the hills. The paved road ended, turning into a dirt track. We began to doubt whether we were in the right direction. Then suddenly, we were standing in front of the gate. We were the first to arrive. As always. A deep bass voice called out from the house,

"Come on in, but close the gate behind you, or the dog will escape!"

The dog was a tiny but utterly adorable Chihuahua named Minouche, who was so excited about our arrival that she raced around the garden fountain like a Duracell bunny. After a few laps, she left the fountain alone and started doing the same around my legs. Our laughter lured the lady of the house out of the kitchen. When she saw what her Minouche was up to, she joined in our hearty laughter. I think that was the moment Anne and I became friends.

I've already briefly mentioned Narbonne. Back then, we had found an apartment on a former vineyard. It belonged to an elderly English gentleman. We jokingly called him our English Lord. Edward had come to France more than 20 years ago with his wife. They had bought the vineyard cheaply and in a dilapidated state, restored it piece by piece, and set up holiday apartments. After his wife passed away, Ed sold parts of it. One flat still belonged to an old family friend who rented it out as a holiday home for two weeks every summer. Ed rented out the rest, but not as holiday homes – that was too much hassle for him – but with the usual French 3-year rental contracts. He had no clue about French rental law. He didn't care where our income came from. The main thing was that we paid the rent. Lucky for us. You know how difficult it is to rent an apartment in France.

We had viewed the flat and signed the rental agreement through an estate agency. The landlord was away. We had only learned from the estate agent that he was British. We found his email address on the rental agreement and sent him a friendly email in English, informing him of our move-in date. Of course, we expressed our hope to meet him then. He was delighted, he replied, and invited us to come over for tea on the day we moved in. And so we did, in our work clothes.

Ed lived on the other side of the main house. There was no doorbell. We knocked. Through the glass front door, we saw him approach. He was a slim, white-haired man in his seventies. Everything about him was British: his checked shorts, the polo shirt, and especially his accent. He was thrilled to have tenants he could speak English with. Just as it came naturally to him. And he did so extensively. While we sat at the large dining table chatting, an Asian-looking woman briefly appeared at the door but immediately turned away when she saw us. Edward hadn't seen her because he was sitting with his back to the door. Only from our reaction did he realise someone was at the door. He turned around, saw who it was, and hurried after her. From the door, he called out to her:

"Come in, they speak English!" And turning to us, he said:

"This is my wife Rose. She's a bit shy; she doesn't speak French very well. But since you speak English, it's all good."

We took to each other immediately. From then on, we regularly sat together for tea, or they came over to us for *apéro*. On one of these occasions, Ed told us about the Lunch Club and asked if we would be interested.

The Lunch Club was organised by Robert, a friend of Ed's, a Brit who came from Hong Kong. Once a month, always on Saturdays, they met at noon in a restaurant that Robert had carefully selected beforehand. The menu was also pre-arranged by Robert with the chef. If you wanted to participate, you had to inform him of your menu choice so that it could be ordered at the restaurant. Next time, we should come along. Ed signed us up.

On the day of the Lunch Club, Ed invited us into his car and drove us deep into the Minervois, which he charmingly pronounced the English way. The restaurant's terrace was already teeming with more or less elderly figures. Most of them were Brits. A few Australians and Americans were also present. Only one Frenchman had ventured into the group. Almost all were pensioners. Some had reached such an advanced age that their mumbling, due to ill-fitting dentures, was practically incomprehensible to us. But that didn't stop one of the old gentleman from talking to me for hours on end. He must have considered me a good listener, as I could contribute little more than the occasional "aha" and a friendly nod to the conversation.

When the standing part of the event came to an end and people began to look for seats, I strategically chose a spot far away from the old gentleman. I considered myself fortunate to have picked the youngest participants by a considerable margin (apart from us) to sit opposite. Terry and Vanessa were an utterly charming couple, still somewhat in the workforce. He was a writer. She worked a few hours a week from her home office for her former employer, contributing a bit more to her pension and because she simply wasn't ready to stop working. They owned a small house in the Minervois – pronouncing it nearly correctly with great effort – and operated a holiday flat there. They also had a lovely pool.

The lunch was good and substantial. The wine flowed even more generously. The menu price, including wine, had been agreed with the restaurant at 25 euros. They always do it this way, Robert informed us. A raw deal for the restaurant! We sat, chatted, and drank. Around four in the afternoon, the waitress came to our table. She would leave us another bottle of wine, but we should all please settle our bills as she was going to close up and head home. She needed a break before her evening shift started at six. We finally left the restaurant at 5 pm. I hadn't noticed anyone abstaining from the wine, yet everyone got into their cars and drove home. Hopefully, the roads were wide enough.

Four weeks later, we met them all again, hale and hearty. Once more, we found ourselves sitting opposite Terry and Vanessa. Already during the greeting – with the for the British uncharacteristically but evidently much-appreciated French cheek kisses – Terry had emitted a soft, contented "Hmm" upon detecting my perfume. Unbeknownst to me, he'd managed to arrange himself opposite me again. This behavioural pattern would repeat itself many times over the coming months. I was, after all, by far the youngest among the female participants. And my neckline was just too tempting for him.

We later learned more about their holiday flat rental business. They offered a very special service for their guests. To take advantage of budget airlines' low fares, guests only needed to travel with hand luggage. Everything they needed in the South, from shampoo to sun cream, would be provided; they just had to specify their preferred brands in advance. And they only needed one set of clothes, in case they wanted to go on excursions. Because on the property, everyone was free to wander around in their birthday suits. They were nudists. When they invited us over, we delayed our visit until we were absolutely certain that the weather would no longer permit a "*plouf*" in the pool. Better safe than sorry.

LOST IN TRANSLATION

I'm often asked whether it makes sense to properly learn French before emigrating to France. And my answer is "YESSSSS!!!!!!!" In capital letters and with lots of exclamation marks. I can't stress this enough. I speak from my own, painful experience. Let me take you on a little journey into the past. When I first came to France in 1999 because my husband had found a job in northern France, I couldn't speak French. Apart from "Bongshour", "Orewar", and "Un baget siwouplai". Heaven forbid someone gave me a reply or, even worse, asked me a question. Necessity forced me to learn the language quickly; today, I speak it fluently, to the extent that the French sometimes mistake me for a Belgian or Swiss. I take that as a compliment.

The first few months back then were difficult for me. I was dependent on help for everything. And when I did venture outside alone, because I couldn't find anyone to accompany me, it ended at best in minor embarrassment and, in worse cases, in total frustration.

I had already started learning French before the move. With little success. I lacked the time; there was always something more important. There was the full-time job. There were the friends. And after all, people need a bit of time to relax. And then the moving date drew closer. There was even less time then. The move had to be prepared. I felt incredibly guilty every time I thought about how little I had learned so far. But that wasn't enough to motivate me to do more. So it happened that I arrived in our new home and could practically speak no French.

The first few days were spent unpacking and running various errands to authority offices, which we tackled together. Then Christian had to start his job and was no longer available to hold my hand whenever I had to go to some authority.

He had accompanied me to the first appointment at the job centre. From then on, I had to go alone. I had "moved" three months of unemployment benefits from Germany. I successfully registered with the ANPE and the ASSEDIC. Now, the French job centre felt it was its sacred duty to find me a job. Of course, that was difficult with my limited French skills. So, first things first, I was put into a French course. One of those integration courses for foreigners living in France. The kind gentleman at the job centre handed me a piece of paper with an address on it. He had scribbled "*Mercredi*" and "*10h*" on it. Even if I hadn't understood a word of his speech, it was clear to me that I had to be at that address on Wednesday at 10:00 a.m. The next day, my husband took the note to work and asked his colleagues if they knew where it was. GoogleMaps didn't exist back then. So, we had a rough idea of where it might be. The city map didn't extend to that neighbourhood.

On Wednesday, I set off at 9:00 a.m. Much too early, in fact, but I wanted to play it safe. Holding the little piece of paper in front of me like a divining rod, I searched for the building. I couldn't find it. In a pharmacy, I showed my little note and received a verbose explanation that I didn't understand. The next passerby on the street got my note shoved under his nose. Again, I received a verbose explanation, but at least I could guess the general direction from the gestures. I decided to follow it, hoping to find enough people to point me in the right direction until I finally stood in front of it. It didn't work. One person sent me this way, the next in another direction. And they all told me something I didn't understand. It was enough to make you cry. And that's what I did, sitting back in my car, long past 10:00 a.m., driving back home. I was angry with myself for not having learned French before the move. I was furious at the stupid French people who had babbled at me in French, even though I'd told them I didn't understand. And I was frustrated because I had failed at such a simple task.

In the evening, when Christian came home from work, he called from the front door:

"So, how was your French course? Did you meet nice people?"

I gave no answer. A sobbing wreck doesn't speak. It sobs.

After I had cried my eyes out in Christian's arms and had calmed down enough to speak in coherent sentences, I told him what had happened.

The next day at the office, he got on the phone and found out that the language school wasn't even where they had sent me. He found out the correct address. In the evening, he drove me there to scout the area. And lo and behold, there was the damn place. It hadn't been difficult to find at all. You just had to have the correct address.

With a delay of one week, I started my first language course the following Wednesday. It was more of an integration course than a language course, indeed. We learned the basics like "*je m'appelle*" and "*je suis Allemande*" and so on. Every time a new fellow sufferer joined the class, we started again from square one. I quickly realised that I couldn't learn conversational French this way. But the class was at least good for making friends among the fellow sufferers. Knowing that you're not the only person in the world who apparently isn't destined to ever learn the French language is somehow comforting.

One of them was named Eva. Eva was from Poland and had followed her husband to France. He was French but apparently had no talent for teaching his wife anything about the French language. I met him later on; he was an odd duck. Anyway, Eva told me the following story one day: Wanting to socialise a bit and because she enjoyed dancing, she had set her mind on taking a dance class. Her husband had no interest in such things. When he came home from work in the evening, all he wanted was his beer and some peace and quiet. Dancing didn't interest him. Knowing this, she didn't even bother him with her plans and set off on her own. When she had picked up her little son from school, she saw a notice advertising a course in "*la danse classique*". She grabbed one of those tear-off slips with the phone number. The next day, when her husband was at work and her son was at school, she mustered all her courage and called. She managed to find out the location and time of the course, albeit with difficulty. Finally, the first class date arrived. She had managed to persuade her husband to accompany her at least the first time, so she would have an interpreter. When they showed up, the dance teacher greeted them warmly, her face beaming with joy.

"And where is the child?" she wanted to know.

"What child?"

"Well, the one who's supposed to take part in my dance class."

No, not the child; it was Eva who wanted to learn to dance.

"Ooooh!" said the dance teacher, her eyes widening. Well, why not. The class was actually for children, but sometimes mothers would participate along with their children. So, if she wanted to, that could be arranged.

"Have you ever practised la *danse classique*, *Madame*?" she asked, turning to Eva.

Eva shook her head.

"*Mais...*" she said, pausing because she probably wasn't sure how to phrase the question. "Do you think you should start la *danse classique* at your age?"

Eva looked at her husband, puzzled, as he translated the question. Because not only had he translated the question, but he had also added his own:

"You want to learn ballet? What gave you that idea?"

"Why ballet?" Eva now asked.

That's when it dawned on her husband, and he burst out laughing.

"What did you think la *danse classique* was?" he asked.

"Well, the classics, standard dances, waltz, tango, and so on..."

"I thought so", he said, laughing. "You thought you were going to learn the waltz, but *la danse classique* is ballet! You should have asked me beforehand."

That was too much for Eva. She didn't dignify him with another word and stormed off.

We had bought a television. Either the TV or the radio was on all day so that I was constantly bombarded with the French language. I was learning with a self-study course. I registered at the library and regularly borrowed *"Tintin et Milou"*. With a hefty dictionary on my lap, I translated every single word that had been put into the speech bubbles for Tintin or Captain Haddock. Every new word – and almost every word was new – I wrote down on a small card. With these cards, I learned such useful vocabulary as *"hurluberlu"* or *"hippopotamus"*. Captain Haddock's curses are world-famous; one simply must know them. And I somehow liked the hippopotamus, so it was easy for me to remember. In this way, I made small progress. Really, just small.

One day the doorbell rang. I was still in my initial weeks of frustration. I had made it a habit in such cases to pretend that no one was home. So, I didn't make a peep and hoped he or she would go away. Most of the time, it was just people who wanted to sell something or followers of some sect who wanted to convert me. I could do without either. The doorbell rang again. This one apparently didn't want to go away. When it rang for the third time, I concluded that it must be something important and went to the door. Outside stood a man in overalls with a toolbox in hand. We hadn't ordered any artisan.

"*Bonjour*", I said, looking at him quizzically.

A long stream of endless words that I didn't understand followed my unspoken question.

"*Je ne vous comprends pas*", I said slowly. I don't understand you. That was a sentence I had memorised right from the start.

Now this person started talking again, only louder and slower.

"*Je ne parle pas Français*", I interrupted him, hoping to finally silence him.

"Aaaaah", he said. But instead of perhaps trying another language so that I could understand him, he began to throw individual words at me, slowly, loudly, and very clearly:

"E-lec-tri-cien… re-le-vé… comp-teur…"

I didn't understand him. I couldn't make heads or tails of his gestures.

"Do you speak English?" I asked.

A bewildered shake of the head was the answer.

I gestured for him to wait, went inside, grabbed the phone, and dialled Christian's number at the office.

"There's some sort of artisan here trying to explain something to me, but I don't understand him. Ask him what he wants", I said into the phone and held the phone out to the supposed artisan. He quickly understood what was going on, took the phone, and was glad to have finally found a human being who spoke the only language of humans. Then he handed the phone back to me.

"He's from EDF and wants to read the meter", said Christian.

"And why doesn't he just read the meter?" I asked. The meter was outside the house next to the entrance. He didn't need me for that.

"Don't know", said Christian.

"Then ask him", I said and handed the phone back to the EDF man.

"He just wanted to be polite, so he doesn't scare anyone by creeping around the house", Christian said when I had the phone again.

Great. My nerves were frayed because he wanted to read the meter and asked for permission beforehand so that I wouldn't be startled.

"D'accord?" said the EDF man, looking at me questioningly.

I answered by pointing with both hands to the meter and left him standing there.

Ten minutes later, the doorbell rang again. The EDF man was back at the door. What was it now? He was doing this on purpose! He held a piece of paper and a pen in front of my nose and said:

"*Sig-na-ture… s'il vous plaît.*" He mimed the action of signing with the pen. Even I got that. I signed and received a copy.

"*Bonne journée*", he said, grinning broadly as he turned away.

"*Au revoir*", I said, hoping for the opposite.

I did my grocery shopping at a large supermarket. Before setting off, I always wrote myself a bilingual shopping list so that I knew what things were called in French once I was there. This time, there were some new items on my list. We were having guests. For the first time. Christian had invited colleagues. I wanted to bake a cake. My first in France. It required ingredients I had never bought here before. I searched the entire store for buttermilk but couldn't find it. In one aisle, a young lad was busy stocking shelves. I mustered all my courage and approached him:

"*Excusez-moi… le lait du beurre?*" I asked.

In response, I got something that sounded like "Shepa", accompanied by a shrug of the shoulders. It wasn't hard to guess what that meant. But I had never heard "*Je ne sais pas*" in this form before. I couldn't find any buttermilk. I settled for yoghurt instead, which worked. Later, years later, I learned that I should have asked for "*lait fermenté*". Whether that would have yielded a better result with the young chap is debatable.

The guests arrived. We conversed in a mix of English and French. When it came to French, I kept my mouth shut and didn't even catch what was being discussed. Nathalie had learned some German in school. She tried a few German sentences to please me. And she had a good sense for the words I was searching for. She guessed what I wanted to say, helped me with the correct French words, and thus helped me make more progress in French than all the hours of French classes had so far.

That evening, I wanted to ask our guests what they would like to drink:

"*Eau gazole ou eau plate?*" I asked, quite proud that I had dared to open my mouth. They looked at me puzzled, then laughed, and immediately apologised for laughing. I blushed, realising I must have said something wrong. But what?

The laughter drew Christian over, who had been busy in the kitchen with his bottle of cola. They told him what I had asked them, and now he too joined in the laughter. I retreated to the kitchen and busied myself with preparing the food. I was embarrassed. I was angry at them for laughing at me. And I couldn't figure out what was wrong with what I had said. I had carefully prepared that sentence in advance.

When Christian came back into the kitchen, he explained that I had asked our guests whether they'd prefer diesel water or still water. I had confused the word *gazeuse* with *gazole*. Oh man, was that embarrassing!

They tried to comfort me. I shouldn't be embarrassed. Such things could happen to anyone. In the end, I had to laugh along. From then on, they always requested diesel water when they came to visit us. I had no choice but to get used to having my faux pas constantly thrown back in my face.

In the weeks leading up to the move, I hadn't managed to get to the hairdresser's. My hair had grown too long and developed split ends. In town, I had seen a hairdresser with "*sans rendez-vous*" displayed in the window, next to a promising "We speak English" sign. I wanted to tame my mane to a moderate extent. When I entered the salon, another customer was still being attended to but seemed to be nearly done. So, I sat down and waited. They even offered me a coffee. When it was my turn, it turned out that the colleague who spoke English wasn't working that day. "English not today" she told me. And that was the extent of her English skills. But she didn't want to let me go when I tried to make my escape.

"*Non, non, non, restez!*" Stay, she said.

I was too shy to break away from her. And I didn't want to fail again. So, I stayed.

Using hand gestures and a few words of French here and there, I tried to make clear what I wanted. I showed her my damaged ends. She nodded understandingly.

"*On y va?*" she said, looking at me questioningly in the mirror.

I nodded.

"*Vous êtes sûre?*" she double-checked.

That should have been my wake-up call. At that point, I should have shouted "STOP!" But I didn't. Instead, I said:

"*Oui.*"

She put the scissors to my hair. "Snip", and the first tuft of hair fell. Before I even realised what was happening, the second tuft fell. Now it was too late for shouting "STOP!" So, I endured. Each snip was a stab to my heart. It would take years for them to grow back.

In the end, I had a super-short haircut. The last time I looked like this was when I was 10, before I decided to grow my hair out so people wouldn't keep mistaking me for a boy. I hardly recognised myself.

I had told Christian that I was going to the hairdresser's. But I had NOT mentioned THIS. How could I? This was not the plan. Help! What would he say?

As I paid, left the salon, and walked back through town to the car park, I bit my lips until they bled, just to keep from bursting into tears. I was truly incapable of managing on my own in this country. I couldn't even go to the hairdresser's. Bloody hell! I pounded the steering wheel. My poor car had nothing to do with it, but I had to vent my frustration somewhere. Then there was a knock on the window. I looked up and was startled. Police!

"*Est-ce que ça va, Madame?*" he asked politely. Are you alright?

I nodded.

"*Vous êtes sûre?*" he asked again.

"*Oui!*" I snapped at him. Was it illegal in this damn country to thrash your steering wheel?

He shrugged and walked away. Poor guy, he probably just wanted to help. But I was beyond help. At least in French.

On the drive home, I made two decisions. First, I never wanted to go to the hairdresser's again. I wouldn't need to for the next five years anyway, until my hair finally grew back to its previous length. And second, I would simply claim that this was intentional. I had always wanted a practical summer cut like this. Wash, towel dry, done. Who wouldn't want that? Only the fact that it wasn't summer but winter was just around the corner made this argument a bit questionable. But, strictly speaking, it wasn't that bad. It didn't hurt. And it would grow back. Christian took it in stride. Such things didn't matter to him.

A colleague pointed out to my husband that the university offered a French course for foreign students. This sounded like a much higher level. Christian found out that the course was offered for free by the city and was open to everyone. To avoid a repeat of the last debacle, he personally dragged me there, filled out the registration form at the reception, and nudged me into the room, which was already half full. I retreated to the back row. More and more seats filled up until finally, every chair had an occupant. I was so intimidated that I didn't dare open my mouth. Yet I should have realised that my neighbours were also foreigners and I could probably have had a very good conversation with them in English. Then *Madame le Professeur* entered and trilled a cheerful "*Bonsoir*" to the room. I sank a few centimetres deeper into my chair.

She chattered and chattered and seemed never to want to stop talking. And she spoke exclusively in French. Occasionally, one of the students would ask a question. When she answered and explained, she did so in French and sometimes wrote something in French on the board. Not a single word was spoken in another language all evening. I didn't understand a word.

At some point, she distributed sheets of paper, which were passed through the rows. It was a fill-in-the-blank text. She started with the first person in the front row with the first blank. His neighbour had to fill in the next blank. And so it went through the rows. There was one word that seemed to fit into every blank. This word was *"passer"*. Eventually, I realised that anyone who didn't know the answer used this word so that the cup would pass them by. I had learned my first genuinely useful word that evening. When it was my turn – it was a damn long text – I said *"passer?"* with a question mark; *Madame* just nodded, and the next person was up. Phew!

This course took place twice a week in the evenings. It took a while, but eventually, I started to understand something. The more I understood, the further forward I moved in my seat choice, leaving the last rows at the back to the newcomers. Here, I learned French.

Later, much later – I had then attended an advanced course with her – she told me how much joy it gave her to see how the newcomers initially hid, completely frightened, in the back row, ducked their heads when she asked a question, and softly and shyly said *"passer"*. And how they gradually lifted their heads, ventured further forward as they became a bit more confident. And how happy she was when someone finally dared to sit right in the front row and look her in the eyes, because then she knew she had succeeded. She did this job for moments like that. *Merci beaucoup, Madame Blazek!*

By now, we speak fluent French and understand an estimated 80% of what reaches our ears. Christian thinks it should be 90%. So, let's say 80-90%. Nevertheless, even today we still encounter French terms we don't know or misunderstand. So, if you're still struggling with the French language, don't be disheartened. You're in good company.

And then there are those delightful mix-ups or misunderstandings when the French pronounce something so oddly that we still can't understand them, even if we know the words. I'm thinking, for example, of the "Odie" from our friends in Aubagne. Or Rishahr Share, the famous actor that everyone should know.

We've got into the habit of not giving out our landline number to anyone anymore. These days, everything is done with mobile numbers. And yet, the landline keeps ringing. And you can be 99% sure that it's another one of those marketing calls. Only because of that one percent, which might perhaps be an authority wanting something important, do we still pick up the receiver.

So it was this one time. The phone rang. I answered. A friendly lady was thrilled to speak with me. She knew my name, even though I'd only answered with the customary French "*Allo*". She even knew my address. How do they do that?

"*C'est pourquoi?*" I asked, to cut to the chase. It's the equivalent of asking, "What do you want?" It's equally as impolite, to be honest.

She wasn't deterred. Probably used to it. She was calling on behalf of *Esmo* and wanted to introduce their product range and offer me a trial package that I surely wouldn't want to refuse. Had I heard of *Esmo*?

"*Non*", I replied.

You don't? I hadn't heard of *Esmo*? Well, it was about time then. She'd detected a charming accent in my speaking. Could it be that I wasn't French?

"Yes, that's possible", I answered. She was starting to get on my nerves. I never like giving out personal information on such calls.

"Could it be a German accent?" she insisted. She was either really slow on the uptake or really good.

"*Oui*", I answered.

"Aaaah, I thought so! But then you must know *Esmo*. It's a German company."

"Never heard of it", I said.

"May I send you some information by post?"

"*Oui*", I said, just to get rid of her.

That worked. She thanked me for the pleasant conversation and promised I'd receive mail from her soon. Could she call me again in a few days?

"*Non*", I said. "If I'm interested in your offer, I'll call you. Otherwise, you can safely assume that I'm not interested."

That finally ended the conversation. A few days later, I found a thick envelope in the letterbox. When I opened it, I was quite surprised. Of course, I knew the name "Eismann" from Germany. It took a few seconds for me to realise that this was the mail from the friendly lady from *Esmo*.

Ah, and then there are the so-called "false friends". Words that we think we have in our language too, but their usage is entirely different. We have lots of French words in German. And you would think you could just use them in French as you used them in German. But no! As you are reading the English translation of this book, I may just give you some examples for English-French false friends. Take this, for example: "*votre bras*" means "your arm", the limb between your shoulder and your wrist. It has no connection whatsoever with female undergarments. The French word for "a bra" is *un soutien-gorge*.

This one is a very common false friend: "*Une journée*" is "a day", so if somebody wishes you "*bonne journée*", they are saying "have a nice day". It doesn't mean they think you're going off on a journey. I'm sure you can think of a few more examples. And as you are thinking of it, imagine now, how much I must be confused speaking all three languages and having those false friends even crossing over from French to German to English. This ends up in what is called Babylonian language confusion.

We had discovered a "*Château d'Eau*" on the map, quite close to where we lived. A castle surrounded by water! That sounded charming. Our next bike ride was planned to go there. When we arrived at the spot marked on the map, there was nothing resembling a castle. We scoured the entire area. Sometimes such map entries aren't precisely located where they should be. In the end, we found ourselves back at the initial map position. We wanted to search more closely there. Perhaps it was just a ruin with not much left to see. Nothing.

What was there, however, was an ugly concrete tower with a bulge at the top. A water tower. Yes, exactly, those things that in France are called "*Château d'Eau*". Embarrassing that it hadn't occurred to us sooner.

And while we're on the subject of castles that turn out to be not quite as grand as their names suggest… Did you know that the French build their castles in the air in Spain? Over here, they're called "*châteaux en Espagne*".

FEELING LIKE A GERMAN

Just as with our friends in Aubagne, whom we henceforth called *les Aubagnais* because their many names confused us too much, it has often been the case in the past and will likely continue to be so in the future. At the beginning of an acquaintance, you're stamped with a label. And our label was "German". Nobody did this with malicious intent, and many even associated positive traits with it. Germans are punctual, reliable, and they build good cars.

We continually find that, as Germans living abroad, we are seen by the people around us as exemplars of the country from which we come. On one hand, we must conform to the image they have of "the Germans". On the other hand, they observe us and infer from our behaviour that of "the Germans". This makes us feel more German abroad than we ever did back in the old homeland. Strange, isn't it? This might get on our nerves, as we left Germany because we prefer our new chosen home and feel more comfortable here. It might amuse us when we once again encounter old, stubborn prejudices. Regardless, we have to live with it. And we must live up to this responsibility.

What I'm describing here relates to the expectations and behaviour at the beginning of our relationship with new acquaintances. Once they get to know us a bit better, the label quickly disappears. Then, at some point, we are no longer "the Germans", but the friends who... (whatever comes to their minds about us).

The fact that we didn't like beer often caused confusion. Frequently, our acquaintances, wanting to give us a special treat, would get beer when we were invited for *apéro*. And, of course, they were initially disappointed when we declined. We regularly defused the situation very successfully by retorting that we hadn't fled from Germany to the country that makes the best wine in the world just to continue drinking beer. That might be a bit exaggerated, but it worked. To stay in the language of stereotypes: if you praise something French to the skies in front of a French person, their heart swells.

When we had invited new acquaintances to our home back in Germany, we never gave much thought to what we'd put on the table. It had to be tasty. And any food intolerances had to be clarified. That was it. Most of the time, we served something Mediterranean because we like it and because it was always well-received.

Now, when we, as Germans living in France, invited new friends – and they weren't also German – then we felt obliged to serve something German. At least in the first few years. These days, I don't do that anymore; I cook what I like and what tastes good to us. It's a colourful mix, with perhaps a few German influences still present, but mostly consisting of the best flavours that have tantalised our taste buds from around the world. Whatever we like, I recreate, tweaking here, simplifying there where it's too complicated or I can't get the ingredients, and letting my creativity run wild. The result is rarely something our guests had expected. But I can live with the surprise from our guests à la "you're not cooking German at all", and I reply: "No, but tasty!"

What I will definitely never change are my grandmother's baking recipes. A proper homemade pie with a shortcrust base, sour cherries, and lots of crumble – that's something "the French" can't do. And so, I've still managed to bring something typically German to the table. And the fact that it is delicious is a point of delightful agreement across all nationalities.

When we're together with our French friends and chatting, the conversation inevitably turns to politics sooner or later. The French absolutely love debating politics. We often have all the trouble in the world keeping up. We're happy if we can even list all the French presidents since the Second World War. The ministers currently in office are a greater challenge, as they change frequently. But it often doesn't stop there. A former minister under Hollande is mentioned, who is now being charged with tax evasion. What, you don't remember him? He was the one who... And then follows a detailed account of the minister and the whole affair, which finally allows us to join in the conversation should the topic come up again.

Next time, we suddenly find ourselves in the midst of recent French history because there's a ship naming ceremony in the harbour tomorrow, where even the granddaughter of the minister whose name the ship will bear is supposed to attend. This minister has contributed significantly to French culture. What, you've never heard the name? Can't imagine! And once again, we're thoroughly taught.

So, every meeting with our French friends is also always a bit of a history, politics, and culture lesson. We make a genuine effort to remember it all. But it's hard; we lack the context; we didn't live through the times when these ministers were active.

Just when we think we're starting to get an overview of the key players in recent French politics and have a rough idea of what's being discussed, the next time we dive into the Third, Fourth, and Fifth Republic because the new play at the town's theatre has a historical background. What we learned in school about the French Revolution is far from sufficient. And once again, we're left rather clueless and have to be educated. But our friends enjoy doing this; they have a whale of a time bringing us clueless folks up to a certain level of education. We take it all in good humour and have long given up thinking they could be equally interested in German politics. It gets easier the longer you live in France.

And then there are those comparison conversations, as I call them. Do you know what I mean? Something in French politics isn't going the way the people would like. And there's always something going wrong. In such instances, the French like to look across the border and often enough discover that, for example, the German economy is doing much better than the French one. Or the French healthcare system isn't working. Or the French educational system is terribly poor. So, the Germans must be doing something right. "Why can't we French do it like the Germans?" we often hear.

Caution is advised here. Such comments about the oh-so-poor French system, whatever it may be, should not be understood as an invitation to join in the chorus and start complaining about everything that has been annoying you for years in France. Quite the opposite! Only the French are allowed to grumble about France. Everyone else has no right to. Anyone else is welcome to go back to where they came from if they don't like it. They are welcome guests here, as long as they behave decently and appreciate the hospitality. And a good guest doesn't criticise their host.

When we're drawn into such a conversation, diplomacy is required. Of course, we might agree with one point or another and we do say so. But to emphasise it and rub salt in the wound rarely goes down well. And let's be honest, not everything is going swimmingly in Germany either, and we do say that too.

Sometimes we're also asked, "And what do our German neighbours think? What impression do they have of us? What's being said in the news?" Then we're supposed to act as ambassadors for our country and reflect the general opinion of the Germans, even though we haven't been concerned with German politics for years and haven't followed German news for ages. Initially, this was still quite easy, as the connection to Germany was still there. The last political events were still fresh in memory. But the longer we live in France, the harder it becomes to answer this question. Honesty being the best policy, we usually say we have no idea because we're simply not interested anymore. We live here now. This is what interests us. After making it clear that Germany no longer interests us, which is met with astonishment but then a certain degree of understanding, they may ask, "So what do you think about the current situation in France?" And there we are, back to what I said earlier.

Let's always remember on such occasions that we are in this country voluntarily, that we chose this country when we had the choice of any country in the world. We chose France. When we point this out to our French friends, their mouths usually hang open for a few seconds. Until they realise what a colossal, galactic compliment that is for their beloved France.

"*Rien à ajouter*", someone once said to us in response. Nothing more to add.

« Fin »

Epilogue

The move to La Ciotat was our first real emigration. All the other moves before that were job-related relocations, where our employers helped us find a flat and paid for the move. We stayed in La Ciotat for two years. Just two years, you'll say now. Yes, unfortunately, our business idea didn't work out. It was a venture, but it was worth taking the risk. In the end, money became tight. The rent was eating into our savings. About six months before we would completely run out of money, we made a decision. One of us had to take a job again. We both applied. Whoever found something first had lost. We would have loved to stay in France, but it wasn't to be. Christian had the misfortune of being offered an employment contract, so it fell to him. And unfortunately, this job was in Germany, in the middle of nowhere. We endured it there for two years. Long enough to replenish the coffers. Oh yes, and to re-register the car. And more than long enough to fuel our yearning for the South of France. We must have watched the film "A Good Year" at least a dozen times, dreaming of the sunny South. And then a headhunter called to offer my husband a job in Monaco…

This book may end with a failure, but don't let that sadden you, dear reader. For this is not the end of our story. Sometimes life just has a way of taking the plans we make and tossing them aside because it has something else in mind for us. One might even call it a higher plan. Or as my friend always puts it: "You never know what it's good for." How right she is. Since our adventures in La Ciotat, we've moved several more times. Some of those moves were also within France. We ended up in Nice, for the job in Monaco, because living in Monaco was something we couldn't afford. Later, we found ourselves in Narbonne, or more precisely, in its surrounding area. And even later, we moved further south, almost to the Spanish border. How did that come about?

How did things go for us afterwards? You'll find out in my next book.

Now, a few remarks on my own behalf.

In this book, I recount our own experiences. These are not tips that you can implement one by one, and I take no responsibility for any potentially incorrect information. Many things will have changed since then anyway. So, before you make an important decision based on something I've said, please consult the relevant authorities for the current correct procedure.

As an author, I've taken the liberty of exaggerating, downplaying, adding, omitting, embellishing, bowdlerising, and much more, wherever I deemed it appropriate or necessary. Not everything written on these pages actually happened that way. But most of it did.

Some names of the individuals involved have been changed for their own protection or mine. Any similarities or even matches with people you may know are purely coincidental.

At this point, it's time to say thank you to all the friends and companions who have supported us with advice and action, or simply with understanding. I won't mention any names here, as I don't want to risk forgetting anyone. Those I mean know that I mean them. So, THANK YOU!

A very special thanks goes to my beloved husband Christian, who has put up with all this nonsense and continues to do so. Although, actually, it's more like I'm the one who has put up with all his nonsense and continues to do so. But with us, you never really know. My mother always says, "The two of you really found each other." And for once, I completely agree with her.

A very heartfelt thanks goes to my dear friend Christine Brice. Without her, the English version of this book would not be out there. She has done a fantastic job as my proofreader. Thank you, Christine!

And last but not least thank you, dear reader, for making it to this page. I hope I've been able to encourage you to pursue your dream of immigrating to France. Or of any other bold dream. If you have any questions or comments, feel free to virtually drop by at https://ines-sachs.de/en (the author's website). I look forward to meeting you.

Printed in Great Britain
by Amazon